FIND
ANOTHER *You*

RJ Layer

BELLA
BOOKS

2018

Bella Books, Inc.
P.O. Box 10543
Tallahassee, FL 32302

First Bella Books Edition 2018

Editor: Ann Roberts
Cover Designer: Judith Fellows

ISBN: 978-1-59493-599-2

Other Bella Books by RJ Layer

Judge Me Not
The Real Story
Dreams Unspoken

Acknowledgment

Thank you to my publisher and the incomparable team at Bella Books. Bella's dedication to bringing queer literature to readers is coveted, and I count myself fortunate to be part of the Bella family. Thanks to my incredible beta readers, Sue Hilliker and Ann Etter, for their valuable input. Thank you to my editor, Ann Roberts, for her gentle nudging and expertise.

Thanks to my family and friends for a lifetime of love and support. The biggest heartfelt thank you to my readers for keeping me motivated to write the next book.

And, Lori—my one, my all, my forever.

About the Author

Born and raised in the "heart" of the Midwest, RJ still resides there with her spouse of twenty-eight years and counting, and their two feline bosses. She loves writing lesbian stories that capture the heart of the romantic. In addition to traveling to new places, RJ can be found in the rolling hills along the water. Their hideaway is the perfect setting for dreaming up engaging characters and moving stories. She also loves taking photos and reading every free moment she can find.

Dedication

For Lori—because I'll never find another you.

CHAPTER ONE

Abby cracked open an eyelid. The bedside alarm clock read one fifty-two a.m. There wasn't any doubt about Selena's nakedness when her hardened nipples pressed into Abby's back. Abby groaned when Selena's hand slipped under the satin of her nightshirt and she kissed the side of her face.

A sweet citrus scent mixed with alcohol immediately assaulted Abby's senses as Selena breathed, "Hey doll." Her hand moved slowly up Abby's hip.

"It's almost two and you've been drinking."

She kissed Abby's neck. "I had a beer on the way home." Her hand traveled with purpose to Abby's breast and caressed the nipple to erectness between her fingers.

Abby grabbed her wrist and pulled her hand away. "Don't think for a minute if you get picked up for DUI, I'll be able to get you out of it."

She kissed Abby's neck again. "You worry too much. It was only one beer."

"It took you two hours to drink a beer on your way home." It was simply an observation, not a question.

"They asked me to stay over for an hour." She took Abby's earlobe lightly between her teeth.

"What is that ungodly smell?"

Selena stiffened momentarily, and then moved her hand over Abby's hip. "I stopped by the mall before work. Tried a new perfume. You don't like it?"

"You smell like a sixteen-year-old. No, I don't like it."

Selena always smelled sexy and exotic, but this smelled like a teenager's fragrance. Her hand moved once again over Abby's hip and when Selena tried to wiggle her fingers between her legs, Abby caught it.

"Selena, not tonight." Selena resisted her grasp. "I should say this morning."

She ran her tongue up Abby's neck and stopped at her ear. "Come on, baby. I'll melt you in my mouth like a sweet piece of chocolate." She wrenched her hand from Abby's grasp and reached for Abby's breast again as she pressed herself firmly against Abby's back.

Abby wasn't the least bit aroused and felt bound by Selena's hold. "Please stop! I didn't get home from work until almost nine. I had your laundry to do, and I had to pick up the mess you left in the living room. I didn't get to bed until eleven and was awake until midnight wondering where you were. You could have called."

Selena kissed her ear. "I'm sorry, baby. Let me make it up to you."

She tried to slip her hand between Abby's legs from behind so Abby rolled away. "I told you no. I have to get up in less than four hours and be in the office early at seven to assist the wicked bitch on some big court case. Please just let me get some sleep." Abby dropped her head onto the pillow. She had no problem getting along with every other prosecuting attorney she'd worked with. But she worried how things would go with Blair Stanton given the gossip in the assistants' pool and the nickname "Wicked Bitch."

Selena moved closer. "I'm sorry. I just get this craving for you sometimes and I can't help myself." She raised Abby's chin and pressed her lips to hers. When she tried to snake her tongue into Abby's mouth, Abby pushed her away.

"Since the hotel decided it was time to screw around with all of the assistant managers' schedules, I'm off tomorrow night. I'll fix us a romantic dinner and then I'll pamper your panty hose off you," Selena promised. She currently worked at one of the national hotel chains out in the suburbs, which is how they met.

Although Abby's brain was mush, she remembered her other commitment for tomorrow. "I'm doing my volunteer time at the hospital after work so I won't be home until probably seven." And also recalling the last time, she warned, "No cooking for you. We'll go out somewhere. Okay?" The last time Selena cooked it had taken Abby hours to clean up the mess after Selena had already worn her out in the bedroom.

"Okay." She flopped over on her back. "Night, Abs."

"Goodnight, Selena."

Exhausted when the alarm went off, Abby hit the snooze button and nine minutes later dragged herself, bleary-eyed, from the bed. Selena was standing in front of the coffeemaker waiting on her. She placed a mug in Abby's hand when she stepped beside her.

"What are you doing up this early?"

Selena's arm snaked around her waist as she filled Abby's cup. "I feel bad that I kept you awake last night."

She didn't pour any coffee for herself, letting Abby know she'd be returning to bed the second Abby left.

"We're still on for tonight, right?"

"Hmm…"

"Dinner tonight, you and me. Remember? Followed by pampering." Selena turned toward Abby and winked.

"I have to—"

"Volunteer at the hospital, I know. How about I make a reservation at Fernando's for seven?"

"That's fine." Selena started to pull her in, but Abby backed away. "I've got to get in the shower or I'll be late."

Selena raised her hands in surrender.

Standing under the hot spray, the fog in her head slowly began to lift. She recalled Selena coming home late last night, smelling of booze and some ungodly perfume. Her persistent attempts to engage Abby in sex and a side trip to the mall equaled Selena wanting something. There was every likelihood she would be finding out tonight what that something was. She rushed to get out the door on time, leaving Selena sitting at the counter. As Abby pulled onto the street, she saw the lights go out upstairs, which confirmed Selena was indeed headed back to bed. After four years together, Abby could read her like one of her favorite books.

Rushing through the early morning traffic, Abby walked briskly from the parking garage to the courts building. She hurriedly shrugged out of her coat and dropped it on her chair. In her peripheral she caught movement in the doorway between the offices.

"I was going to give you five more minutes, and then send out the hounds." Blair's voice sounded harsh.

Abby glanced at the clock on her desk as she gathered files and a notepad. She was only late by two minutes. *I should have guessed she'd know if I was late by twenty seconds.* She feigned a smile and apologized. "Sorry." She sensed she was in for a grueling day and felt an awful lot like something the cat dragged in.

Blair waved Abby past her into the lion's den. "Let's get busy. We have a lot to go over today and the trial starts Thursday."

The "lion" was Abby's new boss since her most recent assistant quit without notice. The lion was taking a toll on the pool of assistants in the prosecutor's offices, of which Abby was one. Apparently Abby was the big lottery loser this time around and now assigned to Blair Stanton, a.k.a. "The Pit Bull," as she was so fondly referred to by any defense attorney that had faced her in court. The assistants in the pool had another name for her. "The Wicked Bitch of the Midwest." At five-foot-six in her three-inch stilettos and perfectly highlighted blond hair, Blair

Stanton didn't appear as terrifying as all the assistants had made her out to be.

Blair pulled out a chair at the table that fronted the window. "Would you like coffee?"

"Yes, please." *And while you're at it maybe you can inject it straight into my veins.*

At the opposite end of her massive office Blair poured coffee. Abby tried to psych herself up for the day by thinking about her stress-relieving trip to the hospital after work to read to the sick kids on the pediatric floor. And of course there was also dinner and pampering by Selena to look forward to after that. If that couldn't relieve Abby's stress, she was in big trouble.

Blair handed Abby the coffee and pulled a chair around to sit beside her. Midmorning arrived quickly, the coffee was gone and so Blair graciously allowed Abby a break. When she returned from the ladies' room, Blair was making more coffee. Abby took her seat and closed her eyes, taking deep breaths. It turned out to be the most relaxing thing she could do during stressful workdays. She allowed her mind's eye to see Selena naked in bed.

"Abby."

Certain she had only just closed her eyes, Blair's voice startled her. Blair stood across the table looking at her inquisitively.

"I'm sorry. I was trying this relaxation technique."

She slid the mug toward Abby. "It must be some technique to make you smile like that." Blair's gaze lingered as she raised her cup and took a drink. "Are you ready to get back to it?" Blair offered a smile that Abby had never seen before. It looked, well…It looked human.

"Of course."

At one o'clock Blair tried to get her to join her for lunch at the restaurant downstairs, but Abby declined in lieu of taking care of a few personal matters during the break. She actually ended up taking advantage of the couch in Blair's office. Abby was certain her eyes had only been closed mere minutes when she opened them to see Blair watching her from her desk. When Abby checked her watch, it was clear her eyes had been closed much longer. It was nearing two thirty, and she knew without asking that Blair had been back half an hour because the other assistants that had worked for her said she never exceeded an hour for her lunch. She jumped to her feet, spilling a file full of pages on the floor.

"Oh God, Blair, I'm sorry." She stooped to gather the mess as Blair walked over to help.

"Why didn't you wake me up when you came back?"

Meeting Abby's gaze, Blair handed her a stack of pages. "You looked so peaceful. I didn't have the heart."

Abby knew there wasn't a single assistant who would dispute Blair's statement about lacking a heart, but she caught a glimpse of something warm in her eyes when Blair smiled at her. Maybe she wasn't as bad as Abby's coworkers claimed.

"Is everything okay, Abby?"

She stood with pages poking raggedly from the file and moved over to the table. "Oh sure. It's just family stuff, you know."

"If you ever need to talk, I'm a pretty good listener. Contrary to what most people in these offices might tell you, I happen to know a thing or two about family," Blair said, taking her seat.

Abby experienced the strangest feeling. She didn't doubt Blair's sincerity. It was quite clear in her eyes and the tone of her voice.

"That's dirty laundry I'd rather keep home in the hamper, but thank you." She began to organize the file she'd destroyed.

At five thirty she stood and stretched. "Blair, I have to leave. Tonight's my night to volunteer at the hospital."

"Oh yes, I'd forgotten."

If she left that minute she'd only be five minutes late, barring any major traffic problems.

"Just ten or fifteen more minutes, Abigail, and we can put this to bed."

Now that was the wicked woman with the reputation everyone knew and detested. She worked quickly, and ten minutes later she was running out the door pulling on her coat. While racing across the parking garage, she called the nurses station on the children's floor to offer her apology for being late. She assured the bubbly Nurse Tiffany that she would be there and not disappoint the kids. She cursed Blair when she got stuck in a traffic snarl and left Selena a message that she would meet her at Fernando's. She couldn't possibly pick Selena up and make the reservation in time.

She didn't arrive at the hospital until twenty after six and was informed by Tiffany as she rushed past, "They're waiting impatiently for you."

Abby entered the activity room to frazzled looks from nurses and aides, but applause from the kids. Joy filled her heart and made the entire day worthwhile.

Tossing her coat aside and taking her designated seat, she said, "Why thank you. I don't think I've ever received such a warm welcome."

The kids chattered on as the adults were trying to shush them.

"Okay," she began, "for those of you new to our special group, my name is Abby and I'm here to have some fun reading stories. For those of you that have been here before, well, I'm sure you'll be getting to go home soon."

She settled her eyes on little redheaded Jenny in the wheelchair, front and center, and gave her a wink. Seven-year-old Jenny had been in a car accident that shattered bones in her right leg from her hip to her ankle. Even more unfortunate was that her twelve-year-old brother had died in the accident. Abby had been informed by a couple of nurses that little Jenny had more surgeries and rehab. She'd become Abby's special friend.

"So now that everyone knows my name, how about if our new visitors tell us old-timers your names?"

Most of the kids proudly boasted their names, and only a few timid ones needed a little encouragement. She began reading from the book the kids picked out last week, but within a few minutes was distracted by whispered voices in the back of the room. When Abby glanced up, a woman with dark hair and bright eyes wearing the standard doctor's white coat, stood looking intently back at her while listening to one of the nurses.

She offered an apologetic smile and Abby continued to read. When she looked toward the door moments later, the doctor was gone.

Dr. Samantha Christiano had heard a number of people raving about the children's storyteller, Ms. Collins, and thought it might be beneficial to check this woman out. She slipped into the back of the activity room to witness a bunch of silent children, their attention riveted on the woman up front. Nurse Erika Walker stepped over beside Sam and began whispering, but she wasn't listening. Sam's attention was on the woman at the front of the room. Ms. Collins glanced up from her book looking toward their whispering voices. Sam gave what she hoped to be a smile of apology and then ducked out of the room feeling like a child who'd been scolded for talking in class. Out in the hall she sucked in a deep breath. The scolder was one beautiful woman. Her gaze alone had taken Sam's breath away. She couldn't remember a time that she'd been so…so…well, so captivated by a woman, or even if she'd ever been. Ms. Collins had auburn hair tied back at her neck and light-colored eyes, maybe hazel. She looked to be a few years older than Sam and quite stylish in a silky blouse and business skirt. Sam guessed that she probably ran one of the city's banks or brokerage firms.

Sam had never denied her attraction to women. She'd known for sure at the young age of ten, when asked by one of her older sisters what boy in her class she would most like to kiss. Sam couldn't come up with a single boy's name, but she had quickly thought of a half dozen girls she'd like to kiss. She kept it under wraps, though, trying to fit the norm. She didn't want to be defined by her sexuality. She didn't want to be part of a "special group" and she didn't want to disappoint Momma. She dated a few boys in high school and attended the usual dances and prom, but she didn't develop interest in any serious relationships, instead concentrating on her schoolwork. Once she went off to college, she was of course free to pursue relationships of her choosing, and in fact had a girlfriend during her first year. Brittany Greer was a beautiful and charming woman. Sam had fallen head over heels in love after going to bed with her the first time. But, the longer she and Sam were together, the more controlling Brittany became. Her first relationship with a woman had ended worse than any nightmare Sam could have imagined.

Because medicine was an exhausting and demanding field, she shifted her time and effort toward her future and hadn't been interested in anyone since. Sam closed her eyes and saw in her mind those intense eyes that had gazed at her moments earlier. She smiled. She'd see those eyes in her sleep...if her shift ever ended.

Concluding the night's reading thirty minutes after beginning, Abby called Selena's cell as she rushed to her car. She had to leave a voice mail and said she'd be at the restaurant as quickly as she could get there, but she knew she was going to be at least fifteen minutes late.

She found Selena seated with a near empty drink glass. Her expression belied her mood. She was upset, and knowing that Selena would require several drinks to lighten up, Abby asked the maitre d' to locate their server on her way to the table.

When the waiter left, Selena gulped the last of her martini. "So glad you found time to join me."

Abby leaned close. "I'm so sorry to keep you waiting. I'm here now. Can't we make the best of our time together?"

Sitting back Selena crossed her arms. *Apparently not.* She was going to be a tough nut about this, but Abby had plenty of experience with her moods and fully intended to crack her before the night was over. Selena sulked throughout dinner and despite having three drinks, Abby still couldn't get her to smile. While Selena polished off her drink and they waited for the waiter to return with Abby's credit card, Abby slipped off one of her heels and slowly worked her bare foot up Selena's calf. She focused on Selena, which only yielded her a glare. Working her foot between Selena's knees and then her thighs, Abby finally touched her toes to Selena's center. Selena's thigh muscles tightened on Abby's foot and she slid down in her chair pushing herself against it. Abby gave a tiny smile as she worked her toes against Selena's heat. Selena's eyes drifted closed for a moment and when she opened them, Abby saw only lust. Selena slid her hand under the tablecloth and onto Abby's foot, her lips curling in a wolfish smile.

Abby had her. "Are you ready?" she asked.

"Oh yeah." Selena squeezed her foot.

Abby slipped her foot back into her shoe and leaned close again. "I don't want you to drive."

Selena's lips curled again. "I can't now."

In the car, Selena took Abby's hand and pressed it to her lips. "Your hand is cold. Let me warm it."

Selena's hot breath on her skin made other parts heat up. She held Abby's hand for another moment, and then placed it between her legs. Images of her hand in Selena's pants played through her mind the entire drive home. On the elevator ride from the parking lot, Selena pinned her in the corner with a long passionate kiss. And the second they stepped into the loft and closed the door, Selena kissed her again all the while tugging at her coat until it lay in a heap at their feet. She pulled Abby's blouse loose and moved one hand up to her breast while the other one slid inside her panties before Abby could stop her.

Selena's lips traveled across her cheek to her ear. "I see you're ready for me. Do you want me to take you to bed?" Selena asked, her voice low and raspy.

Abby pushed Selena's fingers deeper into her wetness.

Selena jerked her hand out. "No doll, you have to tell me what you want."

Abby couldn't get enough air to breathe, let alone talk, but she managed to say between gasps, "Please take me to bed."

"And do what?" she asked with half-lidded eyes.

Abby pulled her within an inch of her lips and put her other hand between Selena's legs. "Make love to me like there's not going to be another tomorrow."

Selena kissed her briefly and then tugged her toward the bedroom, garments strewn along the way.

CHAPTER TWO

Abby slept like a baby. Granted it was only for six hours, but she was sure she must have been unconscious, because the last thing she remembered before the alarm sounded was telling Selena she loved her and kissing her. She rolled out of bed with a smile on her face and a bounce in her step. Selena opened her eyes long enough to tell her last night was over the moon, and that she would see Abby when she got home from work. Abby gave her a kiss and Selena rolled back over.

Abby didn't need to go in early, their normal start time was eight, but she arrived a little after seven thirty. At fifteen of eight she started Blair's coffee, expecting her to blow through the door promptly at seven fifty-five. You could set your watch by her arrival.

"Well, you really must teach me this relaxation thing you do. It looks so enjoyable."

Abby wasn't aware her mind had wandered so far away until Blair's voice came out of nowhere. "Excuse me?"

"You were wearing that smiling, faraway look again." She waved a hand. "Never mind." She stepped into her office. "You made coffee already. Are you bucking for a raise?" Abby followed her in. "Because if you want one, I'd sign off on it." Blair hung up her coat.

"No, I'm not."

Abby pulled out her chair, but before she could sit, Blair continued. "I brought muffins." She raised a paper sack in her hand. "I thought we'd treat ourselves before we get started."

Blair was being exceedingly nice, making Abby wonder who this person was in Blair's office, and what she'd done with the real Blair. Or, maybe she was after something.

Blair joined her at the table bringing two mugs of coffee and the muffins. Taking the seat across the table, she asked, "How was your volunteer thing at the hospital?"

"Fine."

Blair helped herself to a muffin. "So what exactly is it you do there every week?"

She was acting—human. Maybe she'd gotten laid too. Abby shivered. The thought of Blair getting laid conjured up a picture of some unsuspecting guy tied to her bed and her with a whip in hand. According to coworkers, Blair Stanton couldn't care less about anyone's life outside the job. Abby had worked with enough people at the prosecutor's office who'd confirmed that tidbit about Blair.

"Abby?"

"I'm sorry. What were you saying?"

"I asked what you do at the hospital. Is everything all right?"

"Sorry. Yes, I'm fine. I read to the kids on the pediatric floor."

Blair munched on a bite of muffin. "You like kids?"

"I love kids. I can't wait to have my own."

Abby felt her clock ticking away at thirty-four. She and Selena had discussed kids, and while Selena hadn't said no to the idea, she hadn't seemed overly enthused about it either. Of course Selena was only twenty-seven and Abby didn't think her clock had started yet. Her resolution for the New Year was to get Selena fully onboard with having a baby. What a way to begin a New Year. And even though Selena never brought up the topic of kids, Abby knew she had a large family. She couldn't imagine Selena wouldn't want a family of her own.

Everything Blair needed for her trial that began the following day was finished by five. Before Abby could get away from her desk, though, Blair asked if she minded staying long enough to listen to her opening statement to the jury. Since Blair was paying for her time and Selena was working, she didn't see any reason to rush home to a microwave dinner and an empty loft. Blair might be a lot of things, like bitchy and self-centered, but she had a brilliant legal mind. It was no surprise she'd earned the reputation as the toughest, "hard as nails" prosecutor in Dawson, Indiana. She knew the law inside out and she was better than good at putting the bad guys away for breaking it.

"It moved me. I'm sure it will move the jury," Abby told her honestly.

Blair closed the file and dropped herself into her chair. "Speaking of the jury, I'd like you to be in court with me tomorrow."

"Court," Abby repeated, as if she'd not heard Blair correctly. "Why would you want me there?"

Blair tossed the file on her desk. Leaning back in her chair she formed a steeple with her fingers and looked at Abby a long moment. "I think you have good instincts about people. I'd like you to observe the jury during opening statements and let me know if you see anything I should worry about."

"But…"

Blair raised a hand. "I know you studied law for a while. You're much smarter than any assistant I've ever worked with, and again, I think you have good people instincts."

"I don't know. Your confidence in me is far greater than my own."

"Don't worry. If we lose, which is highly unlikely with this case, I'm not going to fire you." Blair's expression became stoic. "Because you've chosen to be just an assistant, I can't require you to do this, but I am sincerely asking for your help."

She actually sounded sincere. "All right." Abby sighed. Blair had never smiled quite like she smiled now.

"Excellent! Court starts at nine. We'll meet there and don't worry about coming here first."

Wow! The boss was going to let her sleep an extra hour tomorrow. Blair stood and began stuffing her briefcase.

"Thank you for helping me out on this," she said as Abby stood to leave.

"Sure, Blair." Abby only made it a step toward the door.

"Hey, Abby, would you like to join me for dinner? I know a place that serves the finest filet in the city."

Abby made sure she was wearing her best poker face before turning around. "I can't. I already have plans, but thank you for the invitation."

Blair nodded. "Another time perhaps."

Abby had plans all right. A frozen microwave dinner, her nails, and now she had to come up with something to wear to court tomorrow—as if someone might notice the prosecutor's assistant seated in the gallery and what she was wearing. As she gathered her things, she pictured Blair in only the finest, most expensive restaurants in the city. It would be nice to be treated to a lavish meal. Selena's idea of lavish was Fernando's, which was okay as restaurants go. But then Selena thought it fancy because they had tablecloths and candles.

Abby stepped into the doorway as she pulled on her coat. Blair was again seated at her desk with a file open in front of her.

"I thought you were going to have dinner."

She looked up. "Oh, I've actually got a few other cases I need to look over."

Abby buttoned up her coat and leaned in the doorway. "I know I should mind my own business, but you should get a life outside the office, you know like dating. You might find Mr. Right and he might steal your heart away from this ball and chain."

Blair's expression hardened. "You're right. It's not your business," she snapped. Then like Jekyll and Hyde, she transformed. Her jaw muscles relaxed. "I'm sorry. I don't know where that came from."

I do. It's inbred in your genes. It's who I've always heard that you are.

"You obviously have a life outside this office," Blair stated in a softer tone.

Abby wasn't sure if she was fishing or making an observation. "I'll see you in court."

"Yes. Have a good evening."

As she walked the cavernous hallway, Abby wondered why Blair wasn't attached, or engaged, or married. She was certainly attractive and probably considered one of the most eligible catches in the city, personality aside. Maybe she was one of those "career first and have a life later" kind of women.

Abby regretted every minute she spent alone in the loft that night and wished she'd taken Blair up on her dinner offer. But, she didn't really want to be seen with her. She worried if something like that got around the office, her coworkers would think she was sucking up or consorting with the enemy. She suspected they were already speculating why she'd been assigned as Blair's new assistant when there were others with less seniority, and therefore, better candidates to be stuck with the worst boss.

Selena had come home so beat that she barely kissed Abby before falling dead asleep. Abby was enjoying her extra hour this morning, sitting in front of the big living room windows, sipping her coffee, and looking out into the city as the day's rat race began. A lady of leisure, she took her time getting ready to leave. Once it was time to go, she sat on the edge of the bed and pushed back the dark locks that covered Selena's face. She kissed the corner of her mouth.

Selena moaned softly and cracked open her eyes. "You smell delicious. Come back to bed." She tried to slide her hand under Abby's skirt but Abby caught it.

"You look dreamy lying there and I wish I could, but I've got to go to work."

Selena again attempted to get her hand under Abby's skirt. "You look especially nice this morning. You have a hot lunch date or something?"

"I'm sitting in on a court case."

Selena yawned and stretched her arms over her head exposing her breasts. The sight made Abby want to crawl into the bed, but instead she pulled up the sheet.

"Is this a promotion?"

The sight of Selena's breasts had stamped an image in Abby's mind and she would have played hooky today were it not for her obligation to Blair.

"No, just a request by the boss."

"You're not having a thing with the boss, are you?" Selena asked seriously.

"Oh, please. She was voted most likely to be hated by everyone in the office, including the other prosecutors. I wouldn't consider such a thing if she were the last woman alive." She shivered and laughed.

"And why would you? She could never satisfy you like I do."

"Stop. This whole conversation is becoming repulsive. I've got to go." She gave Selena a quick peck on the lips and moved away before Selena could get her hands on her. "Go back to sleep. I'll see you tonight."

The conversation with Selena stayed on her mind during her drive to the courthouse. She wondered why she painted Blair in such a bad light to Selena after seeing a more human side of her yesterday and realizing she may actually possess a heart. Selena was insanely jealous, which was why when Abby first volunteered at the hospital, Selena insisted on going with her, no doubt to make certain Abby wasn't having a fling with one of the nurses. When they first started dating Selena admitted that she had issues with abandonment and jealousy. It took quite a bit of convincing on Abby's part for Selena to believe that she was the only woman for her.

The corridor outside courtroom four was packed with people. She finally spotted Blair standing with her second chair. He was fairly new to the prosecutor's office and by appearances, fresh out of law school. Enthralled in conversation, their foreheads almost touched. Blair checked her watch and then looked into the crowd gathering in front of the courtroom doors. Her gaze eventually landed on Abby. Smiling, Blair gave her a wave.

"Nice outfit. You look like you could be my second chair." She winked before looking at the young man beside her. "No offense. This is Jeffery White, and this…" She looked at Abby and smiled, "is my assistant, Abby. I don't know if you've had the chance to work with Jeffery yet."

"No, I haven't." Abby extended her hand, accepting his handshake.

"He's only been with us a few months. I'm sure you'll have a chance to work together if he stays around long enough." Blair glanced at her watch again. "Let's go in. I want you to have a seat with a good view of the jury."

When Jeffery opened and held the door, Blair placed her hand lightly on Abby's back and waved her ahead with her briefcase.

"This should be fine here." Blair stopped at the second row and motioned to the seat on the aisle.

Abby slipped off her coat and settled in, hoping she could stay awake. It reminded her of sitting in a lecture hall in law school, fighting to keep her eyes open during a few of her classes. She was pretty sure that by the last quarter of her first year she had mastered the art of sleeping with her eyes open. She had also decided she didn't want to spend five more years in school and have to pass the bar simply to please her parents. Lawyers spent too much of their lives on display. What she wanted was to live a simple life away from the spotlight and societal obligations.

A few minutes later people filed in and filled the seats. Abby stood at least six times to allow people into the aisle. When she glanced over at Blair and Jeffery, Blair looked back and mouthed, "Sorry."

When Blair stood before the jury and began her opening argument, Abby found it difficult to concentrate on the jurors. Blair's tailored suit with its slim lines gave her the look of a polished politician. Blair was a very striking woman with graceful movements and eloquent hand gestures to emphasize her words. Abby struggled to concentrate on the jury and not be distracted by Blair's smooth public speaking voice. She could definitely be a politician.

Abby was looking at Blair and not the jury when Blair turned to face the spectators and met Abby's gaze. There was a noticeable moment of dead silence before Blair turned back to the jury and continued. Knowing what was coming with the close of her statement, Abby focused all her attention on the jurors. Abby was convinced of the perpetrator's guilt and certain all but possibly one of the jurors would be as well. When Blair finished, she and Jeffery put their heads together at the prosecution table. Once the defense attorney completed his opening, the judge adjourned court until after lunch. Abby waited in her seat until Blair and Jeffery gathered their things and stood.

Abby handed Blair her steno pad. "I hope you find my notes helpful."

Blair glanced at it. "Join us for lunch and we can discuss them."

Abby picked up her coat, which Jeffery helped her put on. "Thanks Blair, but I have something I really must take care of."

Blair dropped the pad in her briefcase. "Well then, I'll see you back at the office if we don't run too late this afternoon." She offered a forced-looking smile and walked off.

The quiet in the office was a nice reprieve, but the afternoon dragged. Abby didn't dare leave a minute before five and prayed when she did, she wouldn't run into Blair before reaching her car. Blair had been her old moody self when Abby declined the lunch offer. She couldn't imagine an afternoon court battle would have improved Blair's mood unless the defense simply threw in the towel. Victory appeared to be the only thing that raised Blair's spirits, and even that was generally short-lived.

With Selena working the second shift indefinitely, Abby had many a solitary evening to look forward to. At times the quiet was too much, even for a homebody like her. *Maybe I should get a dog…or, a baby.* She smiled.

* * *

The lights were on in Blair's office when Abby arrived a few minutes before eight the following morning, so she poked her head in. "I didn't expect to see you here."

Blair looked up from the papers. "I had some notes I needed to get down for another case, and I think better in the solitude here than at home."

"I'll leave you to it then."

"No, I'm done." She scooped the pages into a file. "There's coffee. It's only about a half an hour old. Help yourself."

"Thanks." Abby stepped over to her desk and dropped her coat before entering Blair's office with her coffee mug.

Her back was to Blair when she spoke again. "I didn't thank you for your help yesterday, so thank you."

When Abby turned around, Blair was wearing a pleasant expression. Not so much a smile, but she didn't look like she was ready to chew someone up and spit them out.

"Jeffery and I discussed your observations and both agree that you're very intuitive. The notes were helpful. Thanks again."

Abby approached her desk. "Is there anything pressing you need me to work on today?"

Blair handed her the file she'd closed. "Just these notes for this new case, if you don't mind." She said it as though Abby could decline her request and do something else.

"Sure. Anything else?"

"Nothing I can think of, so you can put your feet up and play cards on the computer if that's your thing. Just don't let anyone see you. I wouldn't want your peers to think I'm getting soft."

Abby again asked herself who is this person and what had she done with the real Blair? "I'm not much of a card player so you need not worry. I have plenty of things to work on." Abby returned to her desk to start her day.

Fifteen minutes later Blair rushed from her office pulling on her coat.

"Good luck in court," Abby said and thought she heard a thanks in reply as Blair turned into the hall, but she might have imagined it.

It was amazing how much she could accomplish when there wasn't someone barking every ten minutes. Abby had been making great strides when Blair came bursting into the offices trailed closely by Jeffery.

"Abby, my office, please," Blair called as she blew past Abby's desk.

With some apprehension, Abby grabbed the files from her desk and followed. Blair dropped her briefcase and coat into a chair and dropped herself behind her desk. Abby remained just inside the door and watched Blair exchange a smile with Jeffery. Maybe they'd exchanged something more on the way back to the office.

"We won!"

Abby took a few steps closer. "Congratulations! How?"

"I put on my star witness after lunch and watched the jury as she testified. I had them, and Jeffery could tell the lead defense attorney saw it too. He couldn't break my witness, so when the judge called the afternoon break, I went to him again with a deal. He knew it was a no-win case. He convinced his client, the dirt bag, that he should take the deal, so he pleaded out. Mr. White here has his first official criminal court case under his belt. A winning one at that."

Jeffery was wearing a permanent smile.

"Again, congratulations to you both." Blair leaned back in her chair. Abby stepped over to the desk and placed down the files she'd been clutching to her chest. "These are finished, and I only have the Simon file left."

"Excellent! We're going to Marty's down the block for dinner and drinks. I want you to join us since you were so helpful on this case."

"I can't…"

"I won't take no for an answer this time. Call your boyfriend and tell him you have plans."

Abby wondered if Blair would change her mind if she knew the "boyfriend" was a woman. She felt the flush start in her neck.

"Now, shoo. I need to make some calls." Blair waved them away. "We'll meet outside the office door in half an hour, and close that door if you will."

Jeffery motioned her through the door, closing it behind him. "The rumors have her painted as pretty wicked, but I haven't seen that yet."

Abby shrugged. *Patience my boy, sooner or later you will.*

"I've got to run down to my cubicle. I'll be back," Jeffery said.

Abby wondered why she hadn't fought Blair harder on the dinner invitation. The last thing she wanted to do on a Friday night was to be exalted with war stories by the boss and her sidekick. Precisely thirty minutes later they were walking to the elevator.

"Either of you mind walking?" Blair asked as the elevator descended.

Jeffery shook his head.

"I can use the exercise," Abby responded.

Blair frowned at her. "You look perfectly fit to me. I should look so good."

Abby hoped not to faint from shock. Blair had actually paid her a compliment in front of a nice-looking guy. But the more she thought about it, the more she suspected it was Blair trying to impress Jeffery with her kinder, softer side.

Blair and Jeffery walked at such a brisk pace that Abby had to take long strides to keep up. In the restaurant, Blair spoke briefly with the hostess before leading them to a spot at the bar.

"I'll have my usual, Carl, and these two are on my tab."

Abby ordered a white wine and Jeffery requested a dark ale. Picking up the short drink glass Carl set before Blair, she raised it toward them.

"If there were more competent people like the two of you, the world would be in much better shape."

They drank to Blair's toast. Abby nursed her wine, not wanting to take a cab home and return tomorrow to pick up her car, even though she'd done it before. Her mind flashed back to her first date with Selena. Selena had driven nearly three hundred miles and they'd met at the theater for a show and then gone out for a late dinner. Abby came to realize the show had been Selena's attempt at trying to impress her. At dinner, Selena had plied her with too much wine and cast some kind of spell over her, because Abby had let Selena take her back to her hotel room for lovemaking like Abby had never experienced before.

"Abby… Please promise you will teach me this relaxation thing you do."

"Pardon me?"

"You were trance-like and smiling. I assume in your Zen place."

Thinking of Selena did put a smile on her face.

"We're having another drink. You need to catch up." She motioned for Carl and ordered a drink for Jeffery and herself. A minute later, Jeffery's phone rang.

"Excuse me, ladies." Stepping toward the back corner, he covered his ear to listen. When he returned, he didn't take his seat at the bar. He did take a quick drink of his fresh beer. "Ladies, I'm sorry but I'm going to have to pass on dinner." He pulled on his coat and looked at Blair. "I look forward to my next opportunity to work with you. Thanks for the drinks." He gave Abby an apologetic smile and left.

Blair moved over to Jeffery's seat seconds before the hostess appeared.

"Your table is ready, Ms. Stanton. Please follow me."

Abby kicked herself as they crossed the restaurant. *Why did I let her talk me into this? What on earth are we going to talk about? I might as well be having dinner with my mother.* Their waiter arrived promptly after they were seated.

"We're going to start with the escargot. Ms. Collins will have another glass of wine and I'll have another Glenlivet. Would you ask Carl to go easy on the water and heavy on the rocks? Thank you, George." When he'd gone, she said, "You'll love Philippe's escargot."

"Escargot?"

Blair looked puzzled. "Escargot." Abby shrugged. "Little snails."

Abby wrinkled her nose. "You ordered snails?" Although she knew what escargot was, she detested the delicacy for palates of the rich.

"He prepares them in a buttery cream sauce. They melt in your mouth. You'll like them."

George soon returned with their drinks and the appetizer. Abby ate one to appease Blair. They were far too rich, but admittedly better tasting than any she'd tried before. Blair devoured them like she hadn't eaten for days. When George returned again, Blair sent her compliments to Philippe and ordered filet mignon. Abby ordered the largest salad on the menu and asked George to surprise her with a dressing that had a lot of garlic.

Blair touched his arm before he got away. "George, cancel the filet. I'll have the same as Ms. Collins." When he left, she asked, "A lot of garlic?"

"To keep the vampires away." She put the wineglass to her lips to hide a smile. Not that she considered Blair Stanton some kind of blood sucker. *Well...*

They talked mostly about food and restaurants while they ate. Abby continued to nurse her glass of wine after dinner while Blair swirled the small amount of amber liquid in her glass before polishing it off.

She crossed her arms on the table and leaned over them. "Abby?"

"Yes."

"No, I mean why Abby and not Abigail?"

"My *mother* calls me Abigail."

"You two don't get along?"

"To say we've had our differences would be an understatement."

"Sorry I brought it up."

Abby waved. "Don't worry about it. We hardly talk anymore and I rarely think of her."

Blair nodded. "So, Ms. Abigail Collins, as in the wealthy Collins family that dates back to the mid-eighteen hundreds and practically founded our fair city. Daughter of socialite Millie and deceased billionaire father Richard." She gave a sly smile. "I like to know who's working in my office."

Heat rose in Abby, and it wasn't the kind that Selena stirred. But she was not about to appear shaken or belittled by Blair's show of authority. She tipped her head, locked her eyes on Blair's and asked in an icy tone, "Is there a question here, Counselor?"

Blair sat back and steepled her fingers, as she so often did when she was thinking. "Why an assistant, a glorified secretary? You have all that money and power, and you could do anything or nothing at all. And yet, you're a...a secretary."

"I work for the good guys. You put the bad ones away." The choices Abby had made were none of Blair Stanton's business.

"That's very noble. Like your hospital thing."

"I don't consider it nobility. I work on the right side of the law, and as far as the 'hospital' thing," she said, making air quotes, "that's pure selfishness on my part." Blair's brows furrowed. "I get more out of it than the kids. I love being around children. Giving my time to them is one of the best things I've got going in my life."

"Really...what are the others?" Blair cocked her head.

There weren't enough horses to drag any more personal information out of Abby. She set her wineglass aside and placed her napkin on the table. "I really have to be going, Blair." She picked up her purse. "Thank you for dinner and drinks."

"It's the least I can do for all your help. Won't you stay? It's Friday night, and I must admit I enjoy talking with you. I'll make sure you get home safely." She smiled. "You know, safe from the vampires."

"I can't. I really do need to get home."

"Right." She nodded ever so slowly. "Don't want to keep the little man waiting."

Abby kept her expression impassive as she stood. "See you on Monday."

"Yes, yes you will. Have a nice weekend, Abby."

Abby saw the loft lights on and Selena's little red Mustang in the parking garage. She was sure Selena had said she was off tomorrow night. She walked in and found her seated at the counter with a half empty tequila bottle. There were candles burning around the kitchen and living room and two place settings on the dining table.

She raised the bottle to her lips and took a drink. "Well, well, look what the cat dragged in."

Abby set her purse on the counter and laid her coat over a stool. "What are you doing home tonight? You didn't quit your job, did you?"

She slammed the bottle down on the counter. "No." Her eyes were slits. "I called in sick 'cause I wanted to enjoy you again. It was so good the other night."

Abby sighed. She had been so looking forward to soaking in the tub and going to bed. Selena grabbed her arm when she walked past.

"Where you goin'?"

"To bed, Selena, I'm tired."

She kept a firm grip on Abby's arm. "Where have you been?" She squinted past Abby. "It's almost nine o'clock."

Abby tried freeing her arm, but Selena wouldn't let go. "I had a dinner meeting with my boss and the other attorney assisting her."

"Really?" she snorted. "Dinner with the bitch boss. You don't say."

Abby managed to pull her arm free. "I'm tired," she repeated. "I'm not going to do this. I'm going to bed."

Abby knew better than to tangle with Selena when she was drunk. And she was very drunk. Selena could cut like a sword with her words. Abby had been down that road a few times before she learned there was no winning. If she simply allowed Selena the verbal slaps, she would lose steam and apologize once she sobered up.

Abby skipped the bath and went right to bed with a book. Sleep found her quickly and she couldn't have guessed at what time Selena stumbled in. She was dead to the world when Abby got up at seven thirty. With any luck Selena would be in bed hours longer, depending on how much more tequila she drank. The bottle sat open on the counter. The smell turned her stomach as she capped it and put it away.

Abby loved the quiet of the loft in the mornings. It was her sanctuary. She settled in the living room with her coffee to watch the sun come up and wondered if Selena planned to work tonight to make up for her sick day off. She'd find out soon enough. And, for failing to read Selena's mind yesterday and knowing to come straight home from work, she would likely be subjected to sulking or a tantrum. She inhaled the coffee's hypnotic aroma and gazed at the sun on the horizon. Life really should be this simple and enjoyable.

By nine o'clock, she was showered and dressed. She took yesterday's mail up to the office above the bedroom. A little after ten, she heard Selena downstairs in the bathroom. She planned to stay put. If Selena wanted to have a fit or yell, she was going to have to come and find her. It wasn't long before she came shuffling into the room with a cup of coffee and the pot. She refilled Abby's cup, set the pot on the coffee table and flopped on the couch. Last night's shirt and socks looked as rumpled as she did. Selena appeared to be paying for last night's drinking, so justice prevailed. Abby smiled inside as she spun the desk chair all the way around and raised the cup to her lips.

"Man, I feel like crap. I don't know why I do this to myself." Selena gulped down some coffee. Abby remained silent, as she didn't want to appear too sympathetic. "Sorry I was nasty with you last night, Abs. That damn tequila makes me mean sometimes."

Only sometimes huh? Abby gave a nod for the apology, as pathetic as it was.

"Can I make it up to you?"

"How will you make it up to me?"

"Let me take you out."

"Out where?"

"Dinner, drinks and dancing."

"Dancing?"

"Is there an echo in here?" Selena shook her head. "Yeah, dancing. We haven't been out partying in a long time."

"Where exactly do you have in mind?"

She shrugged. "I don't know. The city's full of great clubs."

Tread lightly, Abby cautioned herself. "Selena, you know I don't like going out to bars here in the city."

She ran her fingers through her wild dark mane. "Ah, come on. When are you going to quit being ashamed of who you are—of what you are?"

As hard as Selena tried to push Abby's buttons, she wasn't biting. "I am not ashamed of anything. I simply choose to keep my personal life private."

She rolled her eyes. "That's right. I forget."

Abby hadn't ever gone to bars in the city, until Selena came along. She preferred not to be seen in those places. She wasn't trying to hide. Was she? She'd let Selena talk her into it one night not long after they started living together. Unfortunately a clerk at the courthouse saw her. "I assume this knockout is your girlfriend," the woman had commented. Selena had been putting some serious "dirty" into dirty dancing and Abby had feared ever since what the woman may have shared around the courthouse. Abby preferred to keep her work life and private life separate. She didn't feel it necessary to "come out" in her workplace. She assumed the clerk had talked about her being at the lesbian bar and guessed more than a few around the courthouse suspected that she was a lesbian. When she was in college her father had pleaded with her to refrain from displaying her sexuality around town. Out of respect for him and her own personal desire for privacy, she'd kept a low profile.

Abby loved romantic date nights, but it would take some convincing to get Selena on board with going out of the city. She vacated her chair and faced Selena on the couch. When she wouldn't look at her, Abby laid her arm across the back of the couch and played with strands of Selena's hair.

"Let's go to Center City this evening. We can have dinner, then go out to that bar we've been to before." She continued to ignore her, so Abby moved her fingers under Selena's hair and rubbed the back of her neck. Her head dropped back and she closed her eyes. "We can get a hotel room." Abby put her lips close to Selena's ear. "And party into the wee hours of the morning if you want."

Abby's hand slipped under Selena's shirt and caressed her breast. Selena went slack, and Abby took the cup from her hand, placing it on the table before straddling her lap. Very slowly she unbuttoned Selena's shirt. Selena's hands moved to Abby's hips as she thrust herself toward Abby's center. Abby cupped her breasts, massaging her nipples. She lightly touched her tongue to the corner of Selena's mouth and waited for Selena's invitation. Abby might not be a "Latin Lover," but she'd become quite the seductress since meeting Selena. She moved her lips from Selena's mouth to her neck and nipped the tender skin. Selena responded by pulling Abby harder against her.

Abby whispered, "Do you still feel bad?" She allowed her breath to gently caress Selena's ear.

Selena moved her hands under Abby's sweater and fumbled for the clasp of her bra. "Not bad enough to make you stop."

With her bra unhooked, Abby lifted it and her sweater up. Selena tugged her forward to suck a fully erect nipple. Abby felt her wetness against Selena.

Selena dragged her lips from one nipple to the other and then pulled back. "I guess we better take this to the bedroom."

Abby placed her hand in the center of Selena's chest. "You're not going anywhere." She stood, worked off her shoes and jeans and settled back in Selena's lap. The heat radiating from between Selena's legs made Abby grow wetter still.

Selena slipped her fingers inside Abby's panties. "You want me to touch you…" She growled in a raspy tone when she touched Abby's clit. "Here…" When Abby gasped, Selena pulled her within an inch of her lips. "Come for me, *mi caliente amante*," she purred.

Selena entered Abby and all the air rushed from her lungs. She gripped Selena's shoulders and pressed her knees into the couch cushions. Selena had a way of taking Abby's breath away.

They left for Center City around four o'clock and checked into the quaint little hotel on the outskirts of town just after six. Selena immediately raided the mini bar, and after finishing dinner, they headed out to the bar. Abby knew Selena was well on her way to making it two drunken nights in a row, but at least tonight she had no reason to be mad at Abby. Lucking into one of the tables between the bar and dance floor, Selena wasted no time going for drinks. Abby loved dancing with Selena, who happened to be an amazing dancer with enough rhythm for both of them. She wouldn't be surprised if Selena drank herself to the point of passing out. With luck Selena would feel so bad on the drive home tomorrow that she wouldn't push Abby to go out again for quite some time.

CHAPTER THREE

Abby looked forward to the start of the new week and it had nothing to do with going to work. She was more eager than usual to visit the hospital Tuesday evening to read to her kids. She called them "her kids" because when she read, they were a captive audience…her captive audience. And it seemed as though she'd cast a spell over them. She hoped with her own kids she'd possess the same hypnotic power. She was definitely moving ahead with her plans to get pregnant in the New Year, whether Selena was on board or not. She'd come around. Abby felt it in her heart.

Ten minutes into her reading Tuesday evening, Abby felt something stir in the room. When she glanced to the back, she saw the same young woman from last week, the doctor she presumed, looking at her. She gave Abby a smile, and for a second Abby lost all sense of time. To avoid further distraction, she looked only at the kids as she read the remaining pages in the book. Once finished, she gathered her things and only then noticed the lady doctor sitting in one of the kid's chairs at the back of the room.

She stood and smiled when Abby approached. "Hi, Ms. Collins?"

Abby met the deepest blue eyes she'd ever seen that instantly warmed her like rays of sunshine on a winter day. She was slightly taller than Abby was in her heels. Inexplicably tongue-tied, Abby merely nodded.

"Dr. Christiano." She extended her hand.

Abby placed her hand in the gentle grasp. "Uh…it's Abby."

Her smile was welcoming as she held on to Abby's hand. "Okay, Ms. Abby."

"No…uh…it's Abby Collins."

She continued to smile. "Okay then, Abby Collins."

Clearing her throat Abby attempted to collect herself. "I'm sorry, reading children's books for thirty minutes sometimes jumbles my brain. Please, call me Abby." She became fixated on the nametag attached just above the breast pocket of her coat. "Nice to meet you, Dr. Sam." Abby raised her eyes and met the doctor's continued smile. "I was…uh…just reading your tag." She gestured to her own chest.

"Yes, you were."

Abby felt heat rising in her face. She'd been caught, her gaze lingering perhaps a bit too long, in the area of Dr. Sam's nametag. *How embarrassing to be busted staring at a woman's chest.*

"Some of the nurses and parents tell me you have a way with the kids," Dr. Sam said.

"I love kids. They're wonderful little beings."

Dr. Sam nodded. "Yes, they are." She looked to where the few remaining kids were waiting to be taken to their rooms. Returning her attention to Abby she asked, "Would you have time for a cup of coffee?"

"I'm sorry. I can't. I have somewhere I have to be." Selena wasn't working tonight so if Abby made any excuse not to rush home to her, she'd be upset. Selena didn't like Abby "wasting" her time at the hospital because it sometimes conflicted with "her" time. "Perhaps next Tuesday," Abby offered. "If you're here and available." Dr. Sam still smiled a hundred-watt smile.

"Terrific. Then I'll talk to you next week."

Abby gave the young doctor a smile. "Next week."

She stepped aside and Abby left, and all she could think about on the drive home was the young, pretty doctor with the mesmerizing eyes. She didn't necessarily ping Abby's gaydar, but there was something intriguing about Dr. Sam.

Sam stepped out into the hall and watched as Abby Collins walked to the elevator. The thought of having a coffee date with Ms. Collins in a week kept a perpetual smile on her face the remainder of her shift. Granted, the lovely Ms. Collins appeared straight as Sam's shifts were long, it didn't stop Sam from thinking what a wonderful friend she would make. Sam wasn't an easy person to know. She tended to keep all aspects of her life to herself. She lived each day in harmony with her world, on her terms. Yet for some reason she couldn't explain, she wanted to get to know the story teller.

* * *

With the weekend came gratitude. Selena was only off on Sunday, meaning Abby had the loft to herself until four in the afternoon on Saturday. She cleaned, did laundry, picked up the dry cleaning and took a much-deserved soak in the tub. She expected Selena home any minute when the phone rang a little after four o'clock.

"Sorry, babe, but I have to work over a while."

"What time do you think you might be home?"

"I have no idea." She exhaled a deep sigh. "They can't seem to find anyone competent to work second shift."

Abby stood in front of the freezer surveying her options. "If you call me when you leave work, I'll have dinner ready when you get here."

"You're a doll, but I don't know how late it's going to be. Don't wait on me. I'll either get something here or on the way home."

"Are you sure? I'll wait."

"Don't wait. I'm sure I'm going to be stuck here until at least seven or eight."

"Well, don't get stressed out. I won't wait dinner, but I'll be waiting for you."

"Hmm…Now I'll be thinking about that all evening."

Just past seven thirty, after eating a frozen dinner and cleaning up the kitchen, she moved to the couch with a book and glass of wine, waiting for Selena to get home. Then it became eight thirty, and nine thirty, and by ten o'clock Abby was worried. She tried Selena's cell, which went straight to voice mail. After leaving a message she poured another glass of wine and returned to her book. She didn't realize she'd drifted off until she became aware of Selena rubbing her hand across her hip from her position beside Abby on the couch.

"Come on baby, let's go to bed."

She smelled of beer, but Abby couldn't be upset by the fact that Selena obviously had had a long, rough shift at the hotel. She led Abby to the bedroom before disappearing into the adjoining bathroom. Abby stripped off her clothes and slid naked between the sheets.

When Selena returned a few minutes later and crawled in beside her, she ran her hand up Selena's stomach to her breast. Abby teased a nipple hard and then dipped her head under the sheet and circled it with her tongue. Selena didn't respond. Abby slipped her hand down to Selena's mound of curls and still couldn't elicit even a moan. She lifted her head to see Selena's eyes closed.

"Selena?" She had never failed to respond to Abby's touch before. She was Latina and lived for orgasms. "What's wrong?"

She pulled Abby against her side. "I'm so beat. I just need to sleep. Okay?" Abby pressed a gentle kiss to her lips, snuggling in beside her.

Selena was sleeping soundly when Abby awoke, so she climbed carefully from the bed and took her coffee upstairs to the office to get online and do some research. Half an hour later, she heard Selena stirring in the kitchen, appearing moments later with the coffeepot. Filling up Abby's cup, Selena set the pot on a magazine and placed a kiss on the top of her head.

"Sorry about last night. I was just so beat."

Abby patted Selena's hand where it rested on her shoulder. "It's okay to be too tired."

Selena leaned over her shoulder. "What are you reading?" She slid her hand inside the top of Abby's robe and Abby leaned her head back against her.

"Mmm…about making babies."

Selena kissed her neck then placed her lips next to Abby's ear. "We could try that now." As Selena lowered her hand she parted Abby's robe, tracing her fingers inside Abby's thigh.

"Hmm…" Abby's mind was drifting along with Selena's soft touches.

"Try and make a baby."

Selena turned the chair around and knelt between Abby's knees. Pulling Abby to the edge of the chair, she parted her robe completely. When Selena took a nipple between her lips Abby arched against her. Selena trailed her lips and tongue down Abby's stomach. Abby moaned, clenching her legs against Selena's sides.

Her lips were dangerously close to Abby's center. "I don't think it will work, but do try…please." Abby slipped her fingers into Selena's hair and guided her lips to her throbbing flesh.

Selena slid two fingers inside her with ease. "Is this what you want, baby?"

Abby moved with the rhythm of Selena's thrusts. "Yes," she gasped.

She masterfully took Abby over the edge and when she went limp in the chair, Selena stood, kissing the top of Abby's head. "I'm going to jump in the shower."

She picked up her coffee cup and left, leaving Abby sitting like a thrown out empty beer bottle. Abby closed her eyes, savoring the aftereffects of the orgasm, but the sound of running water in the bathroom beside the office encouraged her to her feet. Gathering her robe around her, she went into the bathroom.

The sight of Selena's body behind the steamed glass door made Abby wet again. She dropped the robe and stepped into the shower behind Selena. With her hands holding Selena's slick hips, Abby pressed against her as the warm water sluiced off Selena's shoulders between them. Abby kissed the back of her neck and moved one hand to capture Selena's breast and the other to her mound of wet curls. Selena continued to soap her body as if Abby weren't there.

"Selena, what's wrong?" She laid her cheek against her shoulder.

Selena took both of her hands, raising one palm to her lips. "I'm sorry, doll. All this work stuff has me distracted. Can we do this after awhile?"

The rejection hurt deeply. If Abby had to make a guess, she figured her renewed interest in the "having a baby" subject had turned Selena off. And the sex in the office, well that was merely Selena's attempt at distracting Abby. Selena wanted things her way or not at all. She could be selfish. It was too hard to believe that she was under such an enormous amount of pressure at work that she could be distracted from having sex. Selena lived for sex. No, Abby felt it was the baby business that Selena was avoiding.

The cooling water stirred Abby from her daydream. Selena had left the bathroom, so she pulled on her robe and headed downstairs to the other bathroom. Selena was already seated at the counter with her coffee and the newspaper.

"What's the plan for the day?" Abby asked when she finally entered the kitchen. She poured herself more coffee and looked over Selena's shoulder.

"Nothing planned. Is there anything you want to do?" She seemed unusually intent on the newspaper.

"We can go out for dinner if you'd like."

"Sure babe, that's fine."

Something had Selena so distracted for her to allow Abby to plan her day off for her. Selena spent most of the day in front of the TV in the office. They spent a quiet, uneventful time out for dinner. Abby was eager to roll in the hay when they hit the bed at midnight, but Selena claimed to be tired, asking for a rain check. Maybe she was sick, or again, she wondered if it was the "baby" thing. Abby let it go.

CHAPTER FOUR

For the first time in months, Abby was happy to go to work. She'd been reassigned to work with Daniel, who was the attorney she'd accompanied on the trip when she had first met Selena. Abby had a special affection for the man, a kind and consummate professional, unlike so many of the egocentric male attorneys. Well, actually there was at least one female attorney that fit that description. Of course more than work, Abby was looking forward to going to the hospital Tuesday evening to see her kids and have coffee with Dr. Sam. She only needed to figure out how to best excuse her extended lateness to Selena without raising suspicion that she was doing something she shouldn't, which she wasn't.

Abby saw Dr. Sam for a moment while reading to the kids, but when she looked up again, she was gone, and after she'd finished, still no Dr. Sam. One of the nurses stopped her as she trudged to the door.

"Dr. Christiano asked if you could wait on her. I'm supposed to page her." Abby agreed and followed her to the nurses station.

A few minutes later the desk phone rang. "She's down in the ER and asked if you could meet her in the cafeteria. She said she won't be too long."

Once downstairs, Abby walked outside to call Selena.

"I'm going to be a little later than usual, hon, and I didn't want you to worry."

"Why is that?"

"One of the pediatric doctors wants to talk to me."

"About what?" Selena sounded irritated.

"I honestly don't know, Selena, but I'm going to find out. I have to go. I'll be home as soon as I can." She hung up and turned the phone off before reentering the building.

Scanning the cafeteria and seeing no Dr. Sam, she found a seat and waited. Twenty minutes later Dr. Sam came rushing in. She acknowledged Abby with a glance and a nod, and went straight to the coffee line. She looked completely undone as she set the cups down and dropped into the chair across the table.

"I am so sorry to keep you waiting." Abby couldn't help but smile. "I'm sure you have more important things to do than wait in our drab cafeteria." She gave a brief look around and then settled her gaze on Abby. Her amazing blue eyes seemed to light up the room.

"It's really okay. I understand doctors are busy people." She sat there, only smiling back at Abby. "So…"

Dr. Sam shook her head. "I get so many things going in my head. I sometimes don't know if I'm coming or going, and I've already kept you waiting long enough."

Abby waited again.

"Yes, so…" She took a quick drink of coffee. "I've heard so many nurses and parents singing your praise that I wanted to see if I could solicit your assistance with a particular young patient of mine." She took another drink of her coffee.

"You've certainly piqued my curiosity."

She went on to explain about her nine-year-old patient, Phillip, who was in the final stage of brain cancer. Abby's heart hurt for any child that had to suffer, but to die so young was simply unimaginable. Dr. Sam described how active and vibrant he'd been before getting sick, and what an avid reader he was.

"The cancer has begun to affect his vision, so he isn't able to read his books. And frankly, at this stage, there is little else he has the capacity to enjoy." Her eyes sparkled with moisture. "I know this is asking a lot of a volunteer, but I've seen how the kids respond to you, and…Well, I want to ask if there's any way you might consider spending some time reading to my little guy. He's too sick to attend your group readings, and I really think it would lift his spirits."

"I, I don't know…" Abby struggled not to cry.

"I know…It's a lot to ask, so please just think about it. If you can't, I understand. I just thought…I just wanted…you know, to give him something." She shrugged. "I need to get upstairs. They kept me down here in the ER too long already." She stood. "I do hope you'll consider my request. I can compensate you for your time."

Abby stood with her. "I will consider it, but please don't feel obligated to compensate me. That would take some of the pleasure out of it for me."

She dug deep in her coat pocket. "We can discuss it." She placed a card in Abby's hand, brushing her fingertips over Abby's. "Call me."

Abby wasn't sure she could speak, so she merely nodded and watched Dr. Sam as she strode away.

She called Selena again as she pulled out of the parking lot, deciding to pick up something for dinner on the way home in lieu of cooking. Selena grilled her about what the big crisis was that needed her attention. She became very emotional retelling the little boy's story while Selena seemed completely indifferent to the matter. Abby was in a quandary about more than reading to a very sick little boy.

* * *

The following day at work Abby couldn't get Dr. Sam's pleading eyes out of her mind, nor the young boy's tragic story. She could be one of a few people in this boy's life to give him joy in his final days. What was there to consider? But she knew that answer—an emotional bond that might rip her heart out.

Life was full of them. She'd had more than her share. Still, her maternal longing was tugging her toward this heartbreaking situation. That and a particularly persuasive doctor.

On her lunch break, she called the number on the card and got Dr. Sam's service. She left her office number for a return call.

Hours later the phone rang. "Daniel Black's office."

"Abby Collins, please."

"This is Abby, how can I help you?"

"Hi, Abby Collins! It's Dr. Chris—" she paused. "Dr. Sam from the hospital." Her voice bubbled through the phone and into Abby. "I apologize for taking so long to call you back."

"An apology is not necessary. You're a doctor, and quite busy I would imagine."

"Yes, well, some days are worse than others. So I hope you're calling to make my day?"

The question threw Abby. "Excuse me?"

"My request for your time. Are you calling to make me a happy woman?"

"If you're...uh..." Abby tried again. "If you're referring to my reading to your young patient, then yes, that's why I'm calling."

"Thank you! Thank you! I'll never be able to repay your kindness and generosity, but I'll give it my best shot."

"As I said before, I don't expect compensation. I volunteer my time because it makes me feel good to do so. When would you like me to stop by?"

"You're the one giving your time. You tell me and we'll do our best to work within your schedule."

"I can stop by tomorrow after work around six." She heard beeping sounds in the background.

"Perfect. Just ask at the nurses station on the pediatric floor and they'll find me."

"Then I will see you tomorrow evening."

"Abby Collins, you're an angel for doing this."

"Well then," she smiled inside, "I'll expect to pick up my wings tomorrow evening."

The chuckle that erupted from Dr. Sam warmed Abby's heart. "Compassionate with a sense of humor. I like that."

"I'll see you tomorrow."

The amazing feeling of giving this special boy something in his final weeks faded fast as Abby thought of Selena, and how upset she was going to be for taking more of "her time." She had a tough sell in store for her this evening, but if she went about it just right, Selena would be pushing her out the door.

"Hell, I might as well go back on second shift for no more time than we'll be spending together. Why is this kid more special to you than I am?"

Abby took Selena's face in her hands. "I love you so very much." She swept Selena's hair behind her ears. "I can't help this clock that's ticking inside me. I really need to be with kids," Abby's tone begged.

Selena raised her hands. "Fine, fine, I'm not ready to go there." She kissed Abby's forehead. "You volunteer all the time you need. They're in a bad way for someone on second shift anyway. I might as well be as unselfish as you, doll, and volunteer." She went to the fridge for a beer. "You want wine or something to drink?"

Abby was already thinking about spending more time with another child.

* * *

She kissed Selena before leaving for work. "I'll call you when I'm headed home from the hospital so we can make dinner plans."

Selena nodded. "See you tonight."

Daniel had a busy day for Abby. Once it had sped by, she found herself rushing to bid him a good evening at five o'clock. She felt anxious and apprehensive at the same time as she approached the nurses station. The nurse sent out the page and within a few minutes, Dr. Sam strolled down the hall.

"Abby Collins, hello." She held a patient chart.

"Dr. Sam."

Dr. Sam spoke to the nurse, placed the chart into the nurse's hand and picked up another one.

With the warmest of expressions, Dr. Sam asked, "Are you still sure you want to do this? It's not too late to back out and I would certainly understand if you did." She clutched the chart to her chest.

"I've given it a lot of thought. I think I can handle it and I definitely want to try." She tipped her head. "My inner voice tells me this is something I'm meant to do."

Dr. Sam gave Abby the biggest smile. "Good, because I already kind of spilled the beans and told him that I had someone very special who wants to meet him." She waved to their right and Abby fell in step with her. "He looks fragile enough to break, but I can assure you he has more spirit and fight than anyone I've ever met in my life." She stopped outside a door near the end of the hall. "Ready?"

Abby inhaled a breath. "As I'll ever be, I suppose."

Dr. Sam held the door open. The breath Abby had taken lodged in her chest as her eyes settled on the tiny form in the bed with more machines attached via cables and tubes than Abby had ever seen.

Dr. Sam moved to the bedside. "Phillip, it's Dr. Sam." When she put her fingers to his wrist, his smile lit up the room. "How are you feeling today? Better or worse than yesterday?"

"The same, I guess." His voice matched his tiny body.

She made a note on the chart. "Well, your heart is as strong as a racehorse."

"Who else is here?"

"What makes you think I'm not alone?"

"'Cause you're not." He smiled again.

"Okay, smart guy. I can't get anything past you, can I?" He shook his head and she motioned Abby over to the bed. "Phillip, this is Ms. Collins, the lady that I told you about."

Abby couldn't imagine he could smile any bigger, but he did.

"The story lady!" He reached his hand in their direction, and Dr. Sam stepped back so Abby could move closer.

Her hand engulfed his. "It's very nice to meet you, Phillip. My friends call me Abby." It amazed her how tightly his little fingers gripped her hand.

"What story do you have, Abby?"

She set her bag on the end of the bed. "I have a number of stories, but I'm wondering if you have a favorite."

"I do!" He felt around the bedside table so Abby reached for the book, but Dr. Sam placed her hand on Abby's arm and nodded a "no." When his fingers finally came to rest on the book, he picked it up and held it out to Abby. "This is my new favorite." The book was titled *New Kids on the Rock*. "It's about Josh and Madison. They get to travel all over the world helping other kids. Can we read it?"

His excitement was infectious. "We sure can. I haven't read this one, but I understand it's really good."

"It is! I started to read it a while ago, but...but, I..."

"Phillip's eyesight isn't as good as it used to be, so he needs a little help with his reading."

"Well, I'm excited to read a new book. Where shall we start?"

"Can we start at the beginning again?"

"You betcha! May I sit with you?"

He patted the bed beside his slight body. As she sat, Abby watched his vacant stare settle on her. She glanced up once to see that Dr. Sam had left. About twenty minutes later she noticed his eyes begin to droop and thought maybe she should stop. Dr. Sam returned within a few minutes.

"I think that's enough for this evening you two." She stood very near Abby at the bedside.

"Ah, really?"

"Really?" Abby seconded the question.

She nodded to Abby. "Sorry kiddo, but you need to rest."

Abby slipped in a bookmark and returned the book to the table. He reached out for her arm. "When are you coming back, Abby?"

"Ms. Collins has a job, and I'm sure she is very busy, Phillip."

Abby touched his fingers on her arm. "But, I will come back as soon as I can. I promise."

Fatigued as he was, he managed another smile as big and bright as before.

"It was very nice to meet you, Phillip. I look forward to seeing you again."

He yawned. "Me too." His eyelids drifted closed almost immediately.

Abby stopped a moment outside the door and swiped at her eyes. Dr. Sam dug in her coat pocket and came up with a pack of tissues. They were nearly back to the nurses station before she felt she could speak without breaking into tears.

"How can life be so unfair?"

Dr. Sam shook her head. "I ask myself the same question all the time, and I don't have an answer."

"And he knows he won't be here this time next year?" Dr. Sam nodded. "Of all the people, how does a child accept something like this?"

"Another answer I don't have."

They continued past the elevators to the end of the hall and a window that overlooked the parking lot. Dr. Sam leaned back on the sill and stared down the long corridor.

"He's never gotten upset or angry about any of it. Not the tests, the treatments, the drugs or any loss of function. He was very sad at first, but that's it. It's like he's accepted that his time would be limited, and he's making the best of every minute and breath he has left." Abby could barely stand the sorrow in her voice. "Not just for himself, but everyone around him."

Her words brought Abby more tears, and although Dr. Sam remained collected, Abby could see the hurt and pain in her eyes. Abby would be a basket case, and she wondered how a person dealt with something like this all the time. *She's a doctor… It's what they do. She probably cries herself to sleep at night or has a boyfriend with big strong arms to hold her.* Dr. Sam directed her gaze back to Abby as if reading her mind.

"You don't have to come back. I would certainly understand."

"You think I'm too emotionally weak to do this?" She didn't answer Abby, merely keeping her cool blue gaze on her. "For your information, I'm completely capable of handling this." Abby crossed her arms and breathed a deep breath. "Children are the future, and just because this young boy doesn't have one, doesn't make him any less deserving of the joys every child should have. I made a promise to Phillip, which I fully intend to keep." Her voice rose as she became more impassioned. "I will be back!" She gave a curt nod, but before she could step away, Dr. Sam caught her arm.

"Ms. Collins."

"Abby," she snapped and pulled her arm free.

"Abby," she said contritely. "Most people can't do these kinds of things. They *are* emotionally too weak, and I didn't mean to imply that you are. Quite to the contrary. I only wanted to give you an out if you wanted it. I'm sorry. Please accept my apology." Her baby blues pleaded, her passion burning fierce in them. "Call before you come by to make sure there aren't any conflicts. The nurses station will know."

"Of course."

She turned on her heel and headed for the elevator. She could feel Dr. Sam's eyes on her as she walked and wondered what they were saying. While she crossed the parking lot, she called the house expecting to hear Selena's voice, but she got voice mail instead. She said she was leaving the hospital and picking up dinner because she didn't feel like fixing anything. Dropping her phone and purse onto the passenger's seat, she sat crying for fifteen minutes. She saw Phillip's fragile, smiling face and asked repeatedly how any "God" could take such a young, innocent life? But she knew the answer. He only takes the best. Phillip would be one of the special angels.

Sam couldn't help but notice how purposefully Abby walked to the elevator. She'd known the first time she laid eyes on Abby Collins that she was a very spirited and compassionate woman. In the last two days, she'd also come to realize she was funny, driven and determined, as she'd just witnessed, her green eyes glowing when she'd gotten fired up. The bare ring finger didn't get by Sam's notice either. Turning around, she set the chart on the windowsill to make a few more notes. As she turned to go, she caught sight of the strong, self assured, Ms. Collins crossing the parking lot. Her car didn't leave right away so Sam made the decision to peek in on Phillip, return his chart, and then check back on Ms. Collins. She was already off duty and had been for hours. Sam only stayed around to introduce Ms. Collins to Phillip. She checked the parking space for the black Lexus enroute to her own car and felt disappointed to see it gone. As she started her own car, she considered how it might feel to come to Ms. Abby Collins's rescue. But she banished the thought because a woman like Abby Collins wouldn't ever need rescuing.

CHAPTER FIVE

With Selena working second shift again Abby didn't have to worry about scheduling her evenings, but she missed her. Tuesday night while reading to the kids, she looked up from the book in her lap and saw Dr. Sam standing with the nurses at the back of the room. She smiled warmly, to which Abby responded in kind. She couldn't stop herself from glancing in that direction several more times, a bit disappointed to find her gone. When she stepped into the hall outside the room the voice down the hall surprised her.

"Ms. Collins." Abby turned to find Dr. Sam at the window where she'd left her the previous week. "Do you have a minute?"

Abby took a few calming breaths as she walked the hallway and stopped a few feet from Dr. Sam who looked guilty. Abby waited silently.

"I want to apologize again for underestimating you. Would you have a cup of coffee with me?"

She looked at her watch as if time were a consideration, then replied, "I have a few minutes. Coffee sounds good."

They journeyed to the cafeteria in silence and only after getting cups of coffee and taking a seat at a small table in the corner, did Dr. Sam speak.

"I sincerely hope you can accept my apology."

Abby put her cup to her mouth giving a nod.

Dr. Sam took a drink before placing her cup down on the table and turning it in her hands. "Phillip asks about you every time I see him. He wants to know when you're coming back. I tell him that you are a very busy lady, and you'll return when you can." She leaned closer. "I think he has a crush on you."

"Well I must admit this is a first for me. I'm not sure how to respond."

"I'm surprised. You're a very beautiful woman."

Abby's face heated. "I thought you said he lost his sight."

Sam sat back in the chair and stretched out her long legs. "He can't see you with his eyes, but some people don't need sight to see the beauty in someone."

Abby was sure her face was beet red. "Okay. I'm completely embarrassed."

"Nothing to be embarrassed about, but I'll stop." She cocked her head. "Care to satisfy my curiosity about something?"

"About what?" Abby held her breath. Could she possibly be so perceptive that she sees what most straight women never would?

Her eyes never left Abby's. "How did you get into the business of volunteering?"

Abby's breath slowly left her. "It's a long story, but in a nutshell, I started in the local Big Sisters program and things evolved in the last year."

"So are you a Collins as in the Collins Women's Health Center wing of the hospital?"

Abby tilted her head. "The what?" It wasn't as though Collins was an uncommon name in the city.

Dr. Sam waved her hand. "Never mind."

Abby would never lie to anyone, but avoiding a direct answer to a question that might shed a ray of light on her family had become second nature to her. It wasn't because of the money, but because of her family's narrow-minded, Neanderthal views of lesbians and the gay lifestyle. She steered the focus to Dr. Sam.

"What made you want to be a doctor?"

"Oh, you know, the same thing that inspires every young kid. I found the nest of baby bunnies whose momma had been hit in front of our house, and I took care of them until they were big enough to go out on their own."

"And they grew up to ravage the neighborhood gardens."

"I don't really know." She lowered her eyes to the table. "I always thought if I were a real doctor I could probably help fix people. In high school one of our classmates died of leukemia, so I decided then I wanted to try and impact people's lives in the most positive way possible."

It was so comfortable to sit and listen to her talk. Her eyes slowly closed for only a second.

"And I'm boring you so I'll shut up."

Abby's head shook. "No. You're not boring me."

"You closed your eyes. I put you to sleep."

Abby couldn't help but smile. "No, I...I just remembered something and I need to get going." She stood. "Thanks for the coffee."

Sam pushed up from her chair and stood much too close. "Thank you for graciously accepting my apology and for all that you do for our kids here."

Abby took a step away. "It's what I live for." She got several more steps away before stopping and turning around. Dr. Sam was rooted to the same spot watching her. "I'll be by Thursday after work to read to Phillip if you want to let him know...or not."

Sam rocked back on her heels and smiled. "I think I'll let him be surprised, but I will tell the nurses to expect you. Same time as last week?"

"Yes, around six."

* * *

Abby waited at the desk for the nurse to finish her phone call, which seemed to last an eternity.

"Hi, I'm Abby Collins, here to spend some time with Phillip."

The pleasant round face with rosy cheeks said, "The doctor told us to expect you."

"Is the doctor here this evening?" Abby asked.

"No. Dr. Sam's not on tonight."

Abby heard the TV before she entered the room, and when she was within a few feet of the bed, Phillip snapped off the TV and smiled.

"You came back!" His smile was infectious.

"I promised I would, and I always keep my promises." She couldn't guess how he knew she was there.

He reached for the book on the bedside table and Abby took her place next to him to begin reading where they left off. She knew to limit her time, so after twenty minutes she stopped. Phillip was clearly disappointed, but she assured him she would return again. When she stood to leave, there was a young woman in the doorway who attempted a smile, which failed to reach her eyes. As Abby approached the woman stepped out into the hall.

"Ms. Collins?"

"Yes, and you must be Phillip's mother." The resemblance was uncanny considering his slight and pallid state, and of course, unlike Phillip's brightly shining eyes, hers were dull with pain.

She nodded. "I'm Laura. I want to thank you for taking time for my son." Tears began to fill her empty eyes. "There aren't many people..." The tears flowed freely down her cheeks so Abby gently took her hand and led her away from Phillip's doorway. "It's rare for people to care..." She sucked in a breath. "To care for a stranger like..." She sucked in another breath, but couldn't contain the sob that escaped from deep within.

Abby's arm went automatically around her shoulder. "It's okay to cry. Mothers shouldn't have to let their children go," she said softly. Laura's body shook with her grief as her tears continued to flow. All Abby could do was hold her in an effort to provide some small comfort. She couldn't begin to imagine what it would feel like to lose a child, and she didn't ever want to find out. The longer she cried, the closer Abby's stoic support was to slipping away.

When she finally cried herself out, she looked at Abby. "You're an angel sent from heaven. Thank you."

"It's little comfort, but you're welcome." Abby struggled not to choke on her own emotion.

It was a few minutes before Laura had herself together enough to return to Phillip's room. Caught up in the intensity of the situation, Abby didn't notice Dr. Sam until she neared the elevator. She was leaning against the windowsill at the end of the hall, and she didn't notice Abby immediately. When she did, she pushed off the sill and motioned Abby toward her. Abby struggled to compose herself as she'd been ready to get into the elevator and let go of the tears fighting to get out. They met between the elevators and the end of the hall. This evening there was no white coat. Instead, Dr. Sam wore faded jeans and a sweatshirt. Looking so unlike her usual professional self, she appeared tom-boyish as she held a chart to her chest and leaned against the wall.

"The nurse said you weren't on this evening. I'm surprised to see you here."

She glanced at the chart in her hand. "I stopped in to check on Phillip." She returned her gaze to Abby's. "I see you met his mother."

Abby swallowed the heartache choking her. "She's a very brave woman." She looked down the hall in the direction of Phillip's room and attempted to blink away the tears that were dangerously close to spilling over.

"That's an understatement."

"Yes, I suppose it is." Abby returned to meet her gaze.

An awkward silence fell over them for several long moments. "Listen, I'm on my way out to have some dinner. Would you like to join me?"

Abby felt too emotionally raw. She didn't think she could sit down with Dr. Sam without bursting into tears. "I can't, but thank you for the invitation. Another time perhaps."

Sam smiled. "Perhaps. Do you have plans Saturday evening?"

"Excuse me?" Abby pretended not to hear.

"Saturday evening. Are you busy, because there's this fundraiser for the children's wing? I believe it's at one of the big hotels downtown. It's a hundred dollars a plate, but the cause is well worth it." Her expression looked pleading. "It benefits the kids."

She was tugging Abby's heartstrings. Selena had to work and it wasn't as if Dr. Sam was asking her on a date.

"That sounds like an excellent place to invest a hundred dollars. Where do I get my ticket?"

"Don't worry about it. I'll take care of it."

"You most certainly will not. I'm not making a contribution if you pay for mine.

Sam raised a hand. "Okay, I get it. I believe you can get them online or downstairs in the administrative offices during business hours."

"Where shall we meet?" Abby asked.

"The dinner is at seven and there's an open bar beforehand. How about if we meet around six thirty at the bar?"

"Six thirty it is. I'll get my ticket and see you on Saturday."

Sam left the hospital walking in the clouds. She had a date with the beautiful Abby Collins. Well, not a date-date, but certainly the opportunity to get dressed up and spend a few hours away from the antiseptic-filled air of the hospital socializing with her. Undoubtedly this was just another in a long list of good deeds for Abby, but she intended to make the most of the time they were going to spend together getting to know her better.

Sam didn't believe there was such a thing as love at first sight, but there was some kind of attraction to Abby that she couldn't deny. Heck, she wasn't sure she even knew what love was since the one time she'd thought she was in love turned into a nightmare. A simple crush like all the crushes she had as a teenager, right? Abby was a young and vibrant woman. What was not to like?

As she drove toward home she couldn't recall if her two-year-old suit was recently dry cleaned. She would have liked to buy something new to wear, but she was reminded of all her debt as she entered her cramped apartment. Her parents had helped as much as they could. Sometimes Sam felt like she would be paying for being a doctor the rest of her life. It was worth it though, right? She thought then of Phillip. Helpless little Phillip whom she couldn't fix. A tear rolled down her cheek, and then another as she dropped onto her tiny bed and cried into the pillow.

CHAPTER SIX

Looking the consummate professional in a dark suit, Abby found Sam at the bar when she arrived on Saturday night. It surprised her that there wasn't a line of guys waiting to buy her a drink. They exchanged hellos and ordered drinks. They'd barely started a conversation when a voice suddenly boomed behind Abby. It was unmistakable and she didn't have to turn around to know of the dread she was about to face.

"I thought that was you. What are you doing here?" Millie Collins's tone dripped with disgust and for Abby it amounted to fingernails on a chalkboard.

Abby cringed. Of all the possible times and places to run into her mother, it had to be here, tonight. She hadn't seen her mother since her father's funeral. Abby turned. "It's a fundraiser. I'm doing something good," she replied coldly.

"Well," she huffed. "I can't believe you have the nerve to show up here." Abby glared at her, but she continued. "And what's this?" She waved her hand toward Sam. "One of your conquests?"

Abby's anger surged and her cheeks burned hot. She grabbed her mother's arm and brusquely pulled her out of Sam's earshot. She stopped abruptly and turned her mother so they were face-to-face.

"You are the most self-centered uncaring person on earth, Mother."

She jerked her arm free. "Well, I can't believe you would show up to this with one of your...your..." She fumbled for words. "One of those," she motioned to Sam at the bar.

Abby shook her head. "First of all, Sam is a doctor at the hospital, not 'one of them.'" She curled her fingers in quotations. "Secondly, why can't you just get over the fact that your one and only daughter is a lesbian?"

"That's so disgusting. Why do you have to say that?"

"Because it's true, Mother." Abby wanted to take hold of her shoulders and shake her, but she waited, and when her mother said nothing, she decided to drop a bomb on her. "Daddy finally accepted it. Accepted me."

She looked as though Abby had slapped her. "Your father never accepted who you claim to be. He died embarrassed by his only daughter. God rest his soul."

Abby lowered her head, leveled her mother with a steely glare and with a sneer said, "Oh, but he did, Mother. He had a soul, unlike you." Her mother's head shook violently. "I saw him numerous times in the hospital before he died. We talked a lot."

Tears stung Abby's eyes at the six-month-old memory that seemed like yesterday. Her brother Randall had called her about their father and swore Abby to secrecy. He strongly suggested she bury the hatchet with the old man, as he so fondly referred to their father. "You'll live with regret the rest of your life if you don't," he had cautioned her. He didn't understand Abby's life choices, but he didn't want her to suffer in guilt either. So Abby was able to talk with her father without her mother finding out. They mostly reminisced, but during the second secret visit he confessed to her that he only turned his back on her because of her mother. How could he not love his baby girl? Abby had cried tears not only of sadness, but joy that he accepted her. He had held her for a long, comforting time. The regret they shared in the end was the time lost. Abby couldn't hold back the tears of the sacred memory. With anger she swiped at her cheeks.

"That's not true." Her mother quit shaking her head. "I don't believe you." She squared her shoulders as if they were going to battle over who was right or wrong.

"Believe what you want, Mother," she said matter-of-factly. "I honestly don't care." Her mother had a way of putting the spit in Abby's fire.

"Well," she huffed again.

When Abby leaned close enough to smell her unappealing perfume, she withdrew as if Abby was going to scratch her eyes out. "I'll tell you what, Mother. Let's negotiate the terms for this evening right now. You stay on one side of this monstrous ballroom and I promise to remain far away on the other." Abby felt like her cheeks were going to burst into flames.

She took a step back. "I can only hope God forgives you for your sins."

Abby took quick inventory and decided her only sin was to wish this woman wasn't her mother.

"And when you come to your senses, my dear daughter, I will be waiting to help you get your life in order."

Abby laughed. "Mother, you gave up the right to influence and shape my life a long time ago when you quit loving me… your own flesh and blood."

And with that final word, Abby turned on her heel and walked, head held high, back to where Sam waited patiently at the bar. Sam wore an expression of concern as Abby stepped beside her, took her martini glass and gulped unladylike.

"Are you okay?"

Abby took another drink. "I will be in a minute."

Sam picked at the napkin under her glass of wine. "It's just that you look like…"

When she hesitated, Abby applied a smile and turned to look into Sam's always comforting eyes. "Like?"

"Like…uh…" she stuttered. "You're flushed." She reached her fingers toward Abby's cheek but Abby caught her arm and stopped her. "Are you sure you're okay?"

Abby swallowed the last of the fiery cocktail. "Another of these…" she winked, "and I'll be perfectly fine." She motioned the bartender for another even as she felt the effects of the first one making its way to her brain.

"Who was that, if I may ask?"

Disdain spread through her. "My mother!" She tried to keep the anger from her voice. "Can you believe it?"

Sam gazed past her. "Actually, no." She looked back at Abby, tilting her head. "I pictured your mother as more of a—"

"A mother, instead of a snooty society bitch," Abby interjected. Taking the fresh drink, she looked at Sam over the rim of the glass. Between the alcohol and Sam's intense gaze, she began to feel warm all over.

"That sounds kind of harsh."

Abby placed the glass on the bar. "Yes, and sadly it's true."

Unsteadily, Sam took a sip of wine. "What did she mean about a conquest?"

Abby waved a hand dismissively. "Who knows?" Sam looked at her shrewdly. She glanced in her mother's direction to see her laughing on the arm of one of the hospital board members. "She's not in her right mind half of the time."

Abby's anger flared again at the thought of her mother outing her in front of Sam. There seemed to be some level of respect between her and Sam. She felt she might murder her mother if Sam figured out her sexuality and rejected her because of it. And, as if running into her mother was not enough, who should strut through the ballroom doors but Blair Stanton. She ducked beside Sam hoping not to be noticed. This night couldn't possibly get any worse, and God help her if it did.

She took a quick drink. "I can't do this." She set the glass on the bar. "I have to get out of here. They can feed the homeless from the plate I paid for."

As she stepped away, Sam placed a gentle hand on her arm. "They can feed them mine too." She leaned close. "Let's blow this stuffy affair."

Sam's spontaneous and carefree attitude brought a smile to Abby's face and she managed to slip past Blair, who was now standing at the bar. At the coat check, Sam's hand brushed over

Abby's shoulder as she helped her on with her coat. She wrapped her arms tightly against the night's cold as they made their way to the parking lot.

"Wow! For having spent a hundred bucks on a meal, I feel awfully hungry still."

Abby laughed, stumbled, and nearly fell, grabbing onto Sam's shoulder. They both stopped walking. Sam took Abby's hand from her shoulder and placed it on her arm.

"Here, hold on. I don't want to perform any first aid in the parking lot. I'm a doctor, you know, and I would be required to by my oath."

Abby slid her hand around her arm. "A very good one, I've no doubt."

Sam stopped behind Abby's car. "Are you hungry?"

"Actually yes. I agree that hundred-dollar-a-plate dinner was less than filling."

Sam chuckled. "I know a wonderful little place that serves a spaghetti and meatballs to die for." She put her thumb and a finger together against her lips and made a kissing sound. "It's almost as good as Momma's."

"Hmm…pasta and meat sounds fattening and sinfully delicious. Does it include toasted garlic bread?"

Sam nodded. "All you can eat."

"I'm in. Let's go."

When Abby dug her keys from her purse, Sam reached for them. "I don't think you should drive after two martinis." Abby automatically released the keys to her. "I'll drive and bring you back for your car."

Abby simply smiled and followed Sam to her car. She sat, trance-like on the drive, trying desperately to concentrate on what she was saying about tonight's fundraiser and how it would benefit the hospital.

There were a lot of, "Hello, Dr. Sam," greetings when they entered the quaint little Italian restaurant where they were promptly seated and served piping hot bread and a bottle of wine.

Sam touched her glass to Abby's. "To real food and not that fancy fluff they serve at stuffy fundraisers."

"Sounds like you've been to a few."

Sam sipped her wine and said, *"Excelente"* to the older gentleman who had poured it. She looked back at Abby. "Enough." She leaned toward the candlelight, which sparkled in her eyes. "People assume if you have doctor in front of your name you have money, and when you're a resident, you're lucky if you're only in debt several hundred thousand dollars for school loans."

"Ah…the American dream…in debt up to our eyes."

After dinner they were enjoying another glass of wine when music suddenly erupted from a jukebox in the corner that Abby hadn't noticed. People started moving tables and chairs to clear an area in the middle of the restaurant. Then a lot of women, many more than men, some in couples from Abby's age to ones in their sixties, began dancing.

Several of the ladies called, "Dr. Sam, come join the dance." Sam rolled her eyes as they danced closer to the table. "Dr. Sam, you dance and bring your friend. Come on!"

Sam blushed and waved them away, but that didn't stop two of the women from dancing right up to the table and taking both of them by the arm as they shimmied. "Come dance! It's Salsa night." There was no resisting their charm or their sheer determination to pull Sam and Abby onto the makeshift dance floor.

Between the alcohol and resounding vocals, which implied a liking to the way someone moved, Abby's head was swimming. She couldn't look at Sam, instead concentrating on the floor, and she could not get the silly smile off her face.

"Enough for me," Abby stated when the song ended. She followed Sam back to their table. Once seated she glanced at her watch, surprised to see it was after ten. They'd been there for hours. What was the expression? Time flies when you're having fun. Abby couldn't recall the last time she'd felt so carefree and adventurous. Sam must have noticed her checking the time and waved for their waiter.

"Everything to your satisfaction, Dr. Sam?" he asked.

"Everything was perfect, Carlo, thank you."

When he returned with the check, Abby placed her hand on Sam's before she could pick it up.

"No," Sam said as she looked into Abby's eyes.

"You rescued me from a boring evening and the rantings of my mother. The least I can do to repay your kind gesture is buy dinner." Abby tipped her head.

Sam smiled and Abby realized her hand was still resting on Sam's. She pulled her hand away, fumbling in her purse for a credit card. As they stepped from the restaurant, Abby inhaled the cold night air deeply in hopes of clearing her head. The evening was about to end, and she reminded herself that she would soon be home in her own bed, and Selena would be crawling into that bed with her. She rested her head against the seat back and sighed.

"I'm not about to let you drive. I'm taking you home. Where do you live?" Sam asked. Abby recited her address. "That's the lofts between Third and Fourth Streets, right?" Abby nodded. Sam obviously knew her way around town. "So are you able to walk to work when the weather's nice?"

"Yes, I do walk occasionally."

"I love to exercise. I just don't have much time to do it." Sam glanced over at her. "I do have a membership to a health club. Maybe we can go workout sometime."

Abby sighed louder than she meant to.

"Are you okay, Abby?" she said like a concerned doctor.

"I don't usually drink so much, but yes, I'm fine."

Sam pulled in front of her building, turned off the car and pulled her keys from the ignition. "Come on, I'll walk you in."

"Really, I'm fine. It's not necessary, but thanks for offering." She held her hand out for her keys that Sam had confiscated in the hotel parking lot. Sam dropped the keys in her hand and Abby reached for the door handle with hesitation, not quite ready to end such an enjoyable evening.

Sam shifted in her seat to face Abby. "If you call me in the morning, we can get breakfast and I'll take you to pick up your car."

Oh shit! Her car! She didn't have her car, and Selena would know she didn't drive herself home. Abby tried to sound sober as a judge. "I'm pretty sure I've got something going on tomorrow. Don't worry about the car. I'll get it sometime. Thanks again for the rescue. It was fun."

Sam nodded. "Yeah, fun. We'll have to do something fun again."

CHAPTER SEVEN

Tuesday's story time went by quickly. Abby asked a nurse on her way out of the activity room if Sam was working, but she wasn't sure and suggested Abby ask at the nurses station. Abby wanted to thank Sam again for the rescue on Saturday night.

Yes, she was informed at the nurses station, Dr. Sam was working and the duty nurse was kind enough to page her. Fifteen minutes passed without word from her, so the nurse paged again and after another ten minutes, Abby thanked her and left.

The following afternoon when she answered the phone it surprised her to hear the now familiar voice.

"Abby, hi! It's Dr. Sam. I hope I'm not calling at a bad time."

"No, not at all."

"I'm so sorry I missed you last night. I was up to my elbows, literally, with a trauma down in emergency. I can't believe the nurse let you stand around and wait. She could have found out where I was if she'd tried."

"I understand completely. Please, don't worry about it."

An awkward moment of silence fell before either spoke. "So…was there a reason you were looking for me?"

"I'm going to see Phillip tomorrow evening, and I thought maybe we could have coffee after. If you're there and not too busy that is."

"Hmm…What if we had dinner instead of coffee? Would you be free to have dinner with me? I had such a good time just talking and hanging out with you Saturday, well… It would be nice to do it again. What do you say?"

"You're very persuasive, Dr. Sam. Dinner does sound more appealing than hospital coffee."

"Great! Then I'll see you tomorrow evening."

"You know where to find me."

After Abby hung up the phone her mind wandered to what she should wear to have dinner with Dr. Sam tomorrow.

Sam wore a smile she couldn't hide as hard as she tried, and it didn't go unnoticed by Nurse Walker.

"You look like the Cheshire cat. Been getting lucky, have you?" She waggled her brows at Sam.

It wasn't an observation but a question, and the answer was one Sam wasn't about to share with anyone at work. She cocked her head and gave a wry smile.

"I'm not the kissin' and tellin' kind of girl. Sorry."

The nurse shrugged before walking off. Sam basked in the success of her phone call to Abby. While she couldn't call it a "date," it was most definitely a dinner engagement with the lovely Abby Collins, during which Sam would have the opportunity to gaze across the table at her. Those intense green eyes did something to Sam she couldn't explain and had never felt before. Those eyes invited her to see into Abby's soul. This time she smiled at the vision in her mind.

Abby Collins was a beautiful woman, but Sam sensed there was so much more than meets the eye. The "conquest" comment Abby's mother had made kept rattling around in her head. Abby had seemed to dance around Sam's question about it. She couldn't help but wonder if Abby could possibly be gay.

She knew that there were beautiful-looking women that were lesbians. She'd been with one in college. If that were the case, it certainly would shine a different light on her fantasy of Abby. Is she or is she not?

* * *

Abby's work attire leaned to the conservative side. Skirts and blouses mostly, but today she decided on a silky emerald color dress and took the extra time to put her hair up. She still looked professional for the job, but the look would hopefully be suitable for any dining environment.

Abby had only just turned on the coffee in Daniel's office when she heard a low whistle and, "Wow!" She spun around in surprise.

"That dress is simply stunning on you, Ms. Collins." He gave a polite smile. "My wife would kill to have something so… so lovely." His face flushed. Abby suspected that wasn't exactly what he was thinking, but it was politically correct in their law office.

"Thank you. I'll jot down where I bought it and you can surprise your wife on her next birthday."

"Perhaps."

Daniel had Abby review the edits he'd made to yesterday's notes and then type them. He had little else for her to do. The day seemed to never end.

Phillip was excited upon her arrival at the hospital, announcing his "Hello," before Abby made herself known in his room. She read more of his book, and with that charming boyish smile of his, he encouraged her to read on past the twenty-minute limitation.

A moment after Abby turned the next page, Phillip said in an exuberant voice, "Hi, Dr. Sam."

Abby turned to see Sam smiling from the doorway, returned the smile and marked her place in the book. She looked back to Phillip. "How did you know Dr. Sam was here, Phillip?"

He gave a toothy grin. "Same way I know when you're here."

Abby looked at Sam who shrugged and continued to smile, then back at Phillip. "Okay, I give up."

"You smell pretty. Different pretty than Dr. Sam or my mom, but you all smell pretty different." He and Sam both chuckled, and a few seconds later Abby caught his play on words.

"You're a very clever young man and quite the charmer."

"You need to rest, Phillip. I'll see you in the morning." Sam motioned for Abby as she moved out into the hall.

Abby held his tiny hand. "I'll see you again soon, Phillip."

"Thanks Abby."

"You're very welcome, sweetie."

Abby gave his hand a light squeeze, feeling collected as she stepped out in the hall. She found if she only thought about how incredibly smart and lovable Phillip was, she wasn't so saddened by reality.

Sam was wearing a glum expression while still pressing the chart she held to her chest. "I have a bit of a situation. Well, two actually."

Abby waited, fearing Sam was about to cancel their dinner, and the chart she clutched in her hands was the reason why. Then Sam lowered the chart, revealing a rather large stain on her blue blouse and white coat.

She indicated her soiled clothes. "Kids. This is my third shirt today and I'm out of clothes in my locker. I'll have to stop by my apartment and change before we can go to dinner. And this…" She pulled a prescription bag from her deep pocket. "I need to drop this by my folks for my Grand Momma. So if you'd rather do this another time instead of eating so late, I understand."

Abby glanced at her watch. It wasn't quite seven yet. She didn't want to go home and eat alone. "Where do you live?"

"Ten minutes from here." She fidgeted with a button on her white coat and seemed nervous.

"And where do your parents live?"

"Across town."

"And was there somewhere in particular you were planning for us to have dinner?"

"No. Actually I was going to have you choose the place."

Abby smiled. "I'll follow you to your apartment so you can change. We'll take my car and decide on the drive to your parents where to have dinner, and I'll take you home after. Does that work, or will that make it too late for dinner?"

"Are you kidding?" Sam started toward the nurses station. "Some nights I don't eat until after ten o'clock, so your plan sounds perfect." She gave Abby a sideways glance. "Let's get out of here before another kid shares their dinner with me." Sam saw Abby wrinkle her nose. "Sorry, I guess that doesn't make dinner sound very appetizing."

The apartment building looked like every other brick rectangle among a dozen or so in the complex. Sam parked her car in an open spot and rushed inside. Abby turned her car around pulling close to the door and minutes later Sam returned. Sam recited directions to her parents and they discussed possible dinner options on the thirty-minute drive. Sam's family home was in a neighborhood like any other family neighborhood in the suburbs. This particular area was older, probably developed in the forties. The houses were all two-story framed structures with barely room for a drive between them, but all neat and well kept. Abby pulled to the curb behind a small, aging American made car.

Sam mumbled something under her breath.

"Is there something wrong, Sam?"

She exhaled a sigh. "My sister's here."

Abby turned the car off and dropped the keys in her purse. "How bad can it be?" Abby thought briefly of her own family, promptly regretting having asked the question. "Let's just get it over with." She pushed her door open, but Sam caught her arm before she could get out.

"You're going in with me?"

"I'm your excuse to make a quick getaway. They're not monsters, are they?"

Sam chuckled. "A little overbearing maybe, but no, not monsters."

"Because I actually have some experience with monsters." Sam raised a brow. "My mother. Remember?" Abby grinned.

"Ah yes." Sam grimaced. "I promise it won't be that bad."

Sam pushed through the door without knocking, and the second the heavenly smell of garlic and Italian herbs reached Abby's nose, a very round woman bore down on them from the other end of the hall wiping her hands on her apron.

She grabbed Sam before she could utter a word. "Samantha, shame you stay away from your family too long." She squeezed Sam with strong arms and then took her head in her hands and kissed Sam's forehead. "You too skinny, Samantha." She took a step back. "And who you bring for dinner with you?"

Sam rolled her eyes over at Abby. "Momma, this is Abby Collins. She volunteers at the hospital with the children. We're not staying for dinner. We already have plans."

Abby reached out a hand, which Sam's mother ignored and grabbed Abby in a bear hug. "Welcome, Abby Collins. You skinny too."

A woman after my own heart.

She pulled Abby by the arm. "Come, come meet Samantha's family."

Sam caught her mother's hand. "Momma, we can't stay."

Sam's mother looked at Abby. "You come, meet family."

Abby looked at Sam and shrugged. Her mother introduced Sam's father, Nicola, who took Abby's offered hand but also slid an arm around her shoulders and gave a squeeze. Then a woman about Sam's age, Kattiana, who held a baby in her lap, offered a stiff "hello" but nothing more, keeping her hands busy with her child. She was one of Sam's older sisters.

"What a beautiful baby," Abby said.

Kattiana gave a forced smile and Abby heard Sam's father mumble, "Fatherless child."

A teenage girl, fifteen or sixteen perhaps, bounded down the stairs squealing Sam's name. She threw her arms around Sam. "I miss you."

Sam held the girl and kissed the top of her head. "I miss you too, Arianna. How's school?"

Arianna stepped back and looked at Abby. "Oh you know, boring."

"Arianna, this is my friend, Abby. Abby, this is my baby sister."

"Hello," the young girl said.

"Nice to meet you, Arianna."

Arianna rolled her eyes at Sam. "I'm not a baby anymore, you know."

Sam put her arm around her shoulders. "No, you're not. How many boyfriends do you have now?"

"Only one. How many you got?"

Sam put a pout on her face. "None. I don't have time right now. I guess you win."

"Well, I'm not going to be a doctor if you don't have time for boyfriends."

"It won't always be this way, Arianna. I'm just still learning. Eventually I'll have time."

Her sister smirked. "When you're old and wrinkled like Momma."

"Don't talk about Momma like that," Sam chided. "Be respectful."

And as if she'd heard them talking, Sam's mother returned carrying two glasses of wine, shoving them into Sam's and Abby's hands. "Dinner's ready. Samantha, please help your Grand Momma to the table."

Sam tried to push the glass back. "Momma, I told you we're not staying for dinner. We have plans."

Her mother looked at Abby. "You and Samantha stay and have family dinner, no?"

"It's fine with me, Mrs. Christiano, if Sam wants to stay."

She took Abby's free hand and patted it. "You good girl. No Mrs. You call me Momma."

The woman warmed Abby's heart and together they looked at Sam.

"Samantha, you no break your momma's heart."

Sam locked her gaze on Abby. "It looks like I'm outnumbered. I guess we're staying for dinner."

Her mother took Sam's face again in her hands. "You good girl too. Now get Grand Momma, please." She patted Sam's cheeks and moved away.

Abby felt like she'd shanghaied Sam into something she wasn't prepared for. "I'm sorry. Your mother is so persuasive."

Sam rolled her eyes. "No, I'm sorry you got coerced into dinner with my family."

Abby touched Sam's arm. "Don't be silly. Your family is lovely."

"Lovely...hmm..." Sam gazed into her eyes but appeared very far away.

Abby realized she still had her hand on Sam's arm and removed it. "Sam?" Sam blinked several times. "Your grandmother."

"Oh...yeah, right."

Sam started from the room with Abby following. She stopped at a closed door off the long hallway in the back corner of the house and tapped lightly.

"Grand Momma, it's me."

A tender voice called from within, "Sammy, come, come in."

With her hand on the doorknob, Sam whispered, "She doesn't see very well anymore, but she's still sharp as a tack."

She pushed open the door and they stepped inside the room that looked like every grandmother's private sanctuary—the old prints on the walls, a woven spread over the bed, a hand-made quilt folded over an antique blanket chest, the old wooden rocker that held her petite form, and doilies on every surface.

"Who is with you Sammy?"

Sam stood beside her grandmother's chair and placed a hand on her shoulder. "This is Abby Collins. She volunteers at the hospital where I work."

Abby took the thin, frail hand that reached toward her. "It's very nice to meet you."

She gripped Abby's hand in her fingers. "And you my dear." She rubbed her other hand over Abby's. "Such a pretty young lady, no?"

"Yes, Grand Momma, Abby is very pretty," Sam answered. Abby's cheeks grew hot as she looked at Sam's smiling face.

"So what you give free of your time for?" she asked, releasing Abby's hand.

"I read to the sick children."

She placed her hands to her heart. "Oh...I always love reading to the children." She finally reached a hand in Sam's direction and Sam helped her to her feet.

"Momma sent me for you. Dinner is ready."

Sam's grandmother looked in Abby's direction. "You have children?"

"No," Abby answered reluctantly.

"You have husband, no?"

Abby shook her head before realizing Sam's grandmother couldn't see her, and said, "No husband either."

She reached out and grazed the tips of her long thin fingers over Abby's cheek. "You make beautiful children one day, no worry."

Abby's heart warmed with the woman's words. Sam had a rather intent gaze fixed on her.

"Grand Momma always knows of what she speaks." Sam's smile made her eyes twinkle even in the dim light.

They made their way to the dining room table where Sam's mother seated Sam on her right and Abby on her left. Arianna sat beside Abby, and they all held hands as Sam's father said grace. Abby felt tears pressing behind her closed eyelids. This is what family was about, and Sam was a very lucky lady to have so many loving, caring people in her life. They encouraged Sam to share what she'd been up to during the weeks since they'd last seen her. Eventually though, Sam directed the conversation to Abby and what she did for a living.

Sam's mother scowled and asked, "You work for lawyer?"

Abby took a sip of wine for courage. "Yes, but the good ones. I assist prosecutors. They lock up the bad guys."

Momma patted Abby's hand but looked at Sam. "This is good, no?"

"It's good, Momma."

The sisters helped their mother in the kitchen after the meal while Sam escorted her grandmother back to her room, leaving Abby at the table with Mr. Christiano.

"You have a family?" he asked right off.

"Yes, but we're not close like your family."

He shook his head. "Such a shame, but you will have your own family."

"I certainly hope so. There is nothing I want more for my future than to have children."

"Ah yes, children are joy. My Samantha is very good doctor. You need help to have children, she is very smart doctor. My Samantha, she can help." His bushy eyebrows danced.

As he beamed with pride, Abby's mind conjured an image of Sam helping her to have a baby in a non-traditional way. A minute later Sam came back.

"Are you ready to go?"

Abby nodded and Sam's father stood with her. "You come back with our Samantha." He took her hand and gave it a gentle squeeze.

Sam called toward the kitchen, "Momma, we're leaving."

Mrs. Christiano filled the doorway, drying her hands on her apron. "We see you for Thanksgiving next week, no?"

"I'll be by sometime, but I don't know when just yet." Sam's mother took her face in her hands. "Don't wait dinner on me, Momma. I'll be here when I can get here."

Her mother frowned. "Promise Momma." When Sam nodded, she kissed Sam's forehead and hugged her again. As she moved toward Abby, Abby prepared herself for another bone-crushing show of affection. Mrs. Christiano leaned back and said, "You come with Samantha, Thanksgiving."

"I'm sorry, I can't. I already have a commitment, but thank you so much for the invitation and for dinner this evening. It was wonderful."

"You come again with Samantha, no?"

"I'd like that very much. Thank you."

She smiled, brushing a warm hand over Abby's cheek. "Such a pretty girl."

What a wonderful woman to have for a mother. It was obvious where Sam got her charming, warm personality.

"I probably wouldn't be the first one to nominate you for sainthood, would I?" Sam asked in the car.

"You're joking, right?"

"You suffered through this evening with my family."

"Oh Sam, that's just silly. You have a kind and caring family. Do you suppose they'd adopt me?" She gave a sideways glance and saw Sam smile a smile which she clearly inherited from her mother.

"Momma would adopt you. She really likes you."

"Your mother is a wonderful woman and she's raised beautiful daughters."

"Arianna is definitely the beauty."

"I was including you, Sam." Abby briefly touched Sam's arm.

"If you say so," Sam replied with a blush.

While stopped at a traffic light, Abby glanced at Sam again. "You've got the whole package Sam, good looks and personality."

"Now you're just embarrassing me."

"Oh, and I forgot, you're smart too."

"Now who's being silly?"

The light changed and they drove on. Sam seemed more comfortable talking about her family than herself. She spoke of each one with so much love. Abby envied her having such a wonderful family, and she envied her family because of how much Sam loved them. Sam had what Abby wanted her life to be.

"Thanks for enduring my family so graciously," Sam said when they stopped in front of her building.

Abby turned to face her. "I had a wonderful time. We should definitely get together again."

"Then we will. How about next week we actually go to a restaurant for dinner? I owe you one."

"You don't owe me anything, but I would enjoy going out for dinner sometime."

Sam got out but poked her head back in the car. "Good. Maybe I'll see you next week at the hospital."

Abby smiled. "Goodnight, Sam."

"Night."

Abby watched until Sam disappeared through the building's door, and then drove home to her big empty loft, already missing Sam's company. Sam's family was kind and caring unlike her family who were rigid and unaffectionate. Since her mother had caught her during high school with a girlfriend kissing in the pool house, she looked at Abby with disgust and seethed indignation. They hadn't exactly had a special kind of mother-daughter relationship before, but since that kiss, their relationship was toxic.

* * *

Selena was off Friday night and wanted to go out to a bar. "I don't understand what the big deal is. It's not like you're a lawyer. You're a secretary."

The words didn't anger, but they hurt Abby. "I don't need to put my sexuality out there in everyone's face."

"Come on Abby. People grow…people change."

Abby saw the tension growing on Selena's face. And she was right about people changing. Their physical relationship remained hot, but it seemed more often than not like just hot sex. Abby didn't want another argument.

"If you absolutely have to go out partying, then just go."

Seemingly surprised Selena asked, "Without you?"

Abby surrendered. "Without me."

She slammed her fist on the counter. "Fine, I will."

She stomped to the bedroom and Abby walked to the windows searching the night…for something. She wasn't sure what. Selena came back and stood so their shoulders touched, smelling exotic and feeling hot.

"I don't feel right going out without you."

Abby watched her reflection in the darkened window. "Please don't drink too much and drive yourself. Get a cab or call me if you must. I'll come and get you."

Selena put her arm around her waist and pulled Abby against her. "I do love you, Abby." She pressed a kiss to Abby's ear and left.

Tears streaked Abby's face as the thoughts she'd discarded moments earlier returned. Her heart ached. She took a bottle of wine and a book to the couch. As much as she wanted to drink straight from the bottle until it was empty and her head felt fuzzy, she didn't. She'd told Selena she could call her for a ride, so she only poured a glass and drank slowly.

She put herself to bed around midnight, hugging Selena's pillow to her. Selena's sexy smell enticed her senses. She drifted off longing for Selena's touch and the pleasures Selena always gave her. She thought it was a dream, but she realized Selena was pulling the pillow from her arms.

"Abby," she said softly.

"Hmm…"

Selena drew her hand down Abby's back, resting it on her hip. She smelled of booze, smoke, and sweat. She pulled Abby against her and whispered, "I'm so sorry 'bout before. Hey baby, wake up please."

Abby forced her eyes open. "Selena…"

She moved her hand from Abby's hip and touched her fingers to Abby's lips. "Shh…I'm so sorry. I love you, Abby."

In the faint light from the city beyond the dark windows, Abby could see tears glistening in her eyes. She touched her face and pushed back her hair. "I love you, too."

Selena put her hand in the small of Abby's back and pulled Abby close to her heated center. "I want to make love to you."

Selena had a way of taking Abby to places so intense that Abby forgot who she was. She wanted to forget, to go away, even if only for a little while. She leaned in and kissed Selena. Selena pushed her leg between Abby's, guiding her onto her back and took Abby exactly where she needed to go.

CHAPTER EIGHT

Sam didn't make an appearance in the activity room while Abby read to the kids. Abby found her afterward at the end of the hall looking out the window.

"Hi! Is this your office? I always seem to find you here," Abby said as she neared.

When Sam turned around, Abby could see the sadness in her eyes. The same sadness that was there when she told Abby about Phillip.

"Sometimes I need to remind myself there's life beyond these walls."

Abby's heart leapt to her throat at Sam's anguished words. "Oh Sam, it's not Phillip, is it?" Sam shook her head, a solemn "no," and Abby breathed a sigh of relief. "Is there something you want to talk about? I have time for coffee."

"I don't want to dump my work woes on you."

"Don't be silly. We're practically family."

"Do you mean that?"

She gave Sam's arm a little tug. "Come on. Let's get a cup of coffee."

Sam told the desk where she would be and they rode the elevator down in silence.

"You look like you've lost your best friend," Abby said once they were seated in an out-of-the-way corner of the cafeteria. "Is there anything I can help with?"

Sam looked up from the cardboard cup cradled in her hands. "It's a young patient I'm worried about." Her attempt at a chuckle failed miserably. "Big news flash. All my patients are young. It's a teenage girl."

Abby leaned over the table. "For reasons of confidentiality, I know there are things you can't discuss, but if there's anything that you can share, I'm here for you."

Sam forced a smile and sipped her coffee. "It's a fifteen-year-old and she tried to commit suicide last night."

Abby's heart sank. She reached out and covered Sam's hand. "I'm sorry. Is she going to be all right?"

"Physically…yes…this time, but who knows if there's a next time." Her tone was sad and frustrated. She absently picked at the napkin under her cup. "I called for a psych consult, but she wouldn't talk to her…the psychologist."

"Will she talk to you?"

Sam released a heavy sigh. "She did."

"Well, that's good, isn't it?"

"I'm hardly qualified."

"But with teenagers, isn't it good if they feel comfortable enough to talk to an adult, regardless of who it is?"

"I suppose. I'm just not sure if I'm comfortable having her talk to me."

"Oh?"

Sam averted her eyes. "She says she's different. She's confused because she doesn't really like boys."

"Fifteen can be a very confusing age."

"But she asked me if I ever wondered what it would feel like to be with a girl the way boys want to be with girls."

Abby nearly choked on her coffee. She tried to keep her expression unreadable when Sam's gaze met hers.

"How am I supposed to answer a question like that?"

"I'm not sure."

Sam's gaze lingered. "Well let me ask you this." She leaned toward Abby. "Have you ever wondered what it would be like to be with a woman?"

Abby hesitated a long moment, then said, "I think every female at some point has a curiosity, even if she isn't gay and never intends to act on it." She shrugged. "I think we all wonder." Abby noticed a quick flash of something in Sam's eyes and raised her coffee cup to hide.

Sam closed the distance between them and whispered, "I think that Nurse Walker is a lesbian."

"Perhaps, if this nurse is as you say, your young patient might be comfortable talking with her."

"Possibly. You know I can't imagine ever thinking death could be better than anything I felt for someone, regardless of who I felt it for."

Abby also found it inconceivable that anything could make her want to take her own life. *There have been times I could've died of embarrassment, or over-parenting, but...* "Maybe she has an unhappy or difficult home life that's complicating her situation." Abby had had an unhappy and difficult home life, and it had complicated any number of things in her life. "You know, Sam, qualified or not, it can't hurt to let this young girl unburden herself to you, if she's comfortable doing it. As long as she knows you can't advise her. At least *you're* in a position to guide her toward the right kind of help."

"You're right." They were silent for only a moment before Sam's eyes brightened and she said, "Momma called Sunday and made me promise to ask you again for Thanksgiving."

Abby couldn't stop a smile. "I honestly wish that I could spend Thanksgiving with you and your family. I just can't."

Sam nodded. "I only asked because I promised Momma. Now I can tell her I did and stopped just short of twisting your arm." Sam finally laughed in earnest.

"I love your mother."

Sam looked down at her hands on the table. "Well, I'm guessing you're not planning to break the wishbone with your mother, so it must be a hot date."

What are you fishing for, Dr. Christiano? "Mmm, something like that." The only thing that would be hot about Abby's Thanksgiving would be her slaving away in the kitchen while Selena did little or nothing to help.

"I suppose Phillip will miss his time with you this week."

"I wouldn't think of disappointing him. I was going to stop by sometime Friday since I won't be working."

"He'll appreciate it. I know I certainly appreciate what you're doing for him."

Sam seemed more like her usual happy self, and Abby caught the trace of a smile as Sam raised the coffee cup to her lips. She watched Abby closely before setting the cup down.

"What?"

Abby didn't realize the magnitude of her smile until that moment. "Nothing," she said, shaking her head.

Sam pushed her chair back and stood. "I better get back upstairs. Thanks for talking with me. I feel better than I've felt all day."

"I'm glad I could help. Of course now you know if I find a need to unburden myself, you're expected to let me bend your ear." Abby tilted her head.

"You can bend my ear anytime you like. You've got my number. Have a good evening." Sam slowly pushed in the chair never breaking eye contact.

"You too, Sam." Abby remained seated and watched her walk off.

Abby found it interesting that Sam wanted to share her worries about her patient who might be gay. Abby knew Sam's question about being with a woman was a fishing expedition, and instead of dancing around the subject like she did, she should have simply come out to Sam. But, she liked Sam a lot and didn't want to risk their friendship. At the moment Sam was the only person in her life she felt at ease around. Selena's moods had been so unpredictable of late she felt as though she was walking through a minefield when they were together.

Sam was grateful she had only an hour left to work. Her conversation with Abby was still replaying in her mind. She'd been uncomfortable and a little embarrassed to discuss the subject with Abby, but Abby hadn't seemed shocked or appalled. On the contrary. She'd seemed perfectly comfortable when Sam said "lesbian," as if she'd had the conversation before. Sam exhaled in relief. *Well, if we continue to be friends and I come out to her, at least she probably won't hate me.*

Sam stayed in contact with a few friends from high school, but none of them ever knew she had been involved with a woman while away at college. Sam hadn't been convinced she was gay after her first and only relationship had ended abruptly. She hadn't met another woman since then that turned her head—until now. The first time Sam had slipped into the activity room to see the "lady storyteller" the nurses and parents were bragging about, it hit her. She got the fluttery, butterfly feeling in her chest and stomach, all from simply looking at and listening to the woman. And when she got up the nerve to introduce herself and Abby had taken her hand, it felt like lightning struck. Sam got a charge from her head to her toes. Yes, the very beautiful, and by all appearances, straight Abby Collins had rattled her. And she still felt the butterflies every time Abby was around. Sam couldn't help but wonder, though, if the butterflies she was feeling were more about how maybe Abby might be feeling when they were around each other. Was it too much to hope that Abby might be into women?

She wasn't scheduled until late Friday, but she had every intention of stopping in earlier, hoping to see Abby when she visited Phillip.

CHAPTER NINE

Blair was already seated in her office when Abby arrived ten minutes early on Monday. At Blair's request, Abby had been moved back to her office for a high-profile case.

She appeared in the doorway before Abby could get her coat off. "Coffee's already made. Would you like some?"

"Sure." Abby tossed her coat over the chair behind the desk.

"I'll get it." Blair disappeared into her office and Abby followed.

Blair smiled as she placed the steaming cup in Abby's hand. "Let's sit." She motioned Abby to one of the high-back leather chairs across from her executive chair, but instead of sitting behind her desk, Blair took a seat beside Abby.

Crossing her legs, Blair tugged her skirt down and asked, "Did you have a nice long, holiday weekend?"

Abby eyed her carefully for a moment over the cup as she took a sip. "I did, thank you for asking," Abby replied finally. "And—"

"I imagine you have big family affairs."

Blair was being entirely too polite, and curious. "Actually I had a very small dinner at my place. And how was yours?"

"It was…" Blair picked up her cup from her desk. "I find the whole family holiday affair sometimes too much. My date drank too much of my father's twenty-year-old scotch and then proceeded to make an ass of himself. I felt like an ass for having such poor judgment taking him in the first place, so I'll probably be banned from my parents for the Christmas holiday." She chuckled. "Hell, maybe I'll get lucky and be permanently left off the guest list from now on." She looked straight into Abby's eyes. "Do you already have plans for Christmas?"

Abby waited in silence for the punch line. When none came, she muttered, "Excuse me?"

Blair slapped her hand on the arm of Abby's chair. "I was kidding, Abby. You look like I asked you to give up your firstborn child."

Abby attempted a smile. "Of course you were." Blair said she was kidding, but Abby saw something else in her eyes. Something like longing. *Oh lord, is she about to suggest Christmas holiday plans with me?*

Blair stood. "We should get started."

Abby set her cup on the desk. "I'll be right back."

Hurriedly she hung her coat, put her purse away and grabbed a pad and pen. When she returned to Blair's office, she was refilling their coffee cups. As she took the same seat, Blair again sat beside her and picked up her day planner. *Must be the softer Blair.* She certainly didn't resemble the reputation that preceded her as the Wicked Bitch of the Midwest. Abby knew if she shared Blair's behavior with any of the other assistants, they would submit her name for drug screening. Maybe Blair's date had done something more than simply make an ass of himself over the long weekend. It seemed the only likely explanation for Blair's good-natured demeanor on a Monday morning. They got Blair's schedule set in short order and Abby returned to her sanctuary outside Blair's office.

* * *

One of the nurses handed Abby a note as she entered the activity room on Tuesday evening. It was from Sam, asking if Abby would have her paged when she was finished. After story time, the nurse at the desk paged Sam and they waited. While she waited, Abby strolled down the hall to Phillip's room and found it empty. Another five or so minutes passed before the desk phone rang.

"Dr. Sam is down in radiology and asked if you could meet her downstairs."

Abby gave a nod and the nurse directed her to the correct elevator. When she exited the elevator, she found Sam leaning against the wall with her head hanging. Tightness squeezed Abby's chest, as she feared something had happened to Phillip. Sam looked up as Abby neared, the forced smile not quite reaching her eyes.

"Thanks for staying, although I thought they'd have been done with him by now."

"Who?"

"Phillip's down here for a CT scan. I really thought they would at least have him inside by now."

"You're waiting with him?"

"Yes. I sent his mom out for a bite to eat."

"Come on, I'll wait with you."

Sam looked Abby in the eyes. "I have to warn you. A lot has changed since you last saw him."

"Oh?"

"He's losing more and more of his motor skills, and when he's tired, he has difficulties with even the simplest things."

Abby nodded and when Sam pushed off the wall, she followed. The bed seemed to swallow him as he lay pale and motionless. Abby's breath caught. Her head felt light and she grasped the bed's side rail to gain her balance.

Sam caught her arm. "You okay?"

Abby inhaled deeply and then slowly exhaled. "I'm fine." She let go of the rail but Sam quickly took hold of her arm.

"You don't look so fine. You look pale as a ghost."

A few deep breaths quelled Abby's lightheadedness. "I'm fine." Determined, she added, "I told you I could handle this." Abby's voice took on a sharp tone she didn't intend.

Sam's eyes registered surprise. She released Abby's arm and without another word or look at Abby, Sam leaned over the bedside. "Phillip, I have someone here to wait with us." Sam's voice sounded soft as a feather.

Abby took his tiny limp hand and gave a gentle squeeze. His fingers twitched and the corners of his mouth turned up to his now open eyes. Abby's heart flooded with emotions.

"I've been looking for you. I'm glad I finally found you." He opened his mouth, but no sound emerged. His lips fell into a frown. "I thought I could read to you while we wait. I don't have your book with me, but I have another I've been reading I think you'll like just as much. Would that be okay?" His fingers curled around Abby's hand and his frown disappeared.

Nearly a half hour later they prepared to take him in. While Sam exchanged a few words with one of the technicians, Abby told Phillip she would be by to see him tomorrow evening.

Once he was inside, Sam said, "You made his day and this," she motioned to the wide steel door, "easier to deal with. Thank you."

"You don't have to thank me. I only wish I could take him in my arms and make him better." Sam handed her a tissue for the tears she was only now aware had escaped her eyes.

"I have just enough time for coffee while he's in there. Would you like to join me?"

"Sure. I could use a cup of coffee," Abby replied, shoving the tissue in her pocket. They made the walk to the cafeteria in silence. She pushed the images of Phillip aside and once they were seated, she asked Sam, "How's your teenage suicide patient?" Sam's eyes were locked on Abby's, but they looked blank and she didn't respond. "Sam?"

Sam blinked. "Um…I'm sorry. What did you say?"

Abby rested her arms on the table and curled her hands around the warm cup. "I asked about the teenage girl you were trying to help last week. But if there's something else on your mind you want to talk about…" She abandoned the cup, interlocked her fingers and rested her chin on them. She kept her gaze on Sam.

"I think the teenager will be fine. She and her mother are seeking counseling, and she has my number if she needs it."

So compassionate. No wonder you became a doctor.

"Can we talk about anything other than patients and this place?"

"Okay. Tell me how you ended up with the name Samantha in an Italian family?"

"They were convinced before I was born I was a boy. No question… They knew it. They already had two girls. They were convinced I would be Papa's little boy." She smiled for the first time, relaxing back in her chair and stretching out her legs. "He started calling me Little Sam about six months into Momma's pregnancy. So…instead of Samuel they named me Samantha." She chuckled. "Of course he's never called me Sam a day in my life."

Abby sat hypnotized by the sound of her voice.

"You have family other than that mother of yours I saw at the fundraiser?"

Abby couldn't help but laugh.

"What's so funny?"

"The way you said 'that mother.'" She tipped her head. "Like you know her and know that she's a real mother, if you get my meaning."

Sam's head bobbed. "Ah, yes." She smiled again.

Abby held her breath, hoping Sam wouldn't pursue further family questions she'd have to avoid answering. And as luck would have it, Sam's ringing phone saved her. Sam looked down at the screen.

"Radiology. They're finished with Phillip. I have to go."

Abby stood with her. She needed to get going herself. If Selena was her usual jealous self, she would have already called home and left a message, asking why Abby wasn't home yet.

"I told Phillip I'd be by tomorrow evening," Abby said outside in the hall.

"Thanks again for being so selfless with your time. I'll see you soon."

Abby arrived home to a surprising message that Selena had left at six-o-eight p.m. "Hey doll, I guess you're running late at the hospital. I miss you. I'll see you when I get off, if you're still awake."

At nearly nine o'clock Abby was too tired to think about dinner. She kicked off her shoes, grabbed a yogurt and apple, and then settled on the couch to relax in the quiet. She kept seeing an image of Sam in the dark living room window, how Sam's eyes had stared blankly back at her in the cafeteria earlier. She pushed away worried thoughts about Sam's obvious distraction and went to the bathroom where she soaked in the tub until the water cooled.

* * *

Blair called Abby into her office to go over notes on a case before Abby typed them. At the mention of someone named Phillips, Abby's mind wandered away with thoughts of her small friend and how heart-wrenching it had been last night when he wasn't able to speak to her. She'd researched Phillip's type of cancer and knew his chances of beating it were equal to the odds of winning the lottery. Regardless of those facts, Abby continued to say a prayer for him every day. *The beginning of the end.* She thought about her own relationship.

"Abby!" Blair's voice startled her. She moved quickly around her desk and sat beside Abby. "Are you all right? You suddenly got a faraway look in your eyes and your face is very pale."

Abby took a moment. "Do you ever wonder why sometimes life is so unjust?"

Blair leaned back and crossed her legs. "How do you mean?"

"For the innocent ones."

"I hope you're not referring to the ones we put away."

Abby felt tears threaten to spill over her lashes. *Of all the people, please do not let me cry in front of her.*

"Abby what's wrong?"

Abby's resolve failed her and a few tears escaped to create blood-red streaks down the front of her rose-colored blouse. Blair scrambled from her chair and knelt beside her.

In a voice so soft Abby didn't recognize, Blair asked, "Did something happen? Did someone hurt you?"

Abby blinked away the tears and looked at her. The compassion in her eyes nearly made her sob. "No."

"Are you sure?" Blair placed a comforting hand on her shoulder.

Abby nodded. "I just…I don't know…"

Blair returned to the chair beside her. "I want you to know that you can talk to me, Abby. I know everyone in these offices believe that my heart is carved from a block of ice, but I do care about things, about people. I think we've developed a good working relationship and I do care about you."

The women down in the break room would fall out of their chairs laughing if Abby shared this conversation. They simply wouldn't believe it. When she looked again at Blair, her eyes still showed compassion. What harm could it do to tell her? She wiped the wetness from her cheeks.

"There's a young boy at the hospital who's dying." She had to take deep breaths to steel herself against her building emotions. "I saw him last night and he's progressively worse than just last week."

"Now what exactly is it you do at the hospital?"

"I read stories to the children who can't be recovering at home."

"So this young boy is a part of your audience?"

"No." She dropped her head and stared at the floor. "He's too sick to participate. I'm going back to see him tonight."

Blair reached over and touched Abby's arm. "I have an idea." Abby held her breath. "Why don't you take a few minutes to get yourself together, and then we'll get this work knocked out so you can take off early today."

That was it. Abby *had* stepped into an episode of *The Twilight Zone. This is not Blair Stanton, but a very good rendering of her.* She intended to take advantage of Blair's good nature while she was offering it up. She rushed down the hall to the ladies' room and made herself presentable again. True to her word, Blair let her leave around three thirty. Abby didn't call ahead, deciding instead if she had to wait to spend time with Phillip, she would find something to do.

Phillip's mother was sitting at his bedside, her head tipped to one side. She was asleep, but Phillip was not. His eyes were looking toward the ceiling.

Abby took his hand gently, leaned close and whispered, "Your mom is asleep. Let's not wake her, okay?" He nodded, but in spite of how quiet Abby thought they were, she woke.

"I'm sorry. I must have nodded off."

Abby placed a hand on her shoulder. "I'm sure you must have needed the rest."

She smiled weakly. Her blue eyes were a dull shade of gray and set in hollow sockets accented by dark circles underneath, her color ashen, which gave her a ghostly appearance. However wrong it was, Abby thought it a blessing that Phillip couldn't see how frail and fragile his mother looked.

"Would you like to take a break? Get some air and something to eat? I'll stay with him until you get back."

Laura nodded and kissed his forehead before shuffling from the room. She reminded Abby of Sam's grandmother, shoulders drooping in an arthritic posture—only Phillip's mother was at least forty years younger. She turned around and saw Phillip struggling helplessly to reach his book where it lay on the bedside table.

"Phillip, do you want to continue reading from your book, or would you like me to read from the new one we started yesterday?" As she spoke, hoping her voice was enough of a distraction, she slid the book so his fingers could touch the edge of it.

"We'll have time to finish my book. Don't worry," he said in his tiny voice.

Tears immediately sprang to Abby's eyes. He intended to hang on a while longer and Abby prayed that his words traveled straight from his lips to God's ear. She picked up the book.

"Of course we do, sweetie." The words trembled past her lips as she attempted to rein in her emotions.

"You don't have to be sad for me, Abby." He stretched his hand toward her.

Dear Lord, give me strength. "Why is that, Phillip?"

"Mom says I'm going to heaven to be with the angels, and that Grandma is waiting to take care of me." His weak fingers gently squeezed her hand, prompting Abby's tears to flow freely. "I'm not scared anymore."

She gave a tortured cough and said hoarsely, "I'll be right back, Phillip."

She bolted from the room and down the hall, pulling tissues from her pockets as she went. Slipping into the empty activity room she let out a sob. *Dear God, how could you give him the strength and wisdom of an adult and then take this young angel from life?*

"Ms. Collins, are you okay?" An unfamiliar voice startled Abby.

She turned to see Nurse Walker in the doorway. "I'll be fine. Thank you."

She showed the same compassion Abby saw often in Sam's eyes. "He's a little sweetheart. It gets to me sometimes too. If you need anything, I'm on til eleven."

Abby nodded and she left. Sam had been right in her suspicion that Nurse Erika Walker was gay. She pinged Abby's gaydar. Abby gathered herself and returned to Phillip's room.

"I'm sorry about that, Phillip."

"It's okay. It happens to my mom sometimes."

Abby pinched her eyes shut and took a deep breath. She couldn't begin to imagine how often Phillip's mother was overcome with unbearable grief. She settled beside him on the bed and began reading. After twenty minutes or so his eyes began to droop so she stopped.

They popped open. "Please don't quit. I'm okay. I promise." The little smile he flashed tugged at her heartstrings.

Abby couldn't help but feel a tiny thread of hope since he appeared to be better than the previous evening. "Just a few more minutes." She took his hand in hers so she could feel when he slipped into slumber, and then sat at his bedside for another hour before his mother returned.

She motioned Abby into the hall. "I'm sorry for being so long. I ran home to take a shower and change."

Abby gave her hand a quick squeeze. She looked more like she'd had a good night's sleep, but Abby suspected it was only strategically placed makeup.

"It's perfectly fine. He's such a joy. I'd like to have a dozen just like him." She hoped her words offered some small comfort.

"Do you have children, Ms. Collins?"

"Abby please, and no, not yet."

"Well they are God's special gift to us."

"I don't doubt that." She gave a small smile.

"Thank you again for staying with Phillip."

Abby took a step toward the door. "It was my pleasure." She fished in her purse for something to write on and said as she scribbled, "If you ever need me to sit with him, please call." She handed the slip to her. "I work, but I'm available in the evenings and on weekends. I'd be glad to help in any way."

"Thank you, but you already do so much."

Abby's head shook. "I don't think we can ever do too much for that brave and joyous little boy."

* * *

Blair and Abby were working at the conference table by her office window when the phone rang in the outer office. Abby answered on Blair's phone.

"Blair Stanton's office."

"Abby, it's Sam."

She wasn't prepared to hear Sam's voice. "Oh…yes…"

"Is this a bad time?"

"Uh, yes…I mean no…just a moment please." She put the call on hold and told Blair on her way to the door, "I just need a minute." She picked up the phone in the outer office. "Hi! Sorry about that."

"Is this a bad time for you?" Sam asked again.

"No, it's fine. Is Phillip okay?"

"He's as okay as he can be. Nurse Walker said you were pretty upset yesterday. Did something happen?"

"Nurse Walker shouldn't talk so much. It was nothing."

"Well, Phillip said you two had an awesome time. His exact words." Sam chuckled.

"Yes, and Phillip is an awesome young man."

"He also said you were stopping back again today."

"I am."

"Would you have dinner with me after? I still owe you one."

"Technically you don't owe me a thing." She heard Sam sigh. "But dinner sounds nice, so yes I will." Selena would be working and none the wiser.

"Great! Think about where you'd like to go."

"I don't think there's anywhere in particular I want to go, so you decide. Your choice of a restaurant before was fine with me."

"Are you sure?"

"I'm sure."

"I'll come up with something then. Is there anything you don't like?"

"Not really."

"Okay, so have the nurse on duty page me when you get here and I'll meet you."

"See you later, Sam."

"Yes, yes you will." Abby could hear the smile in Sam's voice.

When she returned to Blair's office, she was leaning against her desk with her arms folded. Her body language spoke volumes. She'd obviously overheard that Abby's conversation was of a personal nature.

"Everything all right?" she asked in a clipped tone.

"It is. Thank you for your concern." Abby put as much sincerity in her voice as possible in hopes of softening Blair's shift in mood.

Blair turned abruptly and walked over to the table. "Let's get back to it then so we don't have to work late."

Abby prayed that Blair was exaggerating about working late, because tonight of all nights, she wouldn't. Blair could fire her if she'd rather.

The nurse paged Sam upon her arrival, and when Abby finished reading to Phillip, she found Sam in her usual spot at the window. She was dressed in khakis and a blue cotton shirt. She looked casually comfortable. Abby wished she were dressed similarly.

"I feel overdressed for dinner."

Sam slowly assessed Abby and then met her gaze. "You look perfectly fine to me." One corner of her mouth turned up.

"Well, if this is appropriate, then you are clearly underdressed," Abby joked.

"Okay. Compared to me, some might consider you overdressed. I'll concede you that point. But I can't imagine you could ever look out of place anywhere, regardless of how you dressed."

Whether Sam had intended to or not, she'd made Abby feel beautiful. And Sam's casual attire gave her a cute, almost boyish look.

"Let's go. I'm starving." Sam cupped Abby's elbow and steered her toward the elevator.

She could feel Sam's eyes on her in the elevator as she stared at the floor lights counting down. "You've already worked today?" Abby asked to break the silence.

"No, I'm on later."

Abby turned to meet Sam's gaze. "You came in just to go out for dinner?" Sam shrugged. "I could have met you at the restaurant," Abby commented as they crossed the parking lot. She unlocked the passenger door of her car.

"And miss being chauffeured in this luxury instead of driving my clunker?" Sam laughed.

"As long as it gets you where you need to go." Abby turned the key to start the car.

"Exactly. It's not like I have to impress anyone."

Sam's comment was a testament to who she was. An earnest kind of woman not out to impress anyone or to jockey for position and status. Abby was pretty sure she had read Dr. Samantha Christiano correctly. Sam had a heart of gold and was as selfless as a person could be. She realized Sam was talking and she hadn't heard a word.

"I'm sorry, you were saying?"

"I was asking if I caused a problem calling you at work this morning. You sounded...I don't know...uneasy."

Abby recalled her flustered state. "My boss can be rather overbearing, but I think I've worked with her enough now that I've tamed the beast...somewhat." Abby glanced sideways.

"Beast?" Sam said in surprise.

"It's a long story for another time when there's not a meal hanging in the balance. I wouldn't want to ruin your appetite." Abby chuckled. "Suffice it to say, I was surprised when you called."

"Like I said, I heard you were upset last night so I was concerned." Abby was without words. "You know I would never think less of you if you wanted to stop spending time with Phillip."

Abby pulled the car into a parking space and turned toward Sam. "I'm sure you wouldn't, but I would think less of myself, and besides, we have to finish his book."

Sam's eyes twinkled. "Let's eat."

She held the door for Abby as the entered Marco's. It looked and smelled very Italian. Candlelight on each table gave it quite the romantic feel. Sam ordered them wine and recommended they share a vegetarian pizza.

"They have the best pizza in the city, if you like pizza. And, you know, vegetables make it healthy." She gave Abby a wink.

Abby laid her menu aside. "Pizza it is."

They talked about everything from music to movies. When Sam asked about her family and college, Abby decided it was time to share.

"When you asked me about the Collins Women's Health Center I kind of danced around without answering. I am one of those Collins. It's not something that I readily share with people. I don't want to be thought of as one of those wealthy trust fund kids." Sam gave a nod. "I have an older brother who lives in Chicago, but we've never been close. One that lives in Florida that I talk to on occasion, and if you're familiar with the Collins name, then you probably know my father passed away six months ago. As for my mother, she doesn't approve of what I've done with my life. She can't accept that I didn't become a lawyer." Abby shrugged. "We haven't had a relationship since I was in high school. She caught me kissing a girl, hence the conquest remark." She leaned in. "I do get the whole sexuality and curiosity thing."

She didn't feel on trial, but rather that Sam was genuinely interested. She looked to be hanging on Abby's every word. Sam's chin rested in one hand while the index finger of her other hand traced around the base of her wineglass. Sam's eyes never left hers. She found Sam's gaze soothing and hypnotic.

When the quiet lingered too long after the pizza and another glass of wine, Sam finally broke the silence. "We shared dinner so we might as well share a dessert." Sam pushed the dessert menu across to Abby. "See anything that tempts your taste buds?"

Abby smiled and laid the menu aside. "You're the Italian, you decide. Your dinner choice was perfectly delicious. I trust your judgment. I can only have a taste. I am stuffed."

They managed to make the dessert last nearly another hour, like two old friends catching up over a dinner. Abby could see herself spending time with Sam on a regular basis. They stepped out of the restaurant into a monsoon. The rain beat so hard on the sidewalk it splashed up onto the step in the doorway where they stood.

"Wow! I didn't know it was supposed to rain like this," Abby said after a long moment.

"I'm sure it'll let up in a few minutes."

Abby noticed that Sam checked her watch. Sam still had to go into work. They waited a bit longer, discussing what else… the weather.

Sam finally held out her hand. "Give me your keys and I'll make a run for it and pick you up here at the curb."

"Don't be silly. You'll be drenched." Abby dug deep in her oversized purse and pulled out a compact umbrella. "It's not very big, but it should keep our hair dry." Sam looked at her curiously. "Well I'm not going to send you into this monsoon by yourself." She popped the pretty lavender umbrella open and brought it over their heads.

After they stepped onto the sidewalk, Abby put her arm around Sam's waist and pulled her close under the tiny shelter that barely covered their heads. Sam laughed when they nearly lost their balance trying to dodge a puddle, and Abby tightened her arm around Sam instinctively. She put Sam in first and then rushed around to the driver's side. Starting the car, Abby turned on the wipers, which seemed to slap in rhythm with the beating of the rain on the roof, and her heart. She pulled down the visor to check for damage in the mirror.

"Like I said, dry hair." She flipped her visor up and looked over at Sam.

Sam reached her hand toward Abby. "You just have this…" She pushed a few loose strands of hair behind Abby's ear. "These got loose." Sam nodded with a smile. "But they're still dry."

Sam leaned so close that Abby caught a whiff of her cologne. It felt like the air had been suddenly sucked from inside the car. She wanted to kiss Sam. She knew it was wrong to even think it, and there was Selena, but she couldn't help feeling an attraction for Sam.

Abby pulled the car onto the street and they said good night at the hospital entrance. Watching until Sam disappeared through the door, Abby thought about the feelings she'd just experienced. "You can't have feelings for Sam," Abby muttered to herself. "You're in love with Selena."

Sam unconsciously whistled as she made her way around the nurses station counter. Nurse Adams, an African-American woman who Sam guessed to be about her own mother's age, and resembled a barrel in both size and shape, raised her eyebrows.

With a wide grin, she asked, "Somethin' you want to be sharin' with me, Dr. Sam? Make my shift a little happier too?"

Sam pulled a chart from the rack. "What are you talking about, Flora?"

She snorted. "'Bout that grin you be wearin'. Child, you look like that cat that done ate the canary."

Sam wasn't aware she was even smiling. "It's a glorious day, Flora, and I'm just happy to be here."

Flora parked a hand on her meaty hip. "It's rainin' like the devil. Ain't nothin' glorious 'bout that."

Sam shrugged and resumed whistling as she sauntered down the hall.

Sam's head was in the clouds as she entered her patient's room. She'd spent the evening with the beautiful Abby Collins. Dinner had been better than wonderful. Although a hotdog at a sidewalk vendor would have been just as wonderful. Then, as if dinner wasn't enough, Abby had wrapped her arm around her under the umbrella. Sam couldn't begin to put words to the sensation. It was…like…well, something she'd never felt before. It had caught her so off guard. Sam was sure she was the one who caused them to stumble. And Abby's tighter grip had literally taken Sam's breath away. "Get a grip girl. You've got work to do," Sam mumbled.

It was the most difficult shift she'd had in a very long time, and just when she thought she'd put the evening out of her mind, something would trigger the memory and she'd be lost in it all over again. Sam hadn't ever had such a powerful crush on a woman. A beautiful, possibly not so straight woman. When Abby had looked into her eyes in the car, Sam felt certain what she saw was lust. Her obsession was confirmed, though, after she dragged herself into her tiny apartment at eight thirty in the morning and fell asleep dreaming of Abby.

CHAPTER TEN

The Curtis trial was set to begin at week's end so Blair had Abby working her tail off the entire day. The second she left for the day, Abby called the hospital to let them know she was coming by to see Phillip. The nurse informed her that she needed to stop by the desk first.

When she got off the elevator the sight of Sam leaning over the counter at the nurses station melted away all thoughts of exhaustion and her bitchy boss. Abby stopped behind her at the desk.

"Fancy meeting you here."

Sam scribbled on the chart in front of her and handed it over to the nurse, picked up another and clutched it to her chest. When she turned around, the most obvious was her bloodshot eyes. *A doctor's life, long grueling shifts.*

"Come with me," Sam said with a forced smile.

She led Abby around the corner and down another hall. Near the end of the hall, she opened a door and waved Abby inside. To describe the room as cramped was understated. The small space had a threadbare sofa, a desk with two chairs, and every surface in the room was stacked with books, folders, papers, or magazines. Most of the floor was covered also with stacks of stuff.

"Sorry about the mess." Sam moved a pile from the end of the couch. "Have a seat, please." She dropped the chart on the desk across from where she indicated Abby should sit and leaned back against it with her hands shoved deep in her pockets.

Abby got a sudden sick feeling in the pit of her stomach. The pain she saw in Sam's eyes caused tears to sting the back of her own. She inhaled a long, deep breath and held it.

"There's no easy way to tell you this." Her eyes glistened with unshed tears.

Abby exhaled. "It's Phillip." It wasn't a question. Abby knew, every part of her knew, that Phillip was gone. "I'm sorry, Sam." She held on to every ounce of self-control she had.

Sam bounced her head. "He took a really bad turn late last night." Her voice trembled and she looked at the floor. "He was tough though. He hung on until early this morning." She met Abby's eyes again. "Of all the kids…" Sam's tears broke free and rushed down her cheeks.

Abby stood. "I'm so sorry." What else could she say?

"I wanted to save him." She inhaled a deep breath and dropped her head forward.

Abby didn't think. She simply put her arm around Sam's shoulder and pulled Sam against her.

"Phillip was very lucky to have you caring for him. I know words are of little comfort, but you have to know you did everything you could for him, and I'm sure you made his last days as painless as is possible." She stroked her hand over Sam's hair. Comforting Sam somehow made it easier for her to accept the news without breaking down. After several long minutes, Sam composed herself and pulled back from Abby's arm. Digging tissues from her pocket she wiped at her face.

"Sorry. I don't usually let it get to me."

Abby shook her head. "I don't know how you do it. And please, don't be sorry for showing emotions. It is what makes us human."

Sam rummaged on the desk under the chart she'd laid there and then handed the plastic hospital bag to Abby. "Phillip's mother wanted you to have this."

The shaking started in her heart and quickly reached her hand as she took the offering from Sam. She didn't need to look inside. She knew what it was, but she opened the bag and pulled out Phillip's book, *New Kids on the Rock*. Abby ran her hand over the cover briefly before returning it to the bag. A single tear escaped, but she reined in the emotions that threatened to take over.

"Do you want to get a cup of coffee and talk?" Sam asked.

Abby wasn't prepared to do…this. Not now, and not in front of Sam. She clutched her treasure of Phillip to her chest.

"I need to go. How about tomorrow? After my time with the kids."

Sam leaned back against the desk again. "Sure. If you don't see me around, have me paged." Abby nodded and as she turned, Sam reached for her hand. "Abby…" Abby faced her, relaxing her fingers as Sam's hand slid so easily into hers. "Thanks for your comfort."

Abby squeezed her hand lightly and tried to smile. "Anytime. I'll see you tomorrow."

It was only when Abby started away from her that Sam let go of her hand. Or was it that she had held on to the comforting contact until the last possible moment? Out in her car, she glanced at the bag beside her purse on the seat and then beat her fists on the steering wheel. "Damn it!" She should have been there to help Sam through Phillip's end. But as she thought about it, she recalled the expression, "The Lord works in mysterious ways," and realized how devastating it would have been to be there and watch him slip away. She said a silent prayer for courage and strength for Phillip's family in their grief.

Abby stepped into the elevator right as Sam came around the corner. She walked to her favorite window down the hall and waited to see Abby exit the building. She watched, noting the downward turn of Abby's head and the lack of the usual confidence in her stride she had always observed. Abby always walked like she had the world in her hand, but not today. Abby's car sat unmoving for at least ten minutes, so Sam decided to only give her a few more minutes before she'd go down and check on her. If Abby was upset, Sam wanted to offer her comfort, the way Abby had for her. Actually, if it were up to Sam, she'd be the only one to hold and comfort Abby, to keep her safe and make her feel secure. She shook her head. *In your dreams.* Just as Sam was ready to go after her, the backup lights lit momentarily and Abby drove away.

It would be another long and sleepless night for Sam. Last night, and this morning, it had been the sight of Phillip's parents holding their son as he slipped away. Tonight's sleeplessness would be a different image. Tonight she'd feel Abby's arm around her, remember the smell of her perfume, and relive over and over the sensations that Abby's touch stirred in her. Pushing Phillip's memory from her mind riddled her with guilt, but it couldn't be helped. She was starved for Abby's warm embrace.

Abby dropped her things on the counter and her tired body on a stool. Pulling Phillip's book from the bag flooded her mind with memories. She ran a hand over the textured surface and recalled her first meeting with him. A tiny smile tugged at her mouth with the image of his beaming smile that lit up everything around him. She flipped open the cover, tracing her finger over the crudely printed letters spelling his name in fourth grader penmanship. And like a tidal wave, the reality of a world no longer graced with the charming magnetic young man hit her. The deep sob sounded foreign to her as she swung her arms wildly across the countertop, scattering everything within reach. She dropped her head to her arms on the counter and cried until there were no more tears. She felt physically sick.

She didn't want to think or feel any longer. She got Selena's bottle of tequila from the cabinet and grabbed the morning's coffee cup from the sink. Pouring the cup half full, she held her breath and gulped a mouthful. It slid like liquid fire down her throat and burned in her stomach. She gagged and almost threw up, but once the feeling passed, she drank again. By the fifth swallow she no longer noticed the burn, the taste barely making her shiver. Pushing the bottle and empty cup aside, she sat staring out the windows into the night. Finally her mind felt empty and fuzzy around the edges. She knew she needed to eat something, but she lacked the energy it took to stand. When it got to be too late to do anything but stumble to bed in her drunken state, she did so. At the bedside she stepped out of her clothes, turned on the alarm and fell onto the bed.

"Abby wake up!" Someone shook her in her dreams. "Come on, open your eyes." Abby struggled, unable to open her eyelids. "Someone was in the tequila. Did you have a party?" Her brain wouldn't focus on Selena's words. "You don't go near that stuff. So who was here?"

The light was blinding. Enough fog lifted from her brain to recall her trip to the hospital. Tears filled her eyes.

"Now you're just scaring me, Abby. What's going on?"

She struggled to sit, throwing her arms around Selena's shoulders and burying her face in Selena's neck.

"Shh…" Selena rocked gently. "It's okay. I've got you. Tell me what's wrong."

Between sobs, Abby managed to say, "He died…" Selena continued rocking.

"Who?"

"The young…" She couldn't catch her breath.

Selena stroked her hair. "Shh… The boy at the hospital?"

"Yes," she whispered against Selena's wet skin.

"Ah baby, I'm sorry." Selena held tight to her, giving Abby what she needed. She pressed her lips to Abby's temple. "If there's anything I can do for you please tell me." Selena kissed her lightly. "Promise you'll tell me?" Abby nodded. "How much did you drink, baby?"

"I…I don't know."

"You're probably gonna feel like crap in the morning."

Abby couldn't think that far ahead. The feel of Selena's lips against her skin was a welcome distraction. Selena lifted Abby's chin and kissed her forehead.

"Be right back." When she returned she placed four aspirin in Abby's hand and held out a large glass of water. "Take these and drink all of it. Trust me on this. It'll make a big difference in the morning."

Abby swallowed the pills and drank the entire glass of water. "Now I'll be peeing all night." She handed the glass to Selena and fell back into the pillows.

"It's better than a tequila hangover, believe me."

Abby stroked her fingers over Selena's cheek. "Thanks."

Selena caught her hand and placed a kiss in her palm. "I love you. And besides, if I don't take care of you, who'll take care of me?" She winked, then kissed Abby.

Selena stripped out of her clothes and climbed under the covers. She pulled Abby into her arms. She stroked Abby's hair and down her back. Abby briefly remembered holding Sam earlier and then drifted off.

* * *

When Abby arrived to work the following morning, Blair was there the second she shrugged out of her coat.

"We have another busy day." Abby tossed her a glance. "Wow! No offense, but you look like the living dead." She turned on her heel and disappeared into her office.

How could Blair make jokes about the dead? Was she really as cold-hearted as everyone said and didn't know that innocent people died every day? Young and innocent children who had done nothing but bring joy to the lives of everyone around them. Has she never loved anyone enough in her life to have her heart shattered by a loss?

Abby tried to put Blair's stinging words out of her mind, but she was in no mood to take her crap. Not today. She always felt a kind of nobility about her job of helping put the bad guys away. *Noble is what Dr. Sam does for kids.* The kids are the future for everyone. She didn't need Blair's negativity in her life. Life, as she'd just been smacked in the face with, was too short for anything but positive energy, like the energy she got from her volunteer time with the sick kids at the hospital. Like she was sure Dr. Sam derived from helping to heal kids. She grabbed up the files from her desk and stormed into Blair's office.

"I quit!" She tossed the files so they scattered across Blair's desk.

"What?" Blair looked at her like she hadn't heard.

"You heard me. I quit! Stick a fork in me because I'm done." She felt tears gathering in her eyes and turned to leave.

Blair sprang up and raced to the door, closing it before Abby could escape. "Abby, please wait a minute. I'm sorry. I—"

Abby raised her hand. "Blair, you can be so damn rude and uncaring, but worst of all, heartless and hurtful. I can't do this anymore, and I won't." Abby planted her fists on her hips, not caring that tears streamed down her face. "As much as I'd like to see what karma has in store for you, I'm not waiting around. Frankly, if there's collateral damage, I don't want to be anywhere near it." She waved one of her hands. "Now move and let me leave." As Abby reached around her for the doorknob, Blair gently placed her hands on Abby's arms.

"Abby, I am sincerely sorry." Abby tried moving but Blair held her in place. "Everything you said is true. I told you last week I'm trying to change." Her tone made her words sound sincere. "I'm trying to change what I've been my whole life. It's no easy task and it's no wonder no one likes me." She looked at her feet. "I thought you did. I thought we were…becoming friends." She sounded meek as a child. "Please give me another chance." When she looked up her eyes pleaded.

Abby dropped her head. What could she say?

"What's going on? I've never seen you this upset."

"The boy at the hospital died," she muttered and swallowed down a sob.

When Blair tipped her chin up, her eyes were blurry with tears. Blair released her arm and pulled her into an embrace.

"I'm so very sorry." Blair whispered against her hair, holding Abby securely in her arms.

She shook once before she remembered whose arms were holding her. *I'm dreaming. I'm at my desk and I'll wake up in a second. I can't be letting Blair see me this vulnerable.*

Blair broke the silence that hung heavily between them. "Abby, if there's anything I can do, please let me know." She relaxed her arms and Abby got the sense that Blair realized the inappropriateness of their position.

She moved out of her arms and went to the desk to grab tissues. Blair was right beside her in an instant.

"If you need to leave, take some time off, it's fine. I'll get a temp."

She shook her head as she blew her nose.

"Are you sure, because it's not a problem?"

"I'm sure. I need to work. It's a good distraction."

Blair briefly touched her arm. "Please accept my apology. I truly am sorry."

She nodded. "I shouldn't have blown up. My nerves feel raw, or maybe it's PMS."

Blair laughed lightly. "That's it. That explains my behavior." She shrugged. "It just affects me on a daily basis." She cocked her head. "Are you sure you're okay?"

"I must look atrocious."

Blair raised her hands. "I'm no dummy. I am not touching that one."

"Let me run down to the ladies' room, and then we can get to work."

"Take your time." Before Abby could get away, Blair caught her hand. "So, we're okay?"

Abby squeezed her hand and pulled away. "For now," she said on her way to the door.

Blair went out of her way to be cordial the rest of the day, but, as Abby drove toward the hospital, her mood swung like a pendulum. She felt light because she was about to spend time with a wonderful group of children, but also dark because Phillip's death was still too fresh in her mind. Perhaps coffee with Sam afterward would help her mood.

Her time with the kids went too quickly, however, it lifted her spirit when she spied Sam at the back of the room shortly before she finished. Sam smiled warmly when their eyes met.

Down in the cafeteria they settled at a table far removed from others. After a long and awkward silence Abby started to wonder if Sam was uncomfortable because of yesterday's physical contact.

"You look a little more rested than yesterday," Abby said as Sam swirled the plastic stick in her coffee, which she'd been doing since they'd sat.

Sam brought her eyes up slowly and met Abby's. "Don't take this the wrong way, but you kind of look a little more undone that you did yesterday. Everything okay?"

Abby patted her cheek. "You mean my makeup isn't hiding it?" She frowned, leaning over the table. "I blew up at my boss this morning, tried to quit, and then broke down in front of her. Will that excuse how I look?" She smiled not wanting Sam to think she'd hurt her feelings. At least Sam had more tact conveying how bad Abby looked. "And all before we started our day."

"Wow! The worst I dealt with today was a six-year-old throwing up on my shoes. You definitely win the 'sucky day' award." She raised her cup in salute and they both chuckled.

"So, tell me about this boss."

Abby sipped her coffee. "You couldn't possibly want to hear about her. She can be so…impossible sometimes, like this morning." The comment elicited another laugh from Sam. This was exactly why she adored Sam. She shared a few details about Blair, including her infamous nickname. "Life's too short and precious to put up with someone like her, and Phillip's situation makes that all too real."

"Life is definitely better when we're surrounded by people who care and that we can care about."

"So true."

"You'll make an incredible mom someday, Abby Collins."

Abby tilted her head. "I'd have to say you'll do a fine job yourself." Sam laughed. "Now what's funny about that?" Sam sat back in her chair, stretching out her legs as she so often did. She held Abby in her gaze.

"No one's interested in more than sex when they find out I'm a poor learning doctor." Sam looked down into her cup.

"And certainly not anything resembling a relationship since it will be years before I earn more than I owe."

"Ah, but you're wealthy with a passion for your work and those children. I find that more attractive in a person than anything money can buy." *Oh heavens, that sounded a lot like flirting.* She raised her cup to hide behind it and hoped Sam wasn't offended.

"If I may be nosy, what is Abby Collins looking forward to in life?" Sam met her eyes again.

"A family with as many kids as I can handle." Abby smiled at the thought. "What about Dr. Sam? What are you after?"

Sam turned the cardboard cup in her hands. "Oh you know, what every girl wants." She flashed a smile. "To find my true love, that special someone and live happily ever after." She sat forward locking her hands around the cup. "Do you believe in love at first sight, or fate, or destiny or any of that?"

Abby swallowed, giving pause a long moment before answering. "I believe there is one person we're meant to be with." She waved a hand wide. "Out there, somewhere." Sam's intense gaze held her own and she would have sworn Sam was looking into her soul.

"I'd sure like to believe that." Silence fell around them, and then Sam jerked and reached in her pocket for her phone. "I've got to go," she said, pushing back from the table. "Maybe I'll see you next week when you come around."

"I'll be here." A bit of disappointment washed over her at the thought of only seeing Sam occasionally. She raised her cup. "Thanks for the coffee."

CHAPTER ELEVEN

Blair hounded Abby the following day until she agreed she might make an appearance at the office Christmas party on Saturday.

"My attendance will be contingent on finding something to wear," she told Blair at the end of the day.

When she told Selena about the party, she didn't seem to care one way or the other about Abby going to a party since she was leaving. Abby didn't RSVP for the dinner, only for cocktails and the socializing that followed at eight p.m. She dug deep into her wardrobe, finding a black tank dress in a sweeping sleek fabric and paired it with a bronze and black print jacket.

Making her way to the bar, Abby ordered a glass of wine, spotting Blair almost immediately in the midst of a group of men deep in conversation. She remained at the end of the bar, sipping her wine and exchanging holiday greetings with people she knew. She noted that Blair moved from group to group with the same attractive, young and athletic-looking blond fellow. She managed to stay off Blair's radar for nearly an hour, but she looked over once again and Blair was watching her. She tipped her drink and nodded. Abby acknowledged with a smile. Blair spoke to the hunky guy then made her way to the bar.

Standing uncomfortably close to Abby, she said, "Well, if it isn't my favorite assistant." Abby could smell the liquor on her breath and guessed Blair had had her share of drinks.

"Hello, Blair. How are you this evening?"

"I am fine. Just fine." She wore a silly grin and moved closer until their shoulders touched. "I have to say that's a knockout dress you're wearing." She wagged a finger. "I knew you wouldn't disappoint. You look marvelous, darling." She winked. "So...can I buy the pretty lady a drink?" She pushed her empty glass toward the bartender.

"Thank you, but no. I already have a drink." Abby tapped a painted nail on her wineglass.

"But you have to let me buy you a drink before the night's over." The blond stepped beside Blair a moment later. "Excuse us." She scooped up her fresh drink and ushered him off.

Abby nursed her wine for another thirty minutes and then set the empty glass aside. As she turned to leave, there stood Blair, as if she somehow sensed Abby's departure.

"Okay, you have to let me buy you a drink now." Blair tapped her finger on the bar.

"No Blair, really. I'm fine."

She raised her glass. "I can't argue that point." She drained the last of her drink. "Not that I'd want to. So come on. Have just one drink with me."

"I've had my limit. I'm driving."

Blair waved a hand. "It's okay. I'm driving too." Her glass landed with a thunk on the bar.

"I don't think that's a good idea. Where's your date?"

She leaned closer and after putting a finger to her lips, quietly said, "That blond cutie is just arm candy. What everybody expects to see. Have to keep up appearances, you know." Abby took a step back. "Anyway, he's gone, had a date or something. So...I'm on my own." She raised her brows suggestively.

"I think common sense in this situation dictates that you let me get you a cab then."

"Oh…no…cabs. It's too early to quit partying." She grabbed her empty glass and waved it to get the bartender's attention.

Abby put a hand on Blair's arm, lowering the glass to the bar. "Far be it for me to tell you what to do, but I think a wise woman would know to call it quits about now. Let me get you a cab."

She wrapped her hand around Abby's forearm. "No, no cabs, Abs." Blair chuckled. "But you can drive me home." She batted her eyes. "Pleeeze…"

Better judgment told Abby to hike up her dress and run like the place was on fire.

"Please, Abby," Blair pleaded again. "I might do something foolish like drive myself home."

Common decency, or maybe it was stupidity, overrode her judgment and she sighed. "All right, but we are leaving *now*." She pushed the glass out of Blair's reach. "No more drinking."

"Agreed," Blair said with a lopsided grin.

"I'm going to get my coat. I assume you have one?" Blair dug in the tiny purse hanging from her shoulder and produced the numbered tag along with some crumpled bills. Abby gave her a stern look. "Wait here. If you're not standing here when I come back, I won't look for you."

Blair nodded and when Abby returned, Blair had in fact remained where she'd left her, but she was tipping back a fresh drink. Abby threw her coat onto the bar.

"One for the road." Blair drained the glass.

"Great," Abby mumbled. *Stupidity wins.* She shrugged into her coat. "Come on Blair. Your taxi is leaving."

Blair grabbed at her coat and it slid to the floor. Hanging on to the bar, she leaned to pick it up and almost toppled over. Abby reached a steadying hand under her arm then helped her on with the coat. Blair swayed as they crossed the ballroom.

"If you fall, I can't pick you up and you'll only embarrass yourself."

Thankfully Blair remained on her feet. As they reached the revolving doors, Abby slipped her arm through Blair's, with high hopes that the night air might sober her up. She propped Blair against the building, and she closed her eyes. After handing over the valet ticket, Abby watched as Blair's steady breaths steamed the cold air. She fell into the passenger's seat and Abby buckled her in.

"Please tell me if you need me to stop," Abby said as she pulled away. "Believe me when I say that you *don't* want to be sick in my car."

Blair waved. "Don worry, I jus fine." Her hand drifted down to settle on Abby's thigh and she dropped her head back against the seat. When Abby returned her hand to her own lap, Blair exhaled loudly and rolled her head to look at Abby.

Once they reached Blair's building and Abby managed to get her out of the car, they rode the elevator from the garage to the ninth floor. After Blair made numerous unsuccessful attempts to get the key in the lock, she took Blair's keys from her and opened the door. She grabbed hold of Abby's arm and pulled her inside.

"Blair, I have to get home."

"No, haf a look round."

She didn't doubt that Blair had a lavish apartment. Taking a step inside, she stopped to pull out the keys dangling from the door lock. When she turned around to hand them over, Blair was there. And too quickly for Abby to move, Blair leaned forward and brushed her lips over Abby's before she could stop her. She put her hands on Blair's shoulders and moved her back.

"Because you're drunk I'm going to pretend you didn't just do that."

She reached a hand toward Abby's face. "So beautiful, I jus—"

"Don't!" Abby jerked the door open and slammed it behind her. She fumed all the way to the parking garage for letting Blair get the drop on her.

* * *

There was no further mention of Blair's Saturday night behavior, and Abby chalked up the kiss to Blair's drunken state, although, it flattered her that Blair might find her attractive.

The offices were closed on Wednesday, Christmas Eve, and by evening Abby didn't know what to do with herself. So, she dressed festively, stopped at the Incredible Edibles Bakery for holiday cookies and went to the hospital's third-floor nurses station. They were delighted to see Abby, but they scolded her with humor for the diet busting temptations.

"By all means share them with the kids if they're allowed to have them," she said to Nurse Adams.

"You just missed seeing 'em all with Santa," Flora told her.

"Shucks! And I have my list all ready for him too." She patted the small purse hanging at her side. She was about to offer to make a coffee run to the cafeteria when she heard the familiar voice around the corner giving some verbal care instructions. Abby couldn't say whose smile was brighter, hers or Sam's, but on a scale of one to ten, her holiday mood suddenly registered at a twenty.

"Weren't you just here last night?" Sam asked.

"I was. I had some free time this evening and wanted to bring some goodies by for the nurses." She gestured at the plate of sweets. "Help yourself."

"Thanks, but I've already had entirely too many unhealthy treats today." When Sam stepped away from the desk, Abby followed. "So, I imagine you're off to a fancy holiday shindig." Sam stopped in front of the door to the activity room.

"I'm in no rush. Did you want to get some coffee or something?"

Sam smiled sheepishly. "Or something."

Abby arched a brow. "You have my attention."

Sam waved her hand. "It's foolish, never mind."

"Sam, tell me." She touched Sam's arm.

Sam looked at her feet. "I have to go to my parents' for dinner, and, well, I thought I might talk you into letting me drag you along for an hour or so, but…" She shrugged. "Like I said, it was a foolish thought and a really big favor to ask."

She found Sam's embarrassment endearing. Masking a smile she said, "Okay."

Sam looked up. "Okay, what?"

"Okay, let me hear you try and talk me into this." She finally smiled.

"My whole family will be there including some aunts, uncles, and cousins. It's only dinner, but Momma will do her best to get me to stay the night. Unless…I have a good reason not to." She shrugged again. "You'd be my excuse, and I know, that sounds so lame." She shoved her hands deep in her coat pockets. "I mean, you wouldn't just be my excuse. You'd be really nice company to have, but anyway, there you go. I'm sure you have other things to do besides bail me out."

"There isn't anywhere I have to be this evening. I would enjoy meeting more of your family." A smile curled Sam's lips. "You're pretty nice company yourself, but I think I may require something in exchange for this big favor."

"Anything, you name it!"

Sam's excitement reminded Abby of a child on Christmas morning. *If luck is a lady, I might have my own little bundle to share Christmas with one of these days.*

"I'll have to think about it."

Sam nodded. "I'll be right back." She rushed back to the nurses station and returned a few minutes later. "I just need to stop at my locker and grab my coat. I'll meet you downstairs."

They met down in the lobby and Sam held the outer door for Abby. "You remember where my parents' place is?"

"Yes, but if I'm supposed to be your excuse, don't you think we should ride together?"

"Oh, yeah." Sam jingled her keys.

"And since you've been working for twelve straight hours, I think I should drive. Do you want to leave your car at your apartment?"

"Here's fine." Sam slid her keys in her pocket.

Sam talked nervously for most of the ride, filling Abby in on family members she would likely meet.

"Momma's going to be so pleased to see you again."

Sam's mother was indeed happy to see Abby, but it seemed, Sam's older sister, Kattiana was less thrilled that she had come with Sam. She made a snide comment about Sam still showing up without a guy. Abby couldn't help but wonder if Sam's sister knew something about Sam that might be of interest to her.

All in all it was a wonderfully festive family affair. After dinner Abby followed Sam as she walked her grandmother to her room. She leaned in the doorway watching them.

"You read, Sammy, please?" She raised a book toward Sam.

Abby stepped in the room. "I can if you'd like."

When her grandmother smiled, Abby took the book and sat on the stool beside her rocker. Sam took a seat on the bed. After no more than ten minutes, Sam's mother appeared in the doorway.

"Samantha, you help your momma please in the kitchen."

Abby continued to read. The smile on Sam's grandmother's face was worth every second of her time.

In the kitchen, Sam's mother pulled two chairs out at the small table. "Sit *mio figlia*." She then poured two glasses of wine. "You so busy, we no talk no more." In a gesture Sam recognized meant to shame, she shook her head. "Your friend Abby, she very nice."

"Yes, Momma, she's very nice."

"She very pretty too."

"Yes, she's pretty too." Sam stared off, seeing Abby's beautiful face in her mind.

"You like her, no?"

Sam returned her attention to her mother. "We're friends, Momma. Yes, I like her."

She took hold of Sam's hand. "You like her, no?" Sam's mother raised a busy brow. Sam averted her mother's eyes. "Samantha, I know you no like boys. I know this for many years."

Sam froze in her seat and the room suddenly lacked enough air. She watched as her mother's lips moved, but couldn't quite get her brain to register the words.

"It is okay, *mio ameno figlia*. Momma loves you for you, my Samantha."

Sam dropped her head and stared at the tabletop.

Her mother cupped Sam's chin and tipped her head up to look into her eyes. "I see how you see her. Momma knows this."

Sam swallowed. "I do like her Momma, but she…she doesn't like me the same way."

"Like woman like a man?" Sam nodded. "I think you wrong, Samantha. I see how she see you."

If only that were true, Momma.

"You know, Samantha, only good things come in time. Like you a doctor. You give time. She will like you same as you like." She patted her hand to her heart. "Momma know this too."

Sam wanted to believe her mother's intuition, but she knew better than to hope. Momma pulled her into a hug and kissed her head.

Abby stopped abruptly in the kitchen doorway. She'd obviously walked in on a tender mother-daughter moment. A moment she envied. Stepping back into the hall she waited until she saw a reflection of movement in the dark window over the sink.

"Am I interrupting?" Sam and her mother stood in silence.

Sam turned around quickly at the sound of her voice. "No… uh…Momma and I were catching up."

"I probably should get going, if you're ready."

Sam turned around and kissed her mother on the cheek. "I'll be by sometime tomorrow after I sleep off today's shift." Her mother held Sam's face in her hands and kissed her forehead.

"Mrs. Christiano, thank you again for dinner."

"Momma." She gave Abby a wide smile. "Thank you, you bring my Samantha." She winked.

They threaded their way through the living room saying goodbyes. Her father bear-hugged them both and invited Abby to return again anytime.

"I'll never be able to thank you enough for this," Sam told Abby more than once on the drive across town. "At the very least I owe you a lavish dinner, your choice, and whatever else you think. I am in your debt."

"I'm still thinking on that," Abby said. "Why did your mother thank me for bringing you this evening?"

"She thinks the only reason I came was because you brought me."

Abby gave a light-hearted laugh. "I can imagine you miss family gatherings for unexpected situations that arise at the hospital. You didn't seem antsy to leave."

"Ah, appearances can be deceiving."

That sounds cryptic Dr. Sam. Abby didn't want to pry. Hopefully she would learn all about mother-daughter moments.

"Do you have big plans for New Year's?"

"I believe so, yes. A party, although a small one." She hoped. "Have to ring in the New Year right. Do you have some special plans?"

"Oh yeah. Sleep right through it. I'm on early New Year's Day."

"Well, lucky for you your kids don't drink."

Sam shifted in her seat. "The young ones, no, but I've seen my share of teenagers with alcohol poisoning."

"I have never understood the allure of getting falling-down drunk." *And still don't, having tried it as recently as last week.* "Where's your car?" Abby asked as she pulled into the emptier than usual parking lot.

"You can drop me at the door. I want to run in and check on something."

"Don't forget to go home and sleep so you can share tomorrow with your family." When Sam opened her door, Abby caught her arm. "Thanks for dragging me along tonight. I enjoyed myself." Sam looked down at Abby's hand on her arm before meeting Abby's gaze. Abby pulled her hand away.

"No, thank you for rescuing me from a sleepover at my parents. I keep trying to tell Momma I'm too old for those now." Sam laughed. "I *really* owe you Abby."

Before Abby could stop herself, she blurted out, "I think I kind of like holding you in debt."

Sam grinned. "Goodnight, Abby. Merry Christmas."

"Merry Christmas, Sam. I'm sure I'll see you again soon."

"I'm sure."

While most were dreaming of Santa and sugarplums, Abby, strange as it was, dreamed about sharing gifts around a

Christmas tree with Sam. She woke longing for Selena's touch, and she finally called Abby a little before noon.

"Hi babe, I miss you."

"I miss you too."

"I can't wait to get back home. I forgot to tell you that I made a bunch of calls while I was waiting at the airport on my flight out. The New Year's Eve party at our place is a go. Invite anyone you'd like and don't worry, I'm going to take care of everything. The food, the booze, and decorations, and well, whatever."

Selena sounded different. Perhaps she'd been drinking or maybe it was the miles between them.

"I love you, Abby. I'll call again over the weekend."

"I love you, Selena. Enjoy your family time."

Abby hung up the phone feeling disappointment that Selena hadn't once said she wished Abby was there with her. And yet Sam, a practical stranger, had wanted to share Abby's company, and for that matter, her family too. The hopes of motherhood loomed large in Abby's mind, and the New Year seemed the right time to make her dream a reality. She only hoped Selena would be as receptive to the idea.

Blair continued to be on her best and most professional behavior, and she had Selena's return home on Sunday to look forward to.

Abby spent Saturday cleaning every crack and crevice of the loft for the upcoming party. She tried to think of one person she could invite, but sadly, she came up empty. Sam was really the only person she could think of to ring in the New Year with them, but she couldn't expect Sam to be comfortable with a group of lesbians. Selena called after dinner to let Abby know her arrival time for the following day. She heard from Selena again on Sunday about an hour before her expected arrival time.

"We're still sitting in the airport. By the time I get in, I'm going to have to go straight to work and I pray I'm not late."

They certainly didn't need Selena to lose her job, considering Abby's plans for the New Year.

"I'm sorry you're delayed." Abby sighed. "I really miss you. Please wake me up when you get in from work okay?"

"You bet, doll. I miss you too."

Selena was dead on her feet when she made it home from work. They took a minute to plan their own Christmas for New Year's Day since Selena wouldn't be working until the evening shift. Kissing briefly, they cuddled closely and Selena fell immediately into a deep sleep.

CHAPTER TWELVE

Abby had twisted Blair's arm until she agreed to let her off on New Year's Eve.

"The deliveries are due between one and three. Are you going to be here?" Selena asked.

"Yes, aren't you?"

"I need to run out and pick up some decorations and stuff. Unless you'd rather."

Abby didn't intend to leave the loft until she had to go back to work on Monday. As a holiday gift to her, Blair had given her Friday off too.

"I think I'll leave it in your very capable hands."

The first guests arrived shortly after eight. A young couple, at least ten years younger than Abby, who Selena introduced as friends of someone whose name Abby didn't recognize. Abby did remember meeting the next arrivals, Carrie and Gina, but she couldn't remember when or where. And they came with three other young women, who Abby didn't think looked old enough to drink. She wondered if she should be carding a few of them. The youngest of them, Liza, wore a fragrance that seemed vaguely familiar to Abby, but she couldn't figure out who she knew that wore it. She just knew she hated it.

By ten o'clock, no fewer than twenty people were jammed inside the loft. She caught Selena at the counter mixing a drink and pinned her from behind as she set her own glass down.

"I thought you said maybe a dozen people."

Selena turned around and placed her hands on Abby's hips. Her eyes already appeared glazed from drinking.

"I guess everybody invited someone else. Sorry, doll. You want me to run them off?"

"Of course not." Abby glanced sideways and saw the very young Liza standing at the end of the counter watching them. When she looked back at Selena, Selena seemed to be looking at the same young girl.

"Hey," she said, regaining Selena's attention. "They all look so young. I just...I don't know...feel like a den mother."

Selena laughed. "Well, you're the hottest damn den mother I could imagine holding in my arms." Selena pulled her close and nuzzled her face into Abby's hair. Her breath felt warm against Abby's ear. "Are you sure you don't want me to run them all out of here?" She pulled Abby's hips firmly against her own.

"No, stop it." Abby gave Selena's thigh a playful pat before giving her a peck on the lips and walking over to Liza. "Can I get you anything?"

"Uh...no thanks." She looked past Abby. "Selena's making me a drink." Abby noted that her fingers were interlocked and she tapped her thumbs together. "Your loft is awesome."

"Thank you." Abby glanced around them.

"It's so open. It gives you this feeling like you have room to breathe."

"Yes, it does." Abby caught the scent of her perfume again and searched her memory for who shared the distinct fragrance. *It'll come to me at three o'clock in the morning.* "Enjoy the party," she said before moving off to mingle with some of the other strangers in her home.

Later, while standing with a young couple admiring the view, Abby briefly thought about Sam, wishing she'd invited her. At least she'd have someone to talk with who she knew, but Sam was probably already home sleeping so she could work her shift tomorrow. Gazing around the packed loft, she noticed Selena going into the upstairs bathroom. She tried, but failed to register what one of the women was saying to her. Her libido unexpectedly urged her to slip into the bathroom with Selena. After several long minutes, Abby excused herself and went upstairs.

She tapped on the door and since it wasn't locked, she pushed it open to poke her head in. Her mouth fell open and the air left her lungs in a rush. Either she'd stepped into another world, or someone had put a hallucinogen in her wine. Selena's jeans were almost off her hips and little blond Liza's pants were bunched around her ankles. Everything moved in slow motion as Selena turned and looked at her.

"Oh, God, Abby! It's not what you think!"

Abby heard her voice, but it sounded like it was coming down a long tunnel. Her peripheral vision dimmed and the instantaneous hot pain in her chest spread to her stomach. She slammed the door. Her hands trembled so badly she thought she'd drop her glass. She felt as though she were going to throw up. Heat suffused her neck and face. Maybe she was only having a heart attack.

On wobbly legs she retreated down the stairs, grabbed a bottle of wine from the counter and rushed into the bedroom, locking both doors behind her. She backed against the bathroom door as tears flooded her eyes. Gulping from the bottle she slowly slid to the floor with her knees to her chest. She heard the bedroom doorknob rattle, and then a moment later, the one on the bathroom door.

"Come on, Abby. You gotta let me explain." Selena tried the knob again.

Every part of Abby wanted to sob, to scream, to strike out at Selena, but she remained silent.

Selena pounded on the door. "Abby, come on. We have a houseful of guests and it's almost midnight." She read the bedside clock through her tears. Sixteen minutes until New Year's. "Abby, you have to let me in sooner or later. Come on. I can explain."

Abby couldn't imagine anything could explain what she'd witnessed. Not now, not ever. She drank more wine, beginning to feel numb, but knowing it wasn't from the alcohol. Then finally the horns, cheers, fireworks—or guns—sounded, all mixed with the sob that erupted from deep within her. She poured it into her hands and pushed up from the floor. At the window she stared into the night. She cried like she had when Phillip passed. It felt the same. She'd lost something she cared deeply about... forever. A hollow emptiness cloaked her in the darkness.

She wanted, she needed, for someone to comfort her, but there was no one. Well, there was Sam. Sam was kind and compassionate. But Sam thought she was straight. If she confided in Sam, it might very well ruin the friendship they were developing. The only friendship she had. She clutched at her chest. She'd have to carry this pain by herself. Given time, though, she knew eventually her heart would heal. And to think she'd planned to have and raise children with *this* woman. A woman she realized now, she didn't know.

She stood in the darkness a long time before noticing the silence. The party was finally over, the guests gone, and hopefully Selena too. *If there really is a God.* She wasn't ready to face Selena, the rest of her life, or starting over. She unlocked the bathroom door, desperate to empty her bladder and wash her face. After returning to the bedroom and pulling on a T-shirt and sweats, she dropped on the bed and hugged a pillow, attempting to exhale the heavy weight pressing on her chest. She needed to sleep. Her body screamed with exhaustion and she knew she'd be more clear-headed in the morning to deal with it all—starting her life over.

Her eyes were closed. She was trying to empty her mind and relax her body when she heard the outer bathroom door. A moment later she saw Selena's silhouette beside the bed.

She swayed as she spoke. "We needa talk, doll." She dropped heavily on the bed. Abby rolled away when Selena reached for her.

"Don't touch me," she barely managed to say aloud.

"M'on babe. I can s'plain." She scooted closer.

"Oh please, Selena. You've got to be kidding? And don't ever touch me again!" She scurried out of bed with the pillow still clutched in her arms. "I'm sleeping upstairs. Just leave me alone." She hurried up the stairs and didn't take a breath until she locked the guest room door. Her body shook. It ached, and she just wanted to shut everything down.

The doorknob rattled loudly. "Abby s-sorry, need you… please…" There was a moment's pause before Selena repeated her plea.

Abby pressed the pillow over her head to muffle Selena's pathetic begging. By two thirty the house was again quiet, and certain that Selena had gone back downstairs, she breathed deeply in and out until sleep finally claimed her.

* * *

Abby couldn't believe she was awake by eight. Tiptoeing downstairs, she found Selena passed out on the bed, fully clothed with a tequila bottle on the nightstand. She pulled the bathroom door closed, grabbed her toothbrush and quietly made her way back upstairs. Entering the bathroom, the unexpected sight she'd witnessed last night hit her like a punch in the gut. On the cold tile floor she dry heaved until she barely had the strength to get up. Trance-like, she cleaned up, pulled her hair back and dabbed on a little blush and lipstick. She changed into jeans and a sweater down in the laundry room.

"Damn," she muttered. Her purse was in the bedroom. *Well, if she wakes up I'm running for it.* She managed to get her purse, keys, and coat, and slip out without waking Selena. Around the corner from her building she picked up a bagel and an extra-large, strong coffee and returned to her car. Pulling from the garage she headed to the park along the river to have her breakfast.

Huddled against the cold on a bench, Abby watched as a family of mom, dad, and three young children walked a puppy along the path—a painful reminder that her dream of having a happy family for herself had been reduced to rubble. With tears stinging her cheeks, she hurried back to her car. For an hour she drove around town, finally ending up in the hospital parking lot. She wasn't sure why she'd come. Sam couldn't fix her life, but without further thought she crossed the parking lot and entered the hospital.

"Would you know where I might find Dr. Christiano?" Abby asked at the nurses station.

The heavyset African-American woman who was as wide as she was tall, with a few spots of gray in her black curly hair, said, "Dr. Sam went home sick as a dog yesterday. Still be home today nursing whatever she got. Somethin' I can help you with, honey?"

Abby's heart sank. "I was hoping to chat with her while I was here. I'll catch up with her another time."

"You want me to give her a message?" Abby shook her head. "You sure, honey?"

This woman was some lucky someone's mother. Abby sensed that if she told this woman her sad tale, she would hug Abby and tell her everything would be okay while Abby cried on her shoulder.

"You okay, honey?" She patted Abby's hand where it rested on the counter.

Abby snapped to attention. "Uh…yes. Thank you." Once back in the elevator she muttered to herself, "Great. Sam's home sick. Could my life suck more?"

She started the car and warmed her hands against the heater vent. *So, Sam is home sick.* She knew where Sam lived. Would she think it odd of Abby to simply show up out of the blue? She drove to the D'lish Diner and picked up some chicken soup. Standing in the lobby of Sam's building, she read the names on the mailboxes. The only listed Christiano was apartment two-ten. She practiced her line as she climbed the stairs.

She knocked and waited, and then an odd thought occurred to her. What if Sam was entertaining company? What if she was holed up in there with someone still celebrating the New Year? Despite her rising anxiety she knocked again, a bit louder and waited. Maybe she wasn't even home.

"Keep your pants on. I'm coming." The door opened a crack.

"If you kept a key hidden out here somewhere, I wouldn't have to drag you from your sick bed to let me in."

"What?" Sam stepped back and opened the door. "Abby, what are you doing here?" She pulled the flannel robe closed over her T-shirt and boxer shorts.

"I heard you were sick. I brought chicken soup." She lifted the bag. Sam's hair stood up wildly. She looked terribly pale, and well, in need of someone to nurse her back to health. "You look like you feel terrible and should probably be in bed."

She turned and trudged across the small living and kitchen space to a doorway. "Don't mind the mess. The maid hasn't been in yet this week," Sam said.

She closed the door and followed her into the bedroom where Sam climbed into her bed and pulled the covers up to her chin. Setting the bag on the corner of the nightstand, littered with half a dozen empty glasses, she sat on the edge of the bed.

"You didn't have to come all the way over here." Sam didn't look her usual self and her voice sounded weak when she spoke.

"Well, I was already out running around, and this works into my New Year's resolution."

One of Sam's brows rose. "And what's that?"

Abby smiled. "Giving more time to the sick and needy. You're pretty sick and look awfully needy right now."

Sam finger-combed her hair. "Atrocious is how I look."

She shrugged. "I was being polite." That got her a half smile from Sam. "So what have you contracted and are you contagious? Are you going to give me something I can take to work and give to my boss?"

Sam offered a weak smile. "I'm pretty sure it's just a bug." Her pale complexion suddenly had color.

"You look feverish." Abby touched the back of her fingers to Sam's cheek and found it quite warm. As she pulled her hand back, Sam took hold of Abby's wrist and placed Abby's palm against her neck.

Eyes closed, she said, "Your hand is cold." She opened her eyes and settled their deep blue on Abby's. "It feels good."

Abby's heart jumped to her throat and her gaze dropped to Sam's hand where it held on to her. She cleared her throat. "You feel awfully warm. Do you have a thermometer?"

"Don't bother." Sam still held Abby's hand against her neck. And Abby wasn't pulling it away. The feel of Sam's soft warm skin under her hand made her feel...something.

"They say doctors make the worst patients. Is that true?"

"What do you think?"

"I think yes. So...do you have a thermometer?"

Sam nodded toward the bathroom door. "In the medicine cabinet."

Abby eased her hand away. Heart racing, she stood before the mirrored medicine cabinet, taking in the added color in her cheeks, mind swirling with question. *What is wrong with me?* Only twelve hours ago she'd caught her girlfriend doing who knows what to some young twit. Maybe it wasn't everyone else that was screwed up. Maybe it was her.

She closed her eyes. *Focus Abby.* Sam only needs your caring friendship. She grabbed a washcloth from the vanity, wet it in cold water, and returned to the bed. Sam had the covers pulled under her arms and several pillows propping her up. Abby shook a mercury thermometer like the one she remembered from childhood.

"Open up," she said, enticing Sam with a smile. She smoothed the cool cloth over Sam's face and neck then placed it across her forehead. After several minutes Abby checked the thermometer. It read one hundred and four. "You definitely have a fever." She turned the thermometer for Sam to see before setting it on a tissue on the night stand. "Any other symptoms?"

Sam slid the cloth over her eyes. "Do you really want to hear about it?"

She plucked it off her eyes. "Humor me. I can hardly nurse you back to good health without all the facts, now can I?"

Sam shook her head. "Vomiting and dehydration for the first eight or so hours. Now it's an entire body ache, some heaviness in my chest and," she motioned to the thermometer, "a low-grade temperature."

Sam's white coat hung over a chair across the small room with her stethoscope peeking out of the pocket. "Can I determine anything with this?" She lifted it from the pocket and then returned to the bedside. She put the earpieces in place and rubbed the silver dial in her hands.

"We can listen for lung sounds that shouldn't be present." Sam pushed the covers to her waist, pulled open her robe, and took Abby's hand, placing the chest piece below her right breast.

Abby's eyes were instantly drawn to the back of her own fingers where they touched the underside of Sam's breast. The stethoscope magnified the sound of her own heart drumming in her ears.

"What do you hear when I take a deep breath?"

Abby strained to hear anything over the noise her own body screamed at her. She shrugged. "What should I hear?"

"Does it sound even and smooth when I breathe in…" Sam took a deep breath, "and out?" She exhaled.

"It sounds… I don't know, quiet."

Sam moved their hands over to her left side and repeated the deep breaths. "No wheezing, rasping or crackling sounds?"

Abby shook her head. "It sounds quiet, in and out." As soon as the words left her mouth she felt a flush start up her neck.

Sam cocked her head. "So what's the prognosis, doc?"

"Elevated temperature but clear lungs. Maybe I should take a listen to the heart to be sure." Sam moved Abby's hand to the upper part of her left breast, keeping her hand firmly on Abby's. Abby heard a steady thump, thump, thump that matched perfectly to the already present drumming of her own heart in her ears.

Sam waited several long moments before moving her hand away. "Well?"

Abby raised a finger. The air in the room was too heavy. Her heart raced faster, but Sam's kept the rhythm. She tilted her head as if listening, struggling to get a full breath. Finally Abby removed the stethoscope and rested it around her neck. "Heartbeat is steady at seventy-two beats per minute. My prognosis is a common flu bug. Plenty of rest and fluids, and you should be good as new in a few days."

She returned the stethoscope to Sam's coat and took the washcloth to wet again in the bathroom, where she attempted to catch the breath that Sam's touch had so easily stolen. Sam's eyes were closed when she returned to the bedroom, but she blinked them open when Abby laid the cloth across her forehead.

"Would you like your soup now or later?" she asked, picking up the bag.

"Later," Sam replied and caught Abby's hand before she turned away. "Thank you, Abby. You make a darn fine nurse."

Abby's insides quivered. "I'll just…put this in your fridge then."

Sam gave a weak smile. After putting up the soup in the matchbox-sized kitchen, she found herself absently straightening things in Sam's tiny living area on her way back to the bedroom. Her eyes were closed again as Abby stood in the doorway watching her chest rise and fall evenly. She wanted to crawl under the covers and wrap Sam in her arms. She wanted an excuse not to go back to her own crumbling life. She wanted to feel needed.

When Sam heard the door close, her eyes popped open. She'd pretended to sleep in hopes that Abby would leave because she didn't think she could have laid there any longer with Abby so close. She wanted to reach out and touch Abby's beautiful face. She'd had an overwhelming desire to kiss her. Sam dragged herself from the bed in time to see Abby cross the parking lot. She could look at her forever. There was no longer a question that this was the worst infatuation she'd ever experienced. She'd feared Abby staying, but that's what she really wanted. There was sadness in Abby's eyes today that she hadn't noticed before.

Abby smiled and tried to make her laugh, but it was there. Sam wanted to make her eyes shine the way she knew they did when Abby was happy. She wrapped her arms around herself against a chill. The pressure stirred the sensation when Abby's fingers had brushed under Sam's breast. She shivered…a wonderful kind of shiver.

As Abby pulled away, Sam wondered how Abby had found out she was home sick. She was an angel disguised as an average woman, although Sam sensed she was anything but average. She picked up the empty glasses from the nightstand and headed to the kitchen for something to cool her burning insides. The neatly stacked magazines on the coffee table didn't escape notice. She also caught the faint scent of Abby's perfume. Dropping onto the old sagging couch, she pressed a throw pillow hard into her lap. She wanted Abby "that way," too much for her own good. She and Abby were developing a friendship unlike any Sam had ever had. It was comfortable and easy to be around her, and they could talk about nearly everything. Sam was not about to jeopardize that. She'd keep her distance except for coffee at the hospital. Well, maybe an occasional dinner, but she couldn't drag Abby off to her parents anymore because seeing Abby getting along like old friends with her momma and papa just made Sam want her all the more. She closed her eyes at the sadness that settled in her heart.

Abby filled the car's tank and drove around again for hours. The way Selena had destroyed the perfect picture of her future life made her nauseous. How had she been so blind to what she now suspected had been going on for some time? Did she have this sudden unexplainable attraction to Sam because her heart had already known she and Selena were over? So many questions. She found herself headed down Blair's street and hurriedly pulled to the curb.

"No," she whispered. Blair wasn't a confidante. Blair was her boss and the last person she could talk to. She drove on, arriving back at the loft around four, exhausted from too little sleep and this drama that had become her life. She pulled into her spot in the garage next to Selena's car, turned off the engine and laid her head against the steering wheel. She didn't want a confrontation. She wanted it over and done with so she could lick her wounds and get on with her life. But now, today, she had to face the music.

Inside the loft she moved about as quietly as possible. To her amazement the place was spotless. Abby pulled the fridge door open and rubbed at her temples. No wine, only a dozen bottles of beer. When she slid out the drawer looking for an opener, Selena appeared. She plucked the opener from the drawer and took the bottle from Abby to open.

"I didn't think you liked beer." The cap hissed and popped off.

Abby cringed at the taste when she sipped. She didn't know how people drank the stuff and wondered if she could drink enough to numb herself. She wasn't ready for this confrontation after all.

"And I didn't know you liked to do teenagers, Selena." She sounded like the smart-mouthed adolescent that always talked back to her mother, and she didn't care anymore now than she did then. She forced down a gulp of beer.

Selena dropped her head. "I deserve that and a lot worse."

"You don't say."

"I'm sorry. I don't know how or why this happened." Selena wouldn't look at her.

Abby took a long breath, tipped the bottle and drained it. After setting it down on the counter harder than she meant to, she said, "Really? Because I'm sure I know." Selena looked up with tears in her eyes, but Abby looked away and continued. "You were not committed to the relationship that we had—"

"But—"

"But nothing, Selena. You knew in the first month we were together what I wanted. You had no intention of fulfilling my need for a partnership, a family, which includes kids." Selena shook her head. "You don't want that. It's not who you are and you're not ever going to want it." When she started to interrupt, Abby raised her hand. "Let me finish. I know you love me, but that and hot sex isn't enough. Not for me." Abby sighed audibly. "Not any more—I want more." She slumped against the counter and Selena stepped around to face her, running her fingers down Abby's arm. Abby jerked away from her.

"We can work through this. I can change…I want to change."

Abby turned back to fully face Selena, tears brimming in her eyes. A tear escaped and rolled down her cheek. "You're just not the one I need. Let's end it now before we end up hating each other."

Selena's phone rang and she crossed to the opposite counter, picked it up, viewed the screen, stopped the ringing and tossed it down. Her shoulders shook as she walked to the bathroom. With the door closed, Abby picked up the phone and checked the call log. The last called registered only as "L," no doubt for Liza. The deep sadness she had been feeling quickly faded to anger. When Selena returned from the bathroom, tissues clutched in her hand, she stood too close so Abby took a few steps back.

"I'd like you to move as soon as possible."

"And where do you think I can just up and move to?"

"I honestly don't care. I will write you a check for a deposit and the first month's rent." Abby crossed her arms. "Find an apartment and please get out of my home."

"I'm not sure I can find an apartment I can afford in this town." Her tone registered distress.

"You should have thought of that before you screwed around on me then." She thought of Sam's tiny apartment. "And there are affordable places, believe me. Get your exchange student to move in and share the expense with you."

"My what?"

"You know, that little blond slut you were exchanging bodily fluids with, and who knows what else, in my bathroom."

"Abby, come on. Isn't there anyway I can make this right?" She lowered her head.

"I'm sorry. I promised myself I wouldn't get nasty with you. But no, there's no going back from here. I can't forget it if I have to see you. This has been coming and this affair didn't just happen."

"But it did, babe. I love you."

"Don't patronize me. It's been going on for months. You should have had your little squeeze wear a different perfume around me." Selena looked surprised. "Tell me, was the first time you came home late from work smelling like her the first time you two were together, or the first time you were careless about fucking someone else?"

"Abby, don't do this."

"Why not? I'd like to know how long I've been walking around with blinders."

Selena shook her head and waved her hand. "You're the one who started doing all the extra stuff for your boss."

Abby laughed. "Oh, please. You can't possibly expect me to accept that as any kind of excuse."

"Why the hell not?"

Abby threw her hands up. "It's ridiculous to think anything could happen between me and Blair Stanton. That goes to show how little you know me. No, you're not going to blame your poor judgment and inexcusable behavior on me. This is all you…babe!"

When she tried to move closer, Abby raised her hands to stop her and Selena stomped off to the bathroom. Abby put water on for tea and prayed for the strength to see this through, not the break up, but having to have Selena there until she found a place to live. Abby was transfixed on the view of the city through the windows.

"Abby," Selena's voice startled her. "Your water's boiling."

The whistling kettle and Selena's exotic fragrance caught her attention.

Selena jingled her keys. "I'm going to get out of your face for a while. I'll be back later." She leaned toward Abby as if to kiss her.

"Don't! Please, just don't." Abby pressed her hand firmly to Selena's sternum.

Selena's eyes were dark like Abby had never seen them, and a moment later the loft door slammed. *Might as well be the door to my heart slamming.* As far as Abby was concerned, her heart was officially closed. Nixing the idea of drinking tea, she grabbed another beer from the fridge and stood at the windows watching as Selena's little convertible pulled out and headed up the street. She didn't care where Selena was going, she told herself. She didn't care anymore.

She moved some things up to the guest room and settled in the bed with a book. Sometime later she woke to the soft sound of Selena's voice.

"Abby." Selena sat perched on the edge of the bed. In the faint light from the bedside lamp, Abby could see the tears that streaked her cheeks. "Please come to our bed and let me show you how sorry I am and how much I love you."

"I'm not doing this. I made myself clear where things stand."

"But…"

Abby could smell alcohol on her breath and was reminded of how very intense Selena's lovemaking could be when she primed herself with a few drinks. Did she prime herself with booze so she could convincingly make love? Abby wondered. *Will I ever feel that kind of all-consuming connection with anyone again?* Selena's hand on her thigh snapped her back to the moment.

"But I love you more than life, Abby. I can't manage without you."

Abby pushed her hand away. "Don't. I have every confidence in your ability to manage without me. You've got all your friends to lean on." *And I have none.* "Look, you don't want kids or a family, and that's all I've ever wanted—"

"I want—"

"No. You don't. We can fight about this for years and I'll still never be any closer to having my family."

"You're already out looking for your co-parent aren't you?"

"No." Abby didn't like the accusing tone of her voice. "And I don't intend to go looking. I wasn't looking for anyone when I met you. If it's meant to be for me I believe it will happen."

Selena stood. "At least sleep in your own bed. I'll sleep up here until I move out."

"I'm settled here. Let's just keep it this way."

She shrugged and left. Truthfully, Abby wanted the comfort of the small room. She wouldn't be comfortable in the bed she and Selena had shared for the last four years as long as Selena still lived there. She tossed and turned all night, never really sleeping. And there was the beer drinking, which necessitated too many bathroom trips.

When Abby got up and went downstairs, Selena had already gone, or maybe she'd not even spent the night. Abby didn't know or care. In her current state of mind, shopping seemed the only thing that made sense. Or drinking. But shopping sounded like a better, healthier kind of therapy. A new wardrobe perhaps. After all, she was single again.

She stayed away until she knew Selena would have left for work, mostly sitting with a cup of coffee people watching to kill time. When it came time to leave, though, she had to make the cold walk to her car twice with all her new purchases. She'd spend a quiet evening sorting through her old wardrobe. Out with the old and in with the new. She gave a little chuckle. If Selena saw all the new clothes, she'd think Abby had won the lottery. She'd kept her inheritance from Selena. It had been her only secret since her dad passed. She would have happily shared with Selena, if they'd actually started their family and she knew she would have her "happily ever after."

As an incentive for Selena to move quickly, Abby left a check for twenty-five hundred dollars on the counter Friday night before she went to bed. If Selena couldn't find a place quickly, the money would, at the very least, keep her comfortable in a room at her hotel.

Sunday morning Selena sat waiting at the counter when she came downstairs. "This is more than enough for a deposit and a month's rent. Why so much? You hiding something from me?" Selena waved the check.

"Exactly what do you think I'm trying to hide?" Abby crossed her arms.

"Oh, I don't know. Maybe a big fat inheritance." Selena's laugh sounded vicious.

"And just what would an inheritance have changed?" Abby countered with her own wicked laugh.

"I don't know." Selena shrugged. "I guess we never will."

"Oh, but I know. You would have made sure you never did anything so stupid as to get caught cheating."

"I'll be out as soon as I can." Selena folded the check and slipped it in her pocket. "And I'll just keep your money. You can afford it."

CHAPTER THIRTEEN

Returning to work in the New Year, Abby promptly submitted a request to work with a different prosecutor, someone who worked lower profile cases with less stress than the cases Blair consistently handled. She felt empty and alone. Her spirits were so low she feared slipping into a depression. Come Tuesday, she called the hospital to report she would not be able to read to the kids, due to a personal matter.

"I'm sorry," was all Abby could manage to get out before the tears came. Selena had not only crushed Abby's heart, but for at least that night, the hearts of a group of expectant children. Her boss, Edward Carlton, was thankfully in meetings all morning and didn't witness her little breakdown. But Blair stopped by to say hello.

She took one look at Abby, closed the door and pulled a chair to the end of the desk. "Abby, are you all right?" She nodded but didn't meet Blair's eyes. "Family again?" When she didn't respond, Blair placed her hand on Abby's arm. "You know if you ever need to talk, I'd be glad to listen."

It wasn't as though she and Blair were friends. She could lie or make up a story, but she gave another nod. "Thanks. I appreciate that."

"I was on my way to lunch." Blair pulled her hand away. "Would you like to join me?"

"I can't. I've got a lot of work to get through." Abby patted the files stacked on her desk. "But thanks for the invitation."

"Another time then." Blair stood, putting the chair back. "I meant what I said about talking if you need to."

"Thanks again."

Abby arrived home Thursday to find a note from Selena. "Abby, I found a place to stay while I continue to look for an apartment. I'll be back for the rest of my things when I find a permanent place." Step one in getting Selena out of her head and her heart was getting Selena out of her home.

Blair stopped again Friday afternoon to check on Abby and invite her to dinner.

"As inviting as it sounds, I already have plans for the evening." And it wasn't a lie. Abby intended to spend the evening with a bottle of wine and see how much of Selena's stuff she could get packed away in boxes before collapsing from exhaustion or an emotional breakdown.

Blair scribbled on Abby's notepad. "If you need to talk, call me anytime. Have a good weekend, Abby."

For a fleeting moment Abby wanted to stop Blair and spill her big secret, but that might be like opening Pandora's Box. Common sense reigned over emotions.

Sunday afternoon all signs of Selena were gone from the loft except the dozen marked and stacked boxes in the utility room behind the kitchen. Abby threw a sheet over them to avoid being reminded of Selena each time she needed to do laundry or get something from the freezer. She could hardly hide their bicycles hanging from hooks and added their sale or donation to her list of things to do.

Blair stopped by again Monday before lunch to invite her along, which Abby declined.

"I'm worried about you."

"It's not necessary. I have a mother."

Blair took the hint and left.

Abby thought she was ready to go back to the hospital for the kids Tuesday until Blair showed once again at lunchtime while Abby's boss was out. She closed the outer door and pulled the chair over to the desk.

"Now what?"

Blair's forehead wrinkled and she paused for a long moment. "I need you to understand that I'm worried about you, and I would never do anything to intentionally hurt you."

Abby swallowed. Her stomach felt like an empty pit.

"I'm in possession of some information pertaining to you, that I probably shouldn't have, but that doesn't change the fact that I have it." Abby sat silently. Blair lowered her head. "I know about Selena Estevez."

"What are you talking about, Blair?" Abby prayed her voice sounded steadier than she felt.

Blair didn't look up, but she shook her head. "I'm sorry. You've been so unhappy lately and I needed...I wanted to try and help. I...I..." she stuttered. "I know what this sounds like, but it's not like that. I...well... My curiosity got the better of me."

"Stop!" Abby raised both hands. "I don't want to hear anymore." Blair knew. She knew her secret.

"There's more I have to tell you." Blair's voice trembled. She glanced at Abby.

"No!"

"Selena is cheating on you." Blair reached for her hand, and Abby smacked it away.

Anger burned inside her like the night Selena had cheated. "How could you possibly know any of this?"

"I...I had an investigator check you out."

"Like a common criminal."

"I'm sorry. I know I shouldn't have, but like I said, curiosity… and I was worried…" She shook her head. "I know how wrong my actions were, and I'm truly sorry you have to hear about this, this way, but I feel you had a right to know."

"Get out!"

"Abby, I'm sorry. Please don't hate me."

Abby stood abruptly pointing toward the door. "Get out and stay the hell away from me!"

Once Blair had gone, Abby paced the narrow space in front of her desk. Her cheeks felt ablaze and she felt violated by Blair's invasion of her privacy.

"Do you feel all right, Ms. Collins?" Edward startled her mid-pace. "You look flushed."

"I may be coming down with something." Abby touched her fingers to her cheek.

He picked up his mail from the corner of her desk. "Perhaps you should take the rest of the day off." He pointed out the pile on her desk. "The filing can wait."

Abby grabbed up her purse. "Thank you. I'm going to go home and crawl in bed."

"I hope you feel better, but if you're still under the weather tomorrow don't worry about coming in, just let me know," he said with a warm smile as she pulled on her coat. "Nothing is more important than your health."

Abby wanted to throttle Blair for turning her life more upside down than it already was. From the quiet of her car she called the hospital with her regrets for having to miss reading to the children again, but she assured them she would return the following week. And she would, unless the world stopped turning.

On the way home she stopped and picked up two bottles of wine, fully intending to take her boss's advice about staying home tomorrow. She didn't want to leave the house again until she returned to work. As the volume of wine in the bottle decreased, so too did Abby's anger. *What fun would life be anyway if it didn't challenge us on a regular basis?*

Although the wine numbed some of her emotions, it increased her thoughts and feelings about Sam. Closing her eyes, she could recall with a precise clarity the feel of the stethoscope in her hand resting on Sam's chest. No touch had ever felt like touching Sam. Emotional and sexual frustration drove her upstairs to the treadmill where she ran for thirty minutes until her legs were on fire. If she ran fast enough could she ditch her past? Exhausted, she stood under the cool shower spray until her body's temperature lowered, and then she slowly warmed the water to relax her aching muscles.

When the alarm buzzed at seven thirty she called the main reception desk, asking Sally to let her boss know she was still under the weather. Shortly before noon, she decided a long soak would do her good, and soon she was comfortably settled in a nice hot bubble bath. The radio piped a sultry jazz, perhaps a few decibels too loud, but soothing nonetheless. Her cup of tea within reach, she closed her eyes, unaware she might fall asleep.

"God...oh...I'm sorry." Abby heard the unmistakable voice before the door quickly snapped shut.

"Sam?" she called over the music.

The door cracked open an inch. "Uh...yeah...it's me. I'm sorry...I thought...I don't know. I thought something might have happened. I couldn't get a hold of you and...and you didn't answer the door. I was worried."

Abby hadn't heard the doorbell, but then Selena probably hadn't fixed it as she'd promised to. So Sam had found her hidden key. A smile tugged at her mouth.

"Sam," Abby called out again. "Could you come in and turn off the music so we don't have to shout?"

The door slowly opened and Sam entered with her eyes directed at the floor. She switched off the music.

"As you can see I'm perfectly fine."

Sam kept her back to the tub. "Oh, I...I didn't see anything."

"Sam, we are both adult women, and if you did get a peek, I promise you I won't die of embarrassment." Abby heard Sam swallow.

"So they said at your office that you're sick. Is there anything I can do? Get you chicken soup or check your temperature?"

It might shock Sam to know that her temperature had risen a few degrees since she'd appeared in her bathroom. "I'm not sick so much as down in the dumps."

"Oh?"

"Yes. And if you want to do something, could you warm up my tea in the microwave for me? Maybe talk with me for a few minutes?"

"Sure. Okay, I..." She cleared her throat. "I can do that." Without looking up from the floor she took the cup from the edge of the tub and disappeared.

When she returned Abby reached for the cup, briefly exposing one of her breasts as Sam placed the cup on the tub. Sam averted her eyes, took a seat on the windowsill, placing Abby's towel in her lap, and fixating her gaze on it.

"You're not working today?"

Sam nodded. "I took a break to come check on you."

"You have to go back to the hospital?"

She picked nervously at the towel. "Yeah...uh...yes. I should go back."

"I feel like I'm having a conversation with that towel in your lap, Sam. Why won't you look at me?"

"I just...uh...I don't want to make you uncomfortable."

"Sam, please look at me. Do I look uncomfortable to you?" She glanced so quickly Abby almost missed it. "Sam, you have sisters." Sam nodded again. "Haven't you ever had to be in the bathroom with one of them?" Another nod. "Well, just pretend I'm a sister. I promise I won't jump up and flash you." Sam's face flushed, but she smiled and finally met Abby's gaze. "That's better. Now I feel as though I can bare my soul to a human instead of that bath towel."

Sam chuckled, keeping her laser-focused gaze on Abby's. "So why down in the dumps? Is it your crazy mother?"

Abby smiled for what felt like the first time since New Year's. "No. If it was my mother I wouldn't be down in the dumps. I would probably be down in the city jail." Sam grinned and relaxed the death grip on the towel. "It's the blues, I suppose." Abby sighed. "Do you ever feel like your life is going nowhere or in the wrong direction?" She paused, but didn't give Sam a chance to answer. "Of course you haven't. You're a doctor. Your life is full of purpose and direction."

Sam's smile faded and her gaze drifted away. When she looked back at Abby, her brow furrowed. "My life is consumed with the doctor thing to the point I sometimes don't feel like my life is my own anymore."

"Really, I would think a doctor's life is all purpose and reward."

"I love helping the kids. It's what I'm destined for. I just feel like something is missing."

"Something?"

Sam looked down at the towel again. "Not something, someone I guess. To share my life with, you know."

Oh Sam honey, do I ever. "Well there must be plenty of eligible bachelors around the hospital."

She shrugged. "I suppose there probably are. I guess I'm not paying attention."

She noticed her bubble cover thinning and without thinking, she sat forward to run more hot water. A sideways glance confirmed Sam was looking at her. A shiver raced through Abby as if Sam's gaze had physically caressed her skin.

"I believe there's a soul mate for every one of us. I'm sure yours is out there." When Sam's eyes returned to meet hers, Abby felt as if they were searching her soul. "Do you need to be getting back to the hospital?"

"Probably so." She turned her watch around on her wrist. "Or I could call in sick."

"You mean play hooky with me?"

Sam smiled. "Why not? There wasn't much going on when I left."

In her excitement, Abby sat forward exposing herself.

Sam looked away as she held out the towel to Abby. "Here, you might want this." She accepted the towel as Sam stood. "I'll meet you out there." Sam hooked her thumb at the door.

Abby dried, dressed, and hurriedly ran a brush through her hair. She found Sam standing at the kitchen counter with her phone to her ear.

"Okay," was all she said and slipped the phone into her pocket as Abby rounded the counter.

"Well, are you off the rest of the day?" Sam looked guilty when she nodded. "What excuse did you use?"

Sam slid onto one of the stools. "I told them I don't quite feel like myself. I don't know what it is, and I don't want to risk being around the kids. It's not a complete lie."

Abby turned around and tipped her head. "Oh?"

"I don't know." Sam shrugged. "I feel out of sorts."

Abby understood the out-of-sorts feeling all too well. "Are you hungry? I can fix us lunch."

"I'm always hungry." She looked over at Abby in front of the fridge. "I have to eat when I can, you know."

She leaned an elbow on the counter and rested her chin in her hand. She looked so darn cute sitting at Abby's kitchen island. Abby wanted to invite her to stay forever. She honestly didn't think so soon after being cheated on by Selena that she would want anything to do with another woman, and yet she did. When Sam sat in the bathroom with her, Abby wanted to reach out and pull Sam into the water. The memory sent another shiver down her spine. Maybe she should tell Sam who she was.

"I have chicken salad and fruit. The chicken salad is low in fat."

"Of course it is, as if you need to lose an ounce."

Abby spun around in time to catch Sam looking at her behind. "It's healthy. I'm much more interested in health than vanity. I want to be sure to live to be a great-grandmother."

Abby poured iced teas, made sandwiches and set a plate of fruit between them. Sam devoured her sandwich like she hadn't eaten in days, and Abby noticed she picked around the blueberries. *The doctor doesn't like blueberries.* Abby committed that fact to memory. It helped ease her weary heart and mind. Sam made her feel worry free and lighthearted, something Abby relished after the last few weeks. It was easy to talk to Sam about anything and joke like they'd been friends forever. It was torture too. Sitting this close to Sam made her feel tingly all over.

The hours passed effortlessly, but eventually Sam pushed off her stool. "I should get going." She set her glass in the sink. "I'm sure you weren't planning to spend your sick day off discussing how to solve the world's problems."

"I enjoy your company, Sam. Besides, I didn't have plans."

Sam looked at the floor where she toed the tile with her shoe. "Just an uninterrupted soak in the tub." Her face flushed.

"Life's full of surprises." Abby threw her hands up. "The key is to not be thrown off by them." Abby smiled when Sam met her gaze.

She dug in the pocket of her slacks and held up a key. "I'll put this back on my way out, but you know, it's not safe to keep your key where anyone can find it."

"I'll keep that in mind." She caught Sam's arm before she pulled the door open. "Thanks for coming by to check on me."

The corner of Sam's mouth turned up. "House calls are my secret specialty, but don't let that get out."

"Your secret is safe with me." The heavy steel door closed on what turned out to be a perfectly lovely afternoon. Abby sighed. *I could use more of these.*

Sam's heart did a little dance as she rode the elevator down, and warmth filled her as she recalled the sight of Abby covered in nothing more than bubbles—an image that would remain with her indefinitely. And having glimpsed Abby's firm full breasts, well, Sam knew infatuation no longer adequately described how she felt. She was in full-blown lust for Abby. She had observed every bit of the loft that she could see without Abby's notice, and there didn't appear to be any signs that anyone else lived there. Of course she understood that it didn't mean Abby wasn't keeping the company of someone special. She felt a twinge of jealousy at the thought of some guy touching Abby's beautiful breasts. Then again, Abby had never made mention of anyone like a boyfriend. Next time, and Sam hoped there would be a next time, she would try and work that into their conversation. At least lusting after a single woman offered a glimmer of hope. Right?

When she reached her car half a block away, all she wanted to do was rush back to the loft and take Abby in her arms. Kiss away her blues. *Yeah, right.* She exhaled a deep sigh as she slid behind the wheel and pointed her car toward home. She'd hug her pillow and hope for dreams of Abby.

CHAPTER FOURTEEN

Excitement filled Abby as she entered the hospital on her way to some spirit-lifting time with the kids. The nurses were thrilled for her return too. "There ain't a soul can hold a candle to you storytellin' to dem kids," Nurse Adams had said.

If her life never amounted to anything more, being a good storyteller was something to be proud of. She understood a child's joy when a reader could bring a story to life. Abby had had a nanny who could transport her into any story she read. She remembered feeling like she would have traded any one of her family members to keep the nanny with them when she left.

The second Abby stepped into the activity room her heart swelled. It was by far the best medicine for heartbreak. She simply needed to surround herself with kids. Well, kids and the presence she sensed about twenty minutes into reading. She glanced to the back of the room to see Sam's smiling face among the nurses. Disappointingly, Sam had already gone when she finished.

"Abby," Sam called out as she stepped into the hall. She rushed up to meet Abby, cupping her hand under Abby's elbow when she asked, "Do you have time for coffee?"

Not wanting to appear as anxious as she felt, Abby made a show of checking her watch. "Sure, I have some time."

"Great!" Sam smiled and rushed down to the nurses station. She returned pulling on her coat. "They just opened a coffee shop around the corner from the hospital that seriously puts the coffee here to shame. She tugged at the straps of Abby's book bag and grinned. "Can I carry your books for you?"

"I'll just drop them in my car on the way."

Sam gave the bag another tug. "We're not going out that way. I know a way out the back of the hospital so we don't have to walk all the way around the block." Abby relinquished the bag and Sam slipped the straps over her shoulder. "Come on."

Sam clipped her badge on her coat and led Abby through parts of the hospital she didn't know existed. She felt like a schoolgirl having her books carried by the cute guy that all the girls drooled over. She imagined there was any number of men as well as women who drooled over the attractive Dr. Sam, herself included. Abby couldn't have said if the coffee shop was nice or the coffee was good. She only noticed her coffee date. She was deep in thought about how she could get Sam back to her loft when Sam's phone went off.

Sam frowned. "I have to get back to the hospital. Do you want to go now so I can sneak you through the back? I hate for you to have to walk all the way around."

"I'm rather enjoying this." Abby indicated her half full cup. "And to be honest, I can use the exercise." She raised the cup. "Thanks for the coffee."

"Maybe next time I won't have to run off."

Sam smiled that smile that Abby adored. Her heart danced at the thought of a next time. "Don't worry about it. I'd want my doctor to respond when called." She gave a wave. "Until next time." She watched Sam leave, trying not to drool in her coffee.

Seeing Sam and being with her made Abby want to see and be with her all the more. It disappointed her that Sam got called back, but the mention of a next time left her feeling hopeful. She analyzed her relationship with Selena and realized that because they rarely spent time together doing things like getting coffee and talking, she really didn't know Selena as well as she'd thought and had been living with blinders on. Never again. Abby intended to take time off from "girlfriends" and catch up on things like reading, painting the utility room, and rearranging her underwear drawer. *God, I sound pathetic. I need some friends and a life.*

Sam cursed under her breath as she walked swiftly through the hospital. She wasn't upset that she'd been summoned for a child in need, only that she had to abandon Abby at the coffee shop. She simply wanted to sit across the table from her and look at her…forever, if that was possible. Concern that she might feel embarrassed at having seen Abby in the tub last week disappeared the second Abby looked up at her in the activity room. Sam felt pumped by the probability of a next time with Abby. *You've got yourself a good crush, Dr. Christiano.* Sam sighed as she stepped up to the nurses station.

"What's up with you Dr. Sam?" Nurse Adams asked. "You look like a lovesick pup."

Sam knitted her brows. "What are you talking about?"

She put a wide hand on a wider hip. "You bounced outta here a while ago like you was goin' off to get you some, and now you look like you just been dumped. So spill. What's up?"

Sam shook her head. "Flora, I've told you I don't have a personal life, so quit prying."

"Hmm… So you keep sayin'. Don't know if your momma ever told you, but you don't lie too good." After leveling Sam with a knowing look, Flora snatched up a chart and disappeared around the corner.

Sam watched as she went, wondering exactly what Flora thought she was showing of herself. She hoped Abby hadn't noticed anything about her behavior. Embarrassment would be mild compared to what Sam would feel if Abby ever thought she had a thing for her.

* * *

Tuesday Abby sat daydreaming at her desk when a faint knock sounded on the open door. There stood Blair, hands raised in surrender. Abby only glared at her.

"Abby, I'm so sorry. Please allow me a minute to apologize."

Abby exhaled loudly. "Close the door." Blair did so and stood across the desk from Abby looking powerless, a look Abby guessed Blair rarely ever wore. Abby crossed her arms over her chest.

"I..." Blair's voice caught and she cleared her throat. "I stopped back last Wednesday to apologize, and you'd gone home sick the day before. I've been in court every day since. I hope everything is okay with your health, and I sincerely hope it wasn't me to blame for your absence."

Blair's words sounded as rehearsed as a closing statement. Abby rolled her eyes. She had no intention of allowing Blair to know that her actions had any impact on her. That would only give Blair power that Abby didn't want her to have.

She continued nervously, "What I did was inexcusable and I don't deny... Well, I think perhaps I was jealous of your relationship." She looked at the floor. "I felt like we were beginning to develop a friendship, and I have completely shot that to hell." She cleared her throat again. "That's the thing that is most upsetting for me. You're a wonderful, caring person and I did a horrible thing. I like you and I hope someday we can get past this."

Her voice oozed with compassion that Abby didn't think even Blair could fake. She relaxed her arms. "I appreciate the apology, and yes, perhaps someday we may get beyond this, but today is not that day."

Blair gave a nod. "I'll let you finish your lunch break." She stopped and turned back before opening the door. "Abby, if you ever need to talk to someone, I promise to treat any conversation between us with lawyer-client confidentiality."

"I'll keep that in mind, Counselor."

"See you around." Blair hinted at a smile.

Blair could be quite charming. Abby had heard the stories about Blair charming judges in one breath—and eating a defense witness alive in the next. If only Blair could be trusted.

She didn't notice Sam at the hospital Tuesday night until she was headed out, and there sat Sam in the window at the end of the hall.

She looked up as Abby approached. "Fancy meeting you here."

Sam's piercing gaze left Abby speechless for a long moment. "Do you want to grab a cup of coffee?"

Sam pushed off the sill. "I'd like to, but I'm the only one on for a few more hours."

Abby nodded. "A doctor's work is never done."

"Something like that."

"Maybe next time."

When Abby turned, Sam touched her arm. "Abby…" Abby met Sam's gaze once again. "Are you busy Saturday night?"

"This Saturday?" Sam nodded. "No, no, I don't believe I am."

"Do you want to go out for dinner somewhere?" Sam jammed her hands in her coat pocket. "I promise it won't be to my folks' house."

Abby chuckled and placed her hand on Sam's shoulder. "Sam, I adore your parents. Don't think if you invited me to dinner at their house I'd decline."

"I was thinking something nicer." Sam swallowed then grinned nervously. "There's a new restaurant a few miles from here I've heard good things about."

"Okay."

"Okay?"

"Okay. We should check this place out. What time?"

"Seven too late?"

"Seven it is. I'll swing by your place and pick you up. Say six thirty?"

"Perfect. I'll see you Saturday evening."

Sam's smile and mesmerizing eyes rendered Abby boneless. She couldn't catch her breath. She barely nodded her head. Perfect would be the word she'd use to describe the woman before her. Abby walked trance-like to the elevator, feeling Sam's piercing gaze on her with her every step down the hall. She stumbled into the elevator when the doors opened. *I just made a date with Dr. Sam.* After the doors closed, she raised her fists with a resounding, "Yes."

Abby glanced back at the building as she crossed the parking lot to her car. It wasn't possible to tell if Sam was still at the window looking out, but Abby got the same feeling she had walking to the elevator and hoped that meant Sam was indeed watching.

* * *

Abby floated into the loft on a high she'd never before experienced and immediately tore into her closet looking for the ultimate outfit to wear Saturday night. Sam hadn't indicated the kind of restaurant they were going to, so Abby decided on dressy casual as a safe bet.

The week dragged by ever so slowly. Things weren't busy at work, making the days endless. Blair didn't stay away either. She popped back in Friday with a lunch date request. It wasn't possible to convince her she was too busy since Blair caught her flipping through a magazine.

"Don't get the idea this is going to become a regular thing. I'm still very upset, and I don't feel like I can trust you out of my own sight."

A tiny smile curled the corner of Blair's mouth as she helped Abby on with her coat. "Maybe you should keep me close more often." Abby turned around glaring at her. Blair shrugged. "I can't help it. You're a beautiful woman." She raised her hands. "But I promise I'll try to behave."

Blair was accustomed to too much power. Someone needed to take her down a peg or two or she'd never find herself a partner. Maybe it was Abby's job to make Blair a likeable human being. Abby laughed to herself at the thought.

"What's so amusing?" Blair asked as they stepped into the elevator. Abby lifted her brows. "You laughed."

Oops. "I hardly know you well enough to share, but maybe someday." Abby made doubly sure the smile she felt wasn't showing.

Lunch turned out to be pleasant with Blair conducting herself like a professional having a business lunch.

"Do you have plans for this evening?" she asked Abby as they made their way back across the skywalk.

"Yes, I have a date."

"Tomorrow evening?" Blair persisted.

Abby continued her lie. "If all goes well this evening, I certainly hope so." She gave what she hoped passed for a coy smile.

"Well, I'm jealous." She lowered her voice. "You've been out of a relationship for what, two weeks, and you're already dating? I haven't had a date, you know..." she whispered, "since I was on vacation over a year ago, and it wasn't exactly a date. More like dinner, drinks, nice to meet you, and we parted for opposite ends of the country."

"Maybe you should stop looking so hard and the right one might just drop into your lap." Abby regretted her word choice instantly, but it was too late to take them back.

Blair stopped abruptly, forcing Abby to turn around.

"Does that ever really happen?"

"I would certainly like to believe it does. What are you looking at?"

"That's her."

"Who?" There were people walking everywhere below them.

"My kind of woman." Blair smiled. "There in the gray coat and boots."

Abby picked out the blonde and could tell even in her tightly closed wool coat she was built to stop men, and apparently women, in their tracks.

"That's what you like, huh?"

Blair sighed. "Well I can't have you so I'd settle for her."

Abby rolled her eyes. "You almost made it back to the office."

"Sorry." Blair tipped her head. "I'll try harder next time."

Abby started walking again. "Who said anything about a next time?"

Blair quickly caught up. "Come on, lunch with me isn't that torturous, is it?"

"I can say honestly that you're not the worst lunch date I've ever had."

Blair chuckled. "So there's room for improvement." She nodded. "I can assure you failure is not an option for me."

"Like I said, don't think this is going to become a habit. I could stay mad at you for the rest of my life for what you did."

She caught Abby's arm briefly before she could enter the building and pulled her out of the pedestrian traffic. "Abby, I will regret what I did every day for the rest of my life, but I will also spend every day making up for it as your friend."

Her eyes reflected a sincerity and compassion that Abby didn't believe Blair capable of faking. But, as she'd thought earlier, someone needed to teach Blair a few things about life, especially people's feelings.

"Don't push it, okay."

"Got it." Blair lifted her hands in surrender.

CHAPTER FIFTEEN

Friday night felt like Christmas Eve had been for Abby as a child. The anticipation of tomorrow brought so much excitement she could hardly sit still. She almost wished she'd taken Blair up on her invite for the evening to fill her time. Instead she settled on a glass of wine and a movie purchased months ago that she and Selena had never gotten around to watching.

She started getting ready at four o'clock on Saturday and spent so much time on her hair and makeup that one would have thought she was dining with a queen. Thinking she had decided on her outfit, she changed out the top twice again before being satisfied. She checked the mirror one last time, pleased with her gray wool slacks and yellow sweater. She threw on her coat, grabbed her purse, and left before second-guessing her wardrobe choice again.

A few minutes before six thirty, Sam answered Abby's knock and then leaned back against the door as she closed it.

"I...uh..." She cleared her throat and started again. "I couldn't get a reservation until seven thirty, so we have some time. I would have called but I only have your work number."

Abby noticed the place was picked up and spotlessly clean.

"We can have a drink before we go if you'd like." Sam caught Abby's coat as it slid off her shoulders and laid it across the back of the small couch.

"That's fine." Sam drifted into the kitchen area so Abby followed and stopped to lean in the opening.

"I have wine. Red or white. Which would you prefer?"

"Either is fine. You choose."

Abby was a nervous wreck and Sam seemed even more nervous. She turned with the wine bottle in hand and their eyes met briefly. Sam was without shoes in a pair of black jeans, which, for all Abby could tell, might have been painted onto her skin and a light blue shirt that left nothing to the imagination as to her fit shape. She'd had her hair trimmed since last Abby saw her on Tuesday. She was the sexiest woman alive.

"I feel overdressed," Abby commented as Sam poured the wine.

Sam turned and fixed Abby with her gaze and a smile. The shirt accentuated the color of her eyes, making them sparkle like stars. "You look amazing. I, on the other hand, am underdressed." She lifted a glass to Abby and motioned to the tiny living area. "I didn't make it to the cleaners, so my wardrobe choices were slim."

Abby took a seat at one end of the couch. "You look great." She settled back in the cushions adding, "and comfortable."

Sam set her glass on the neatly arranged coffee table. "I'll be right back."

When she returned minutes later, she wore a pair of black boots that made her several inches taller, and the whole package was a package Abby ached to unwrap. When the time came to go, Sam held Abby's coat for her, and then she pulled on a black leather blazer. One look took Abby's breath away. It wasn't any wonder why she felt she was falling for Sam. She made it impossible not to be attracted to her. *Of all the lesbians out there in the world, I have to fall for the straight Dr. Samantha Christiano.*

As they stepped outside Abby noticed the ominous clouds hovering over the city and pulled her coat tight against the chill.

"Are we supposed to get snow tonight?"

Sam answered once inside the car. "I don't get to catch the weather often. I can usually look out my window and be as accurate as most of the weather forecasters." She looked through the windshield at the sky. "I'd say there's a better chance than not that we might get some snow this evening. Would you rather cancel dinner?"

"Not on your life, unless you're worried about my driving in it." Sam shook her head.

The restaurant was divine and both she and Sam were appropriately dressed. Two nice-looking guys at the bar kept eyeing them, and the waitress eventually informed them the gentlemen wanted to buy them drinks.

"I can't, but thank you." Sam directed her gaze to Abby. "I have to go in on the graveyard shift."

"Please decline for us and pass along our thanks for the gesture." She directed her attention to Sam. "I don't know how anyone can work different shifts constantly. I couldn't do it. My last…" Abby caught herself.

"What?" Sam asked, leaning forward.

"I'm sorry…"

"You were about to say…something."

"Oh yes. I completely lost my train of thought." Sam tipped her head. "My late father used to talk about his dad, my grandfather whom I never met, and how he worked shift work in a steel mill. My father put in a lot of hours, but he was always home to tuck us into bed at night."

"Your father must have been a young man when he passed."

Abby nodded and blinked back the tears that threatened. "He was, and just like his father," she patted her chest, "weak hearts. I hope it's not a gene I've inherited. I want to live a long healthy life for my children." The smile Sam gave warmed her heart.

After dinner they stepped from the restaurant into a steadily falling snow. Sam clutched her jacket at the neck against the damp cold.

"I can go get my car and pick you up if you want to wait inside," Abby offered.

Sam brushed large, wet snowflakes from her hair. "Don't be silly. Unlike these…" She held out her palm to catch a handful of flakes. "I won't melt." She dusted her hand and hooked her arm through Abby's. "Come on." They slipped and slid to Abby's car. Once inside with the heater blasting warmth, she said, "First real snow of the season. This should have the ER hopping tonight. You think that people would learn to slow down when driving in the snow, but they don't. The statistics show emergency room visits rise exponentially with inclement weather. Especially snow." The car tires slipped a bit on the slick surface. "And the worst part is the folks that can't seem to drive in bad weather, also don't take good safety precautions with their kids." She shook her head.

Abby drove slowly and cautiously for the few miles to Sam's apartment and turned at a snail's pace into the parking lot.

"Shoot!" Sam said.

Startled, Abby stopped the car. "What's wrong?"

"My car." Sam pointed and Abby followed her finger to see Sam's car sitting at a peculiar tilt. "I have a flat tire." Sam dropped her face into her hands.

"I'm sure the road service can take care of it." Abby glanced at the dash clock. It was only a few minutes until ten.

"I'm poor, remember. I don't have road service."

Abby reached in her purse for her phone. "Not to worry. I do."

Sam placed her hand gently on Abby's. "There's not time. I'm sure with the weather they'll be backed up with accidents and cars off in the ditches."

Abby let the phone drop into her purse. "Okay, I'll drop you by the hospital and pick you up tomorrow."

Sam shook her head. "It's not on your way home and I'm not going to be responsible for getting you up at the crack of dawn on a Sunday to chauffeur me home. Besides, the roads may be worse than they are now." She pulled the collar up on her jacket. "I'll change it myself. It's not like it'll be the first time."

When Sam reached for the door handle, Abby caught her arm. "At least let me help."

Sam grinned. "You can hold the flashlight and that little umbrella of yours if you really want to help."

Abby moved her car around so her headlights were shining on Sam's car, blocking the parking lot, but positioned to move quickly if necessary. Sam started what looked like a routine.

Between shivers, Abby asked, "Just how many times have you changed a flat tire?"

Sam kicked the wrench to loosen the last bolt. "More times than you'd ever want to think about, believe me. My car is entering its teenage years." She worked quickly in silence, finishing in roughly twenty minutes. She stood for a moment and rubbed her thighs. "No way that a road service would have even been here yet." She squatted again and when she put her hand on the jack the car suddenly fell to the pavement. "Damn!" she yelled, jerking her hand back and shaking it. She then squeezed it in her other hand.

Abby touched her shoulder. "Are you okay?"

"Yeah. I just pinched it." She pulled the jack out and tossed it in the trunk beside the flat tire. She slammed the trunk before facing Abby. "Thanks for your help. Sorry the evening had to end with you shivering in the cold and snow."

Abby smiled. "Thanks for introducing me to a new restaurant. I really enjoyed it. We'll have to go again sometime." Sam gave a nod. Abby noticed the dark spot growing on the snow-covered ground at Sam's feet and quickly realized it was blood dripping from her hand. "I'm worried about your hand."

"It's nothing. It'll be fine."

Abby took hold of Sam's wrist and raised her hand for a better look. "Really? Is that why you're making a blood pool in the snow?" Sam didn't reply. "We need to see how bad it is. Hold this." Abby put the umbrella in Sam's other hand and moved her car to a parking spot. She pulled every clean tissue from her purse that she had and pressed them into Sam's hand before taking the umbrella back. "Let's go see how bad it really is. You may need stitches."

Sam gripped the tissues in her hand and started for the door. "Well, if I do, you can assist me."

Abby hoped she was kidding. There wasn't any way she could possibly stand to watch someone sew their own flesh. Inside, Sam shrugged out of her jacket, careful not to get blood on the leather. Abby dropped her coat and purse hurriedly on the couch, unbuttoned Sam's shirtsleeve and pushed it above her elbow.

"Where are your first aid supplies?"

"The bathroom."

She led Sam into her tiny bathroom, lowered the lid on the toilet and pointed. "Sit." She got the water warm at the sink and placed Sam's hand under the faucet. "Where are your bandages?"

"Down there." Sam pointed to the vanity.

Abby placed the necessary items next to the sink and took Sam's hand gently in her own. Carefully she rubbed away the already drying blood until she could see the wound clearly. "You're lucky. It only cut a flap of skin on the side of your palm. It doesn't look too deep and I don't think it needs stitches. What do you think, Doctor?" Sam silently agreed. Abby turned off the water and picked up the antiseptic. "This might burn a little." Sam's hand flinched in Abby's grasp as she poured the liquid over the cut. Abby gave it a minute to work and patted Sam's hand dry.

"You're a natural caregiver," Sam said with a smile. "You'll make a wonderful mom."

"Thanks. But sometimes I don't think I'll ever get the chance." It felt as though Sam's hand was melting into her own and Abby wanted badly to lift it and kiss the pain away.

Sam cleared her throat. "You'll meet the right guy and it'll happen."

Abby rolled her eyes sideways to look at Sam. Sam cringed as she rubbed on some antibiotic cream. "I wasn't exactly planning on having a man involved personally in my child's conception."

"Oh!" Sam's eyes drifted away. "So you plan to have children in a non-traditional manner." Her cheeks colored with a blush. "You're going to adopt."

Abby shook her head. "I want to bear my own children, but it's not looking very probable now, and I feel like I'm readier than I've ever been."

"So what's the problem? You inseminate and hope it takes."

"I was hoping to have someone special to help me with it. You know?" Abby spilled before her brain could stop her mouth. *Great. I have now come out to Sam without actually coming right out with it.*

"Ooo…okay."

Abby pulled a couple of bandages over Sam's wound, catching the questions in her eyes. Already embarrassed, she asked, "You're a doctor, and my friend, would you?"

"Uh…would I what?"

Abby took a deep breath. "Help me get pregnant." Sam couldn't have hidden her shock if she'd tried.

"I'm not sure if I'd be the best person to help you with that." She lowered her head and looked at her bandaged hand. "I like you."

Abby smiled at her shyness. "I understand. It's asking a lot."

Sam shook her head. "I'm not so sure you understand, Abby." She swallowed hard. "I mean, I really like you."

Abby heard the words and the nervousness in Sam's voice, but she couldn't believe she'd heard correctly. "Sam, please look at me." She slowly lifted her head and met Abby's gaze. Time stopped for a long moment. Emotions overwhelmed Abby. She barely found her voice to ask, "You like me like this?" Abby brushed her lips over Sam's, her heart aching to press harder, but she withdrew.

She saw the same want she felt reflected in Sam's eyes as Sam reached her good hand behind Abby's neck to stop her retreat. Agonizingly slow, Sam leaned in and pressed her lips to Abby's. Uncontrolled desire coursed through Abby as Sam's lips caressed her own. Passion erupted inside her and warmth spread all the way to Abby's toes. Selena had never kissed her like this.

No one's kiss had ever made her feel like this. With a gasp, Abby finally pulled away. Sam's eyes shimmered deep violet. Abby wanted to dive in headfirst. Abby brushed her fingers through Sam's hair and then across her cheek. Sam's eye lids fluttered and she inhaled sharply.

"I really like you, too, Sam," Abby said softly. She took Sam's face in her hands and kissed her again. Sam stood, pulling Abby into her arms.

Abby held on to her shoulders as Sam's hands slipped to her hips and pulled them closer, their tongues dancing. Abby let her hands wander to the buttons of Sam's shirt and worked methodically to open enough of them to push the shirt off her shoulders. She cupped Sam's small breasts. The kiss grew with hunger. There wasn't any doubt about how much she wanted Sam. She'd gotten an inkling of *something* the first time they met, something she wasn't quite sure of. The caresses of Sam's long soft fingers drove Abby's desire beyond control.

It was only with force that she was able to pull away and mutter, "I want you, Sam."

Her hands moved to Sam's waistband and unbuttoned her pants, but when she slipped her hand toward the elastic of Sam's underwear, Sam caught her wrist and pulled back. The deep sharp color in Sam's eyes was gone. They were hazy—unfocused. Acutely aware of the tension in Sam's touch, Abby took a step back.

"Sam…"

Sam dropped her gaze, gathered her shirt over her chest and stepped farther back. "I'm sorry. I'm so sorry." She rubbed a hand over her face then pushed it through her hair.

"Sam?"

Sam only stood there shaking her head and staring at the floor. Abby's heart sank. Either Sam wasn't ready to come out or she was never going to. It was… Hell, Abby didn't know what it was. She gathered herself as confidently as she could.

"I should go. I hope your hand is okay."

She brushed past Sam, quickly grabbing her coat and purse en route to the door. She pulled on her coat as she rushed down the stairs and replayed the encounter, trying to figure out what she'd misread. She sat for several minutes in the car while it warmed up and tried to make some sense of what happened. She'd been certain Sam was coming on to her. Or was it simply that she wanted Sam to be attracted to her the way she'd found herself attracted to Sam? She tipped her head back against the seat exhaling a deep breath. Her heart ached all over again. Then she remembered a conversation and Sam asking if she ever wondered about being with a woman. Sam was only curious.

Turning off the light, she went to the bedroom window overlooking the parking lot. In the darkness she watched as Abby practically ran to her car. She already hated herself for letting her attraction to Abby get so out of control. She'd simply wanted Sam's help as a friend. "Dammit!" She muttered in the silence. She now wondered if Abby thought she needed to "play lesbian" to get her help?

Sam hadn't felt the sting from her hand. All there had been was the heat created by Abby pressed against her. Like the dream she had often dreamed of Abby. It consumed her. She'd known she would wake as always, alone in her bed hugging her pillow and Abby would be gone. She'd prayed silently for it to last just a little longer.

How long had it been since she'd felt like that? Had she ever? She'd slipped her hand under Abby's sweater. A slow tender exploration of the softest skin she had ever touched, and it led to Abby's breast. Abby had emitted a tiny moan when Sam's fingers tenderly stroked her erect nipple through the flimsy lace of her bra. Sam had instantly grown wet. How many nights had she lain in bed dreaming of this beautiful woman in her arms? And only moments before she'd had her right where she dreamed she would. The sweet taste of Abby's lips made Sam want to drag her to the bed and taste every exquisite inch of her.

Then Abby murmured her name and something inside Sam had shaken loose. Even as her body screamed for a release, her last time with a woman invaded her thoughts. The memories took over. Oh, but a part of her had desperately ached to take

Abby on a long slow journey to ecstasy. It'd been such a long time. If only... But Abby had rushed past her and out the door before Sam could get her brain to communicate with her mouth.

Sam wanted to drink until her mind went numb and fall into her bed. Yeah, fall into bed hugging her pillow and dream. She watched Abby's car as it sat in the parking space for a long time, asking herself how much damage she'd done to their friendship. She felt as though she was falling in love with Abby. If she couldn't get past this absurd desire for Abby, she stood to lose her forever. The car's lights finally came on and Abby drove off. Sam hoped with all her heart that Abby wasn't leaving forever. She grabbed her phone and dialed the hospital to skip her shift, and then she found the bottle of whiskey in the cabinet and took it to her bed.

In the dark, Abby plopped down on a stool at the counter with a bottle of wine. Hypnotized, she watched the snowflakes falling around the city's lights in the sprawling black velvet of the night beyond her windows. With pain in her heart and an empty feeling in the pit of her stomach, she couldn't stop the tears.

CHAPTER SIXTEEN

"Blair, if you don't stop apologizing and being...well, so docile, you'll never be feared by another criminal, defense attorney, or judge again. I promise I won't think any less of you for behaving the way everyone assumes that you do. Besides, people might start to think there's more going on in this office than work." That seemed to get her attention.

Abby enjoyed being with the kids more than she had in weeks. She didn't allow any thoughts of Sam's absence to enter her mind. She read well past her scheduled time and had to be asked by one of the nurses to surrender the kids for bed.

Abby spotted Nurse Walker at the desk as she was leaving and decided she might as well ask if Sam was around. If Ms. Walker was gay, she might be as fixated on Sam as Abby and actually know Sam's whereabouts.

"Ms. Collins, hi! Something we can help you with?" She looked Abby up and down.

"Is Dr. Sam around this evening?"

Her head bobbed. "She is, but was just called down for an ER trauma. She said she might be off the floor for hours. You want to leave a note for her?"

Why not? "I have a question for her." *I want to know what I have to do to fix things between us.*

"Maybe I can answer your question." She smiled flirtatiously.

Abby felt the color rising in her cheeks. "It's personal." Nurse Walker continued to smile as Abby scribbled. "Sam—please call me when you have a minute to chat—thanks, Abby." She included both her cell and home numbers, folded the paper and wrote, "Dr. Sam" on the outside and handed it over. Her request was far too ambiguous for anyone to construe anything of it.

"I'll personally make sure she gets this." When she tucked it in her pocket, Abby said a silent prayer that she would pass it on to Sam, but more importantly, that Sam would call her.

"Thanks."

Sam didn't call that night, or Wednesday or Thursday. Abby thought she might as well cultivate a friendship with Blair while she waited to meet someone that she found interested in dating, because Sam was gone. She came close to asking Blair on Friday afternoon about her weekend plans, but she didn't want Blair to know she was needy for some companionship. Entering the loft she saw the flashing light on the phone indicating she had a message. She went to the bedroom to kick off her shoes and sat on the bed to listen, assuming it would be a message from Selena, wanting to extort more money. The time stamp announced five twenty-six and according to the alarm clock, it was now five thirty-two.

"Abby." The voice made her breath catch. "It's Sam. Sorry it took so long to get back to you, but I've been putting in a lot of hours lately. Anyway, call my cell and I'll try to call you back right away." Sam recited her number.

Abby could only sit stunned. She replayed the message again and then a third time. She didn't want to have hope, but she couldn't stop the racing in her heart. After throwing on an old pair of sweats and a sweatshirt, she used the phone in the kitchen to make the call, then poured a glass of wine and carried the phone to the window where she sat to watch the bustling city. Twenty minutes later the phone rang.

"Hello." Abby held her breath.

"Abby, it's Sam." The silence grew uncomfortable.

"Thanks for calling me back." She didn't know where to start a conversation at this point.

"No problem," Sam replied, her voice flat and emotionless.

Abby took a deep breath and swallowed the lump in her throat. "Sam...we need to talk." She heard a sigh.

"Yes, we do," Sam muttered.

"Face-to-face, not over the phone."

"Okay." She paused. "I'm off at seven. You want to meet somewhere?"

"Have you had dinner yet?"

"No."

"I was going to fix myself some dinner." It was a lie, but only a little white one. "Come by and have dinner with me." Abby wanted this vital conversation to happen without distractions.

Sam hesitated a long, long moment. "Uh...all right. You need me to pick up anything on my way?"

"Just bring your smiling face. I'll see you in a while."

"Okay."

Abby's heart danced as she disconnected the call, and she literally danced her way to the kitchen to scramble for something she could prepare for their dinner. Just two friends having a meal, she reminded herself, keep it simple. She placed chicken in the oven to bake, selected a mixture of vegetables to cook and bread to warm. Shortly after seven, the loft smelling heavenly, she went to change into a sweater and pair of jeans. Skipping shoes, she pulled on a heavy pair of woolen socks. She turned the oven down only a moment before the knock on her door.

"Hi."

Abby opened the door wide. "Hi you! Your timing is perfect. We can eat now or wait."

Sam looked over at the place settings on the dining table. "It looks so formal. Can we maybe eat at the counter like the last time?"

Abby moved to gather the dishes. "Of course." As she began to place them on the counter, she realized Sam had seated herself so Abby would sit beside her instead of across the counter looking at each other. *Oh Sam… What do we need to do to fix this?* She offered Sam wine before pouring more in her own glass.

"I can't. I'm going back in at eleven to cover a shift for someone."

It would be a definite positive if Abby could keep Sam here until then. They ate mostly in silence…a very awkward silence. Sam made a few comments about the food and Abby's cooking, but it felt more like two complete strangers forced to share dining space. Abby glanced sideways often, only to find Sam focused on the plate in front of her. After swallowing the last bite of a second helping, Sam pushed her plate away.

"That was excellent and I'm stuffed." When Abby reached for her plate, Sam placed a gentle hand on her arm. "I've been avoiding you. I'm sorry."

Before Abby could think, her mouth opened and words spilled out. "Really? I guess I hadn't noticed." Sam flinched. "I'm sorry. That was mean," she quickly apologized.

"No, I'm sorry." She hesitated. "What happened that night… that kiss…kind of caught me off guard—"

"I'm so sorry. I obviously misunderstood when you said you 'really' liked me." Abby stared at the darkness beyond the living room windows sensing Sam's gaze on her.

"No. You didn't misunderstand." She hesitated and then cleared her throat. "The truth is I wanted to kiss you more than I wanted air to breathe, but I realized you were responding for a completely different reason. I got scared. I am so sorry for putting you in that position."

Abby turned her gaze on Sam, but she was staring out into the night. It made so much more sense now. Sam was only just coming out. She touched her arm.

"I know, Sam, and I understand." The muscles in Sam's arm tensed. She felt compelled to make her own confession. "Sam, since we're sharing truths, I have one too. That day you showed up here worried about me and caught me in the tub…" Sam's cheeks colored like they had on that day. "It had only been a couple of weeks since I kicked out my girlfriend of four years. I'd gone to work the previous day and had Blair, I've told you about her, come to the office, knowing my boss was in court at the time. She wanted to make sure that I knew my girlfriend was cheating on me, assured of that fact having seen the proof herself. She wanted to protect me from being hurt by my cheating ex. The news was old to me, but it sickened me that she invaded my personal life like that." The hurtful emotions of that day surged back making her voice shake and summoned the tears again.

"I'm sorry." Sam turned her gaze to Abby.

Abby swiped away her tears and looked deep into Sam's kind, welcoming eyes as Sam put a comforting hand on her shoulder.

"It's not your fault, but I do understand how scary it can feel." She tried forcing a smile. "I'm not sure what this is between us. I only know how I feel. Since the first time we met, I've wanted to know you better. You're always in my thoughts." She sighed and turned on the stool, her knees brushing Sam's thigh. "Sam?"

Sam turned around so that her legs were against Abby's. "I have another truth to confess, Abby."

She feared the worst and worried her expression showed it. Sam looked so serious.

"When I said that I really like you, what I was afraid to tell you was that I think I'm falling in love with you."

Abby sat silent, her heart pounding so hard it echoed in her ears. She finally slipped off the stool and between Sam's legs.

"And now?"

Sam brushed her fingertips over Abby's cheek. "Just this…" She kissed Abby tenderly. Abby braced herself on Sam's thighs, welcoming her lips. The kiss was brief, but time seemed inconsequential. Sam leaned back and ran her fingers through Abby's hair. "You are so beautiful."

Abby caught Sam's hand, pressed it first to her cheek and then kissed her palm. Sam's eyes were dreamy. She placed Sam's hand over her racing heart.

"Do you feel what you do to me?"

Sam grinned and took hold of Abby's hand, placing it over her own heart. "Likewise."

Every part of Abby wanted to drag Sam to her bed, but she knew better. "We'll just take our time and see how this goes."

Sam nodded. It was almost painful for Abby to move away from her and back onto the stool. She wanted to touch Sam, and feel her touch, like Sam had said, more than she wanted "air to breathe."

Sam stood and stepped beside Abby's stool, turning her so they were facing one another she took Abby's hands. Sam's eyes were deeper blue than Abby had ever seen.

"What is it?"

Sam's cheeks colored and she glanced down at their joined hands. "When I'm around you, my heart hammers in my chest." She released Abby's hands and rubbed her own hands over her thighs. "My hands get all sweaty and my stomach flips and flops all around."

"Sam, honey." Abby stroked Sam's cheek. "You make me feel the same way."

"Really?" She met Abby's gaze again.

"Really." Abby pushed off the stool. "And I want you to kiss me again."

Sam pulled her closer. Abby tipped her head. When Sam pressed her lips to Abby's, a tiny moan escaped Abby's throat. The kiss turned more ravenous than the last. Abby moved her hands around Sam's neck while Sam's hands traveled up and down her back before settling on Abby's hips. Abby pressed herself against the full length of Sam's body, unable to resist the heat building between them.

Abby ended the kiss breathing hard. "I'm sorry." Sam's forehead creased. "I said we'd take our time and now I'm trying to seduce you."

Sam touched her lips briefly to Abby's to stop her talking, and then leaned her forehead against Abby's. "I want to make love to you." Abby melted into her arms as Sam kissed a tender trail to her ear. "Let me make love to you," she whispered.

Choked on emotion, "Please," was all Abby could manage to whimper.

Sam took Abby's hand and led her to the bedroom where she sat on the bed and stood Abby between her legs. Agonizingly slow, Sam unbuttoned Abby's sweater and unhooked her bra. She cupped Abby's breasts, gently rubbing her nipples until they were fully erect. When Sam's mouth captured a nipple, they moaned in unison. Sam's tongue teased one nipple and then the other. Abby grasped Sam's shoulders, pulling her against her, her legs growing shaky. Abby was soaking wet. Sam stood and pressed their hips together, kissing her with a hungry need as her hands moved to open Abby's jeans. Abby pushed into Sam's hand as she slipped it inside her jeans. Sam's fingers slid into her wetness. Abby groaned. And when Sam stroked her, Abby's breath caught and her legs became so weak she *had* to hang onto Sam's shoulders to keep from buckling to the floor.

Without moving her hand, Sam turned Abby around, worked her jeans below her hips and sat Abby on the bed. Sam sat too, her hand still driving Abby to a breathless frenzy. Sam's lips started below Abby's ear, painting a trail down Abby's neck to the hollow of her throat. She slipped her hand from between Abby's legs and traced a path of kisses down Abby's stomach. Kneeling on the floor, Sam pulled Abby's jeans and panties off in one swift motion. She placed kisses over Abby's bare thighs. She slid her arms under Abby's legs and shouldered her legs apart.

"Oh, Sam…" Abby murmured at the first touch of Sam's tongue against her sensitized flesh. Sam pleasured and teased Abby until her legs trembled uncontrollably. Then she took Abby over the precipice, Abby calling Sam's name over and over again as the wave washed over her.

When Abby's breathing finally slowed, Sam eased her back onto the bed and stretched alongside her body. Fueled by the heat that consumed her, Abby's desire to touch and pleasure every part of Sam overwhelmed her. She ran her fingers through Sam's hair and slid her hand down her back.

"I want you Sam." She tugged at the waistband of Sam's pants. "Could I talk you out of your clothes?"

Sam smiled shyly but rolled off the bed and began to undress. Abby pulled her sweater and bra off, pushed farther up on the bed and watched as Sam removed her clothes, revealing herself to Abby bit by bit. Her tall, well-toned body contrasted Abby's softer, curvier shape. Sam crawled on the bed next to her.

"Tell me what you want," Abby said, still unsure if this was Sam's first time.

"I want to look in your eyes." Sam's eyelids were heavy with lust. "I want to taste your lips and feel you against me."

Abby urged Sam onto her back and slid a leg between hers as she settled her weight on Sam with a pleasing moan. Sam lifted her hips, her wetness coating Abby's thigh. Abby wanted to devour her all at once. She wanted to dive into the deep blue of Sam's eyes and linger, savoring every breath, every touch and every sensation. Abby traced her fingers down Sam's side causing Sam to quiver.

She touched her cheek to Sam's and whispered, "I want to touch you." She pressed her thigh harder to Sam's heat. "Here."

Sam grabbed Abby's hips and rocked against her. "I want…" Sam murmured as Abby slid her hand between them. "Oh, God!" Sam gasped when Abby's fingers found her wetness. "I've dreamed about you, about this," Sam said, her voice raspy.

Her hips jerked when Abby entered her, eyes closing briefly. Sam bit her lip. Abby moved with the rhythm of Sam's hips. Too soon she started to tremble, her hips arching one last time before she went slack. She pulled Abby's mouth to hers, her tongue teasing Abby's lips. She tightened around Abby's fingers, still deep inside her, and began to move again against Abby's hips. She wasn't done. Abby was pleased. She wanted more too.

When Sam's legs trembled, Abby put her lips to Sam's ear and whispered, "Oh…yes."

Sam's entire body vibrated beneath her. She gasped for breath, and her heart thundered in her chest against Abby.

Keeping her hand in the warm embrace of Sam's thighs, Abby propped herself on an elbow.

"Wow!" Sam's eyes looked glazed and a tiny smile curled her lips.

"Yes, wow." Abby smiled back at her. When she started to move her hand, Sam's thighs held tightly.

"Mmm..." Sam moaned.

Abby kissed her temple and Sam's eyelids fluttered like butterfly wings against her cheek. Abby leaned away and gazed into her eyes. "I thought this might be your first time, but I'm guessing not."

The sparkle vanished from Sam's eyes. She shook her head, looked away and reached down to pull Abby's hand from between her legs.

"Sam?" Abby waited a moment. "Sam, please look at me." Sam met her gaze. "I didn't mean anything. You're an incredible lover and I want to be with you. I want to do *this* with you until I can't breathe." Abby kept her eyes focused on Sam's.

Sam finally reached up and touched her cheek. "You're so beautiful." She pulled Abby to her lips and kissed her with a passion that threatened to start the lovemaking all over again, but she ended it just as quickly.

"What time is it?"

Abby checked the bedside clock. "Almost ten."

Sam sighed deeply. "I have to go back at eleven and cover a shift. Remember?"

Abby dropped her head to Sam's chest. "And what if I don't let go of you?"

Sam chuckled. "Will you if I promise I'll come back?" She kissed Abby's forehead.

Abby drew her hand up Sam's side and over her breast catching a nipple between her fingers. When Sam moaned softly, Abby repositioned her weight on top of Sam.

"I don't think I can let you go."

Sam pushed Abby's hair back from her face and stroked it. "I'm on three to eleven tomorrow. I can come back after my shift and we can have a repeat performance around midnight."

She winked a blue eye. "All night if you want. I'm off Sunday."
She wrapped Abby in her arms.

"You're very convincing, Doctor Sam. You may leave my
bed." Being in Sam's arms was more wonderful than anything
Abby had ever experienced. She slid over and lay next to Sam.
"There's a shower in the upstairs bathroom." Sam rolled off the
bed and stood beside it, her body silhouetted by the lights of the
city beyond the windows.

"I think I'd rather wear you around on me all night." She
took a deep breath as she pulled her shirt over her head. "Your
scent will keep me on my toes." She sat down on the side of
the bed and pulled the covers over to partially cover Abby. "It
will definitely keep reminding me of this." She placed a kiss on
Abby's lips. "And keep me wanting more."

She kissed Abby once more with so much passion that Abby
wanted to pull her clothes off and have her again and again.
Abby held Sam's firm upper arms only a moment, and then
pushed her away.

"Sweet dreams. I'll see you tomorrow night."

Abby reached out and briefly caught hold of Sam's fingers
before she slipped away. Grabbing her pillow, she held it against
her chest. She was so far gone over Sam. Lying there for the
longest time, she breathed in Sam's scent, languishing in how
amazing it felt to have Sam's touch on her skin, and simply
unable to get the thoughts out of her mind.

CHAPTER SEVENTEEN

Abby was awake a few minutes past seven, so she started the bath water and went to make coffee. Tuning the radio in the bathroom to soft jazz, she pinned up her hair and submerged herself in the steaming bath. Relaxed to the point of almost nodding off, she barely heard the light rap on the bathroom door.

"I brought breakfast," Sam said. "Do you mind if I come in?"

"Hmm…depends on what you consider breakfast."

Sam cracked the door and reached her hand inside. "Bagels and juice."

"In that case, come on in."

Sam entered and backed against the door to close it. "Whew, it's hot in here." Her cheeks were flushed when she met Abby's eyes. "Or maybe it's just you." She stepped out of her shoes and sat beside the tub. As brightly as her eyes sparkled, she looked completely wiped out.

"Come in and soak with me."

Sam dipped her hand in the water. "You won't melt me, will you?"

The mere touch of Sam's fingers sliding up her arm set a fire burning in Abby's belly. "Not on purpose."

"You look like an angel. How can I resist?"

Abby watched as she undressed. "You know you're pretty cute in those scrubs."

Sam glanced down as she untied the pants. "Thanks. A little one nailed me in the ER and I didn't have another change of clothes at the hospital."

When Sam stepped out of her pants and underwear, Abby scooted forward and she climbed in, sliding her legs on either side of Abby and pulling Abby against her. Sam's nipples pressed into Abby's back. Her kiss on the back of Abby's neck sent a shiver down her spine and she melted into Sam's embrace as Sam leaned them back in the water. Sam's hands roamed over Abby's breasts, then down her stomach parting her legs. Abby moaned with pleasure when Sam entered her.

"Touching you makes me this wet too."

Sam held Abby tightly as she took her to the edge and over. Abby collapsed in her arms and when her breathing returned to normal, she turned in Sam's embrace. Sam's eyes were closed.

"Are you ready to go again?" Sam said, blinking her eyes open.

Abby touched a finger to Sam's lips and kissed them. "Sam, honey, let me put you to bed. You need to sleep. Then we'll see."

Sam's eyes drifted closed. "I can nap right here."

Abby got out and pulled on her robe. Grabbing a towel, she took Sam's hand and gave it a tug. "Come on, sweetie." When Sam got out, Abby wrapped the towel around her and pulled Sam against her. Sam's eyes drooped. "We'll pick up where we left off after you sleep."

Sam dropped the towel, climbed into bed and Abby pulled the covers up, kissing her on the forehead.

Sam caught her hand as she stood. "I don't usually sleep naked."

"Well, we'll see about that." Abby dropped her robe and slipped in against Sam's side. She stroked Sam's hair until her eyes drifted closed. She kissed her temple. "Sweet dreams, my darling Sam." In a moment Sam was sleeping.

As quietly as possible Abby slipped from the bed, gathered her clothes and dressed in the bathroom. She took Sam's breakfast to the kitchen, put the juice in the fridge, and left a note on the counter next to the bagels. Then she ran out to take care of a few errands. Returning an hour later, she sat at the counter, still seeing the image of Sam naked in her bed. Willing herself not to disturb Sam for purely selfish reasons, she forced herself to the laundry room and started the washer. As she gathered towels in the bathroom, she contemplated folding Sam's scrubs and leaving them on the bed, but instead she took them to the laundry room as well. She tiptoed into the bedroom and placed a sweatshirt, flannel boxers and a pair of thick socks on the bed for her when she got up.

Plugging in earbuds, she queued up some music on her iPod and started cleaning the kitchen and living room. More than once she found herself caught up in the music, dancing as she moved. She smiled. The love bug had definitely bit. She couldn't recall a time she'd ever felt so happy to simply share the same space with someone. Around eleven, with the laundry and cleaning done, she settled on the couch with a cup of tea and the book she had started to read months ago. She lowered the volume on the music and switched to something a little mellower.

Abby startled at the touch on her shoulder and kiss on the top of her head. She pulled out the earbuds and tipped her head backward.

"Hey."

"Hey." Sam smiled and leaned over to kiss her forehead. "Someone stole my clothes while I was sleeping."

"Really?"

Sam's hand wandered from Abby's shoulder inside the V of her sweater. The touch was fiery hot on Abby's skin. She moved her hand lower, cupping Abby's breast. Abby's breath left her in a rush and her book fell away. Sam knelt behind the couch and slipped her other hand inside Abby's sweater to her other breast. With her cheek against Abby's head, Sam's breath whispered warmly across Abby's ear.

"We have ways to make you talk."

"I confess... I took them... I surrender. Do with me what you will."

"Your punishment will be long and torturous."

Sam swiftly hopped over the back of the couch to kneel beside Abby and hover over her like a menacing beast. When Abby offered her fisted hands, wrists pressed together, Sam leapt to her feet in front of the couch and pulled Abby to her feet too. Sam released her hands, cupped her face and kissed her fiercely. Her hands went to Sam's hips and pulled her close. Sam moaned and then dragged her lips from Abby's.

"You make me want to forget everything in the world but you."

Abby snuck her hands under the sweatshirt, up Sam's back and around to her breasts. Sam threw her head back, pressing her hips to Abby's. When Abby moved her hand down Sam's stomach to the top of the shorts, Sam caught her hand.

"That's bad. I'm supposed to be torturing you." She stepped back out of Abby's reach.

"You can't imagine how much you are." Abby bit her lip to keep from groaning.

"Oh, I think I do."

Abby tipped her head.

"What?" Sam asked.

"You look adorable in my clothes."

Sam playfully pulled at the hem of the shorts and spun around on her socked foot. "You think so?"

Abby smiled. "Maybe next time I'll put you in one of my dresses."

Sam let go a deep belly laugh, fell onto the couch and pulled Abby into her lap. "Have you ever wrestled a tiger?" Abby shook her head. "Well, try putting me in a dress and you'll find out what it's like." Abby giggled. "If you don't believe me, ask Momma. She quit wrestling this tiger when I was about eight or so."

"Hmm... I think I will..." Sam narrowed her eyes. "Ask your mother," Abby chuckled, "not wrestle the tiger."

Sam pushed Abby's hair behind her ear. "I *really* like you Abby Collins." Abby raised a brow. "Did you understand that inflection correctly?"

Abby chuckled again and kissed her. "Would you like something to eat?" Sam only grinned at her. "Sam?"

Sam blinked. "I was trying to decide if I could sustain myself on you." She slipped her hand under Abby's sweater.

"Seriously, are you hungry?"

Sam teased her nipple through the lace of her bra. "Mmm… hungry for you sweetheart."

"You need real food." Abby got to her feet and pulled Sam after her. "Come on, I'll whip something up."

Sam squeezed her hand and gave a seductive smile. "Or just whip me."

"You're insatiable."

"I can't help it." Sam tugged her hand and pulled Abby into her arms. "I hunger for you." Sam smothered her mouth in a kiss.

She sat Sam at the counter with a glass of juice while she fixed eggs and chopped fresh fruit. She couldn't help stealing glances at Sam in her boxers and sweatshirt. *I could get used to this picture.* Abby placed the plate in front of her and took the seat across the counter.

"Do you always eat so healthy?" Sam asked, digging in with gusto.

"I try."

Sam pointed her fork at the plate of fruit. "No blueberries today?"

"I didn't think you liked them. You didn't—"

"I don't. Can't even stand the smell of them."

"I figured as much."

"So noted. Nothing gets by you."

If that were so I wouldn't have let Selena use me.

"I eat the worst things imaginable. You'd think a doctor would know better. There just isn't time for healthy meals the way we work. The only ones I usually get are the occasions when I visit my folks."

She ate like she was starving. Dr. Sam, always taking care of others first, made Abby want to take care of her all the more.

"When is the last time you ate?"

"I grabbed a vending machine sandwich about three o'clock this morning." Her eyes narrowed. "I think." When she cleaned the plate, Abby refilled it. After finishing a heaping second helping she leaned back with a satisfied smile. "What's for dessert?"

"You had it, honey. Are you still hungry?"

"Not for food."

"The shower's in the upstairs bathroom. Maybe you should take a cold one."

She sauntered around the counter and slipped her arms around Abby from behind. "Only if you take one with me." She kissed Abby on the back of the neck making her shiver. "Besides, I vaguely remember a bath, maybe...this morning when I got here."

Abby wrapped her arms over Sam's. "And it was quite nice, although, I think you slept through it."

Sam turned her around on the stool. "I remember every slippery wet second of it. Afterward you tucked me into bed like a good girl."

Abby put a hand to her cheek. "You are a good girl. That's why your family loves you so much." Sam gave her a look of question. "What?"

Sam hesitated a moment. "You're not planning to tell me are you?"

"Tell you what, sweetie?"

"I saw it in the bathroom wastebasket. You're ovulating." When Abby looked away, Sam hooked a finger under her chin. "Abby?"

"Yes," Abby replied quietly. Sam kept an intense gaze on her. "I'm going to do it after you leave for work."

Sam took her hand. "Would you like my help?"

Abby bit her lip. If she allowed Sam to do this for her, she wondered how it might impact a possible relationship going forward. They barely knew each other, and Abby was pretty sure this was all new to Sam. Sam stepped between Abby's knees and put her hands on Abby's hips.

"They say there's a better chance of conceiving if you're aroused. And I should know, I am a doctor." She waggled her brows.

"Are you saying—"

Sam touched her finger to her lips. "I want to do this for you."

"Oh Sam, I don't know if this is a good idea," Abby nearly whispered.

Sam kissed the top of her head then rested her chin there. "Please, Abby."

Sam's plea, like lava, melted any resolve Abby had. When she still didn't answer, Sam took hold of her hand.

"Come on." She pulled Abby up and to the bedroom.

Sam's fingers brushed across Abby's stomach as she worked the button open on her jeans. Abby stiffened and caught Sam's hands.

"Sam?"

Sam raised her hand to stroke Abby's hair. "Shh." She kissed Abby's lips tenderly. "Please let me do this for you."

Abby's heart hammered. She leaned back to look into Sam's eyes and saw passion, burning wild. Abby kissed her with matching passion.

Sam made love to her slowly. Abby saw blinding white light when she climaxed and Sam's name sounded foreign as it tore from her throat. Sam moved up next to her, continuing the aftershocks with her featherlight touches on Abby's skin.

"I want you Sam," she said between breaths and pulled Sam close.

"I want you to want me, but important things first. Where is it?" Abby looked at her, confused. "Your little contributors. We should do it now before anything else."

Abby felt more nervous than she ever had in her life. She was actually about to try and get pregnant.

"In the kitchen, next to the sink."

Sam set everything on the nightstand and began to slowly undress while Abby watched.

"I need your legs up just like you're in the stirrups at the gynecologist." Once Abby positioned herself, Sam settled between her legs. Touching her thumb to Abby's wetness, she said softly, "Just close your eyes and pretend this is me inside you."

Sam eased the syringe in and released the little swimmers. Abby said a prayer that they would do their job. When Sam removed the syringe, she quickly slipped her fingers in its place. Abby emitted a deep low moan and tightened herself around Sam's fingers. Sam coaxed her legs down and moved beside her again, keeping her fingers buried inside her. She kissed the corner of Abby's mouth.

"Thank you." Abby murmured, opening her eyes to see Sam's smiling face. "I want you. I want you now."

She kissed beads of sweat from Abby's forehead. "Not yet. We need to give those little guys a fighting chance." Sam wiggled her fingers making Abby clench tighter around her fingers.

"Oh…"

Sam laid her head next to Abby's. "Maybe we'll get pregnant on the first try."

Abby's heart melted. Sam had said "we" not you. Like a landslide, emotions swept over her.

"I think I could love you, Sam Christiano." She rolled on top of Sam. "And now I've got you right where I want you." She checked the time on the bedside clock.

"Please don't feel like you have to reciprocate."

"I don't. I want you." She squeezed Sam's thigh between her own. "I really want you, but I don't want to wear you out before work."

Sam brushed Abby's hair back. "I can wait. I don't ever want to feel rushed with you."

Abby smiled at the thought of always making slow, lingering love with her.

"What if I can't wait?"

"It'll be a good test of willpower," Sam replied.

Abby pushed out her bottom lip. "I guess if I can't wait, there are things I can do to relieve the urge." Sam's cheeks turned a rosy hue and she averted her gaze. "Oh, sweetie, what I meant was that I can call you to talk. I can call you, right?"

Sam nodded. "Can we cuddle on the couch until I have to leave?"

Abby traced her finger over Sam's cheek and across her lips. "I'm all yours. We can do whatever you want."

After dressing, Abby led the way to the living room, turned on some jazz at a low volume and settled beside Sam on the couch. Sam promptly moved to the opposite end.

Abby sniffed the air. "I know I took a bath this morning."

Sam grinned. "You did." She patted her legs. "Put your feet up here."

Abby parked her woolen-socked feet in her lap. Sam took hold of a foot and began massaging the bottom of it.

The sensation shot straight up Abby's leg to her center. She clenched her legs.

"Oh, my," she gasped. Sam kept pressing. "Where...how..." She couldn't think.

Sam gave a sultry look. "I learned some massage during one of my internships."

Abby waved a hand. "If you don't stop, I'm going to...oh..." Her brain shut down.

"You're going to what?" She kept Abby locked in her gaze. "Climax?"

Abby dropped her head back on the pillow. Sam possessed her. She couldn't do anything but lie limp as a wet cloth. Sam put her other hand on Abby's other foot and simultaneously pressed into the same spot on both feet. Abby couldn't stop the inevitable. She shuddered.

"That's nice," Sam murmured.

It wasn't a screaming orgasm, but it felt so good. Sam slid her hand up the inside of Abby's thigh.

"I can finish what I started." She wiggled her thumb between Abby's legs and pressed lightly.

Abby grasped her hand. "You've done quite enough, but thanks for the offer." She squeezed her legs together again and tugged on Sam's hand. "Come here."

Sam lowered herself on Abby and kissed her. Abby wanted her right there, with her all the time. She wanted to be pinned under Sam and for Sam to hold her captive. Because if she were honest with herself, she knew Sam had already captured her heart.

"Do you think it's possible we did it the first time?"

"Unless I was having a really vivid dream, I'm pretty sure we did that." Sam waggled her brows.

"I mean get pregnant."

"Oh well, if you're really fertile, I suppose so." She grinned again.

"What?"

She squeezed Abby's legs between hers. "You feel pretty fertile to me."

Abby slipped her hands in the back of Sam's shorts and grasped her firm backside.

Sam's gaze drifted toward the windows and then back to Abby. "Do you think people in those tall buildings downtown can see us?"

Abby looked out at numerous tall buildings within city blocks that towered over her four-story loft.

"I suppose they could if they were looking. Do you want to go into the bedroom?"

Sam narrowed her eyes. "You are a temptress." Her expression softened. "I want to make love to you all afternoon until you're too spent to talk, but..." She pushed up from the couch. "I have to be at the hospital in little over an hour. I don't think I can do what I did last night. My shift was two-thirds over before I could stop thinking about you and think about what I was supposed to be doing." She cocked her head. "What?"

"You just look like an invitation any woman would be foolish to pass up." Abby took in her long, lean legs and thought how much she wanted to dive between them. She absently traced her fingers up Sam's thigh.

Sam sidestepped. "You're so bad." She caught Abby's fingers. "And while I really like bad, unfortunately I need to get ready. Where'd you hide my clothes?" When Abby started to get up, Sam held out a hand. "Stay put. I'll get them."

"In the laundry room behind the kitchen."

Sam entered the space behind the kitchen. Laundry room? It was over half the size of her apartment. You could park a car in it. She found her scrubs hanging on a rack in front of the dryer and pulled them off the hangers. She pressed them to her face. They smelled fresh, like a spring day, and soft as a baby blanket. Her turtleneck and underwear were neatly folded on the dryer. After dressing she laid Abby's loaned clothes on the washer and when she turned to leave, she noticed the large stack of boxes partially covered by a sheet. Written on the sides of the boxes were things like "Selena – clothes," or "Selena – stuff." Selena must be the ex, she thought. What a sexy, exotic sounding name. She shook off a feeling of inadequacy that she couldn't compete with someone hot and sexy. She was only kind of cute in her mind's eye, and even her Italian genes didn't manifest themselves into anything resembling sexy.

But, she reminded herself, Abby had said she thought she could love her. And she knew in her heart, she could definitely spend her life loving a woman like Abby.

CHAPTER EIGHTEEN

It felt like the longest evening of her life waiting for Sam to come back. She delayed her dinner as long as possible and was pacing nervously at ten o'clock. So far every moment she'd spent with Sam had been wondrous. If she were honest with herself, she hadn't been exactly truthful when she told Sam she thought she could love her. She was hopelessly in love with Sam. Abby knew in every part of herself that Sam was her one.

She fell asleep on the couch reading sometime after eleven o'clock and woke just before midnight. Unable to stay awake, she left the lights on, pulled the bedroom door almost closed and crawled into bed. Abby said a silent prayer as her eyes drifted closed that Sam would come back and not run away like she had after their first unexpected kiss. The creaking bedroom door woke Abby. Groggy with sleep, she watched Sam's shadow near the bed and reached for her hand.

"I tried to stay awake," she said around a yawn.

"I'm sorry it's so late. I got caught up with a patient." She sat, leaning over to kiss Abby's lips lightly.

Abby touched her cheek. "It's fine, sweetie. I understand."

Sam took Abby's hand and kissed her palm. "You must be tired."

Abby tugged on her shirt. "Undress and come sleep with me."

Sam stripped off her clothes and slid under the covers. "Hey, no fair, you're not naked." Abby sat up and peeled the long T-shirt over her head. Sam hooked a finger in her panties. "These too, please." Abby laid back and gathered Sam into her arms. Sam rested her head on Abby's chest. "I could get used to this."

Abby put the coffee on, found the sweatshirt and shorts she laundered the day before, and quietly re-entered the bedroom. She placed the clean clothes on the bed and gathered Sam's discarded clothes from the floor. She held Sam's shirt to her cheek, breathing in the scent of her freshly scrubbed skin mixed with the antiseptic hospital smell. In the faint light filtering through the blinds she watched Sam sleeping soundly. *Oh God, I am in love with her.* Panic grabbed hold of her like a bad dream, and she hurriedly slipped again from the room. Was it crazy to feel so in love so soon after ending a four-year relationship?

Sipping coffee at the counter with the newspaper spread out before her, Abby wasn't reading, but daydreaming, when she heard the flush from the bathroom. Moments later, Abby's heart skipped a few beats as Sam pressed against her side and kissed her hair.

"Good morning." Sam dropped her arm across Abby's shoulders.

"Good morning to you." Abby slid her arm around Sam's waist. Before she could ask, Sam picked up Abby's mug and took a drink.

"Ooh, this is wonderful."

"Would you like me to get you a cup?"

"Would you be mad if I drank yours?" Abby shook her head. Sam swiveled Abby's stool and wiggled between her knees. "What if I were to drink in all of you again?" She leaned down and placed a fiery kiss on Abby's lips. Abby gasped when Sam pulled back. "Maybe here, maybe now." Sam's eyebrows danced.

When Sam returned her lips to Abby's, Abby slid her hands under Sam's sweatshirt and up her sides. She moaned into her mouth and pulled Abby's hips to hers. Abby stopped her hands just under Sam's breasts, gently separating their bodies. Sam looked hurt.

"Don't you think we should have some food to sustain ourselves?"

Sam's expression brightened. "I could sustain myself fine on you." She grinned.

She leaned in to capture Abby's lips, but Abby held her off. "I'm serious." Sam pouted. "When's the last time you ate anything?"

Sam tilted her head finally saying, "I don't know...maybe around seven last night."

"Sit," Abby ordered as she got up. "I'll fix breakfast." After filling a mug with coffee for herself, she topped off the one Sam had claimed. Sam hooked her arm around Abby's waist.

"I really could get used to this, but please don't spoil me. I'm afraid I'd have to move back in with Momma."

Abby brushed her fingers through Sam's hair and kissed her temple. "I'm sure your mother wouldn't complain. And, you'd have more room there than in that tiny apartment of yours."

"All true, but I've grown accustomed to living on my own. I don't think I could go back to sharing my space."

Sam's words sparked questions for Abby as she went about whipping eggs for an omelet and cutting fruit. Was this Sam's way of telling her she was not a cohabitating kind of woman? It was too soon to ask. All things would be answered in time. Wouldn't they? Like, Sam obviously hadn't just come out. How many other girlfriends had she had?

Sam dove into the food Abby placed before her. She had as healthy an appetite for food as she had for sex. Abby made a mental note to keep the fridge better stocked in the event Sam might be showing up regularly.

Being with Sam was the easiest, most natural thing for Abby. It felt like she'd known her for years. During dinner they got onto the subject of family, or rather, Abby asked a lot of questions and Sam talked about her family.

"You never talk about your family. Are they criminals or something?"

Abby didn't want to keep secrets from Sam about her family status like she had with Selena. Especially in a budding relationship, if that's what this was with Sam.

"There's not a lot to know. I don't really have a relationship with them. Like I told you before, I have two brothers, but we're not close. My dad is gone, and well… You saw my mother. There's so much bad blood between us that it's toxic. We share a name." She shrugged. "I like to think that I would have eventually had a relationship with my dad if he were still here."

Sam touched her hand. "I'm sorry. Everybody should have a loving family."

Abby forced a smile. "They don't approve of my lifestyle, so I'll probably never have a relationship with them since I don't intend to change who I am."

Sam locked her fingers with Abby's. "I have a rather large family. I'll share." Her eyes sparkled when she smiled.

"That's so sweet." Abby pecked her on the lips. "I may take you up on that offer." Joy… That's what Sam brought into her life and it warmed every part of her. When Abby stood to clean up, Sam stopped her.

"Let me. You sit and enjoy your wine."

"Aren't you going to have some more?"

Sam dropped her head and stared at the floor. "I didn't mention this before because I didn't want to spoil this day with you, but I'm on the midnight shift this week, starting tonight."

"That's so unfair. We've barely had any time," Abby pouted.

Sam returned to the table and placed her finger over Abby's lips. "I know, beautiful." She tipped Abby's chin up. "Boy, do I ever, but it's my life. We'll just have to make the best of my limited time."

A little after ten o'clock, Sam left the bed with a groan, got dressed and returned to Abby's side.

"If I could fit you in my pocket, I'd take you with me instead of leaving you in this bed alone." She ran her hand down Abby's thigh, causing Abby to shiver.

"I'll keep you right here until we're together again." Abby pulled Sam's hand to her chest where her heart pounded fiercely. "Call me."

Sam kissed her tenderly. "You can count on it."

When she'd gone, Abby lay staring at the darkness through the blinds and wondered why Sam seemed different and felt different than any other woman she'd been with.

CHAPTER NINETEEN

"Well, it appears somebody got some over the weekend. That or your mother passed and left you the family fortune," Blair said when Abby arrived in the office Monday morning.

She obviously hadn't hidden her euphoria as well as she had thought. "My personal life isn't up for discussion."

Blair dropped several folders onto the table in front of Abby. "Oh, come on, spill. Maybe I can live vicariously through you since I can't seem to find anyone suitable to tussle in bed with." She placed her hands on Abby's shoulders from behind. "Humor me."

Abby forcibly pushed her chair back to stand and Blair stepped away. "I won't be your source for entertainment, Blair. I met someone and we had a nice weekend. Not everything is about sex." But the sex had been mind-blowing, and Abby felt a twinge between her legs thinking about it.

Blair dropped into the chair Abby vacated. "I'm sorry. I'm starving for some companionship. Let's go out for lunch today. That's all, no funny business. Please..." Abby frowned at her. "Please Abby. It will be strictly professional."

Against her better judgment, Abby agreed.

Blair pulled her car into the parking garage of one of the smaller office towers downtown and they rode the elevator to the fifteenth floor. The lavishly decorated lobby and highly polished mahogany door directly in front of them was rather impressive. Blair pulled a plastic card from her pocket and swiped it over the electronic pad beside the door. It couldn't be a publicized place. Abby had no idea there was a restaurant at this location. Blair pulled the heavy door open and followed Abby inside. Slipping out of her coat, she then took hold of Abby's to help her. A moment later, a short hair, medium-height woman appeared to greet them. She was wearing black pants, starched white shirt and black vest. Abby's gaydar pinged loudly.

"Good afternoon, Ms. Stanton. Your table is ready."

Blair nodded and took Abby's elbow with the lightest touch to steer her across the crowded restaurant. Most apparent was that there were only female guests. Their table at the far side by the windows offered a spectacular view of the city. On one side of the restaurant sat a massive mahogany bar. What Abby thought was a man behind the bar, she quickly realized was in fact a woman...another lesbian. Her eyes traveled around the room searching the faces when she spied a familiar one. It was Judge Thomas, whom Abby only recognized from the election signs that blanketed the city the year before. It thrilled Abby to know that a place like this existed in their town.

Blair touched Abby's arm to gain her attention. "What would you like to drink?"

There wasn't any doubt that their waitress was a lesbian too. They were sitting in an exclusive women's only club, and probably most were lesbians, or at least women who enjoyed the company of women over men.

She heard Blair say, "And she'll have a glass of sparkling water." After the waitress left, Blair asked, "Is everything all right?"

Abby nodded slowly. "These women—"

Blair leaned closer. "Yes?"

"They're gay?"

Blair scanned the room. "Yes, most are, I suppose."

"You brought me to an exclusive restaurant for lesbians?"

"It's actually a club. There's a dance floor around the corner from the bar, and yes, it is exclusively for women. I can assure you it's completely discreet, or I wouldn't be here. Is it a problem?"

"Are you kidding?" Abby arched a brow. "I might get lucky." She gave Blair a grin. "I had no idea our city had such a place."

"Perhaps you should get out more often."

"When I said I might get lucky, you know that I was *not* referring to you."

"I know, I know. You don't have to keep reminding me. I'm happy to simply share your company."

Blair recommended the chef's lunch special, giving Abby the impression she knew the place well. But having said before that she hadn't had a date in a year, Abby wondered if Blair dined there alone.

"Do you know many of the women here?"

"Some of them, yes." Blair scanned the room again. "Judge Thomas for example. I've appeared before her in court several times. We acknowledge each other, but we've never had a conversation to speak of." Blair lowered her voice. "I've only ever seen her here in the company of straight, married women."

Abby glanced over at the judge and the woman seated with her. "You don't say?"

* * *

Sam arrived home shortly after eight o'clock. Her shift had been difficult. She couldn't erase the image of Abby naked and alone in her bed. And it proved even more difficult now that she didn't have the distraction of patients and the hospital. She dropped onto her bed fully clothed, closed her eyes and relived the previous two days. Abby was an amazing lover and she filled Sam with energy she'd never known. A lover… At this point that's all Abby was, though after making love, Abby had stated she thought she could fall in love with Sam. But, Sam knew enough to know it wasn't a guarantee that she would. She could be nothing more than a fling for Abby. Sam wanted to believe otherwise, in spite of her mind's reminder that she should protect her heart.

She hugged a pillow to her chest with a yawn. She'd call Abby before heading to her parents for dinner. Momma had left numerous messages on Sam's home voice mail over the weekend, wanting to know the whereabouts of her long-lost daughter. Sam had called as soon as she could and quashed her momma's tirade by promising to be at dinner that evening. Sam rarely missed Sunday dinner with her family unless she was working, but spending the day with Abby had outweighed any meal her momma could have tempted her with.

* * *

It's astounding how delirious love can make a person. Abby was like a kid waiting for the trip to the amusement park, anticipating the next time she would see Sam. She looked for her Tuesday evening while she read to the kids, and each time her eyes glanced to the back of the room, she reminded herself Sam wouldn't be working until much later. But she continued to look. As she left the activity room, she was delighted to see Sam leaning on the counter at the nurses station embroiled in conversation with Nurse Erika Walker. They were laughing as Abby approached, and a pang of jealously surprised her. Nurse Walker spied Abby first, and then Sam's eyes followed.

A wide grin adorned Sam's face as she stepped toward Abby. "Hi!"

"Hi yourself." Abby reined in her desire to reach for Sam's hand. "What are you doing here so early?"

They walked to the elevator. "I thought I might entice you to have a cup of coffee with me before you head home."

Abby wanted to grab and kiss her. "Is that all the enticing you want to do?"

Sam shrugged. "Maybe…" she said as color painted her cheeks.

Abby punched the elevator button and after a moment they entered the empty car. Sam stood opposite her in the small space and rolled her eyes to the corner above the panels. For the first time Abby noticed the camera and surveillance warning. Not that it came as a surprise. Practically all elevators now had surveillance. Sam punched the button for the lower level, which indicated they were going to the coffee shop around the block instead of the hospital cafeteria.

Abby felt sure she wore a wide grin as she stared at Sam's lips when she talked. Lips, and mouth for that matter, that had taken Abby to places of pleasure she'd never known before. She desperately wanted to feel Sam's lips and mouth on her now. She had a much clearer understanding of sexually frustrated teenage males. After nearly an hour of torture, Abby said she needed to head home.

"I have to show you something," Sam said once they were back in the hospital's lower level.

She grabbed Abby's hand and pulled her through a set of metal doors. The smell of detergent and bleach indicated they were in the hospital's laundry area. It was semi-dark and eerily quiet. "Come on." Sam led her around the corner into a vast space that held enormous washers, dryers, and large folding tables. She stopped abruptly, turned Abby and backed her against one of the folding tables.

Sam's hungry lips found Abby's, and she melted into Sam's embrace. Two days had been too long to be without Sam's touch. Abby eagerly pushed Sam's jacket open and went to work on her shirt buttons. When Abby's cold hands touched the warm flesh of Sam's sides, she jerked and inhaled sharply.

"I can see I need to warm you up," Sam muttered against Abby's lips.

Abby unhooked Sam's bra and cupped her breasts. Sam moaned in her mouth as Abby's thumbs coaxed Sam's nipples hard. Abby moved her mouth to Sam's breast while her hands fumbled to unbutton and unzip her pants.

Abby's fingers slid into Sam's wetness and she groaned. "See what you do to me?" Sam pressed her hips against Abby's hand in a rhythm that didn't stop until she shook. She dropped her head onto Abby's shoulder, kissing her neck. "How am I supposed to work tonight with this on my mind?"

Abby kissed her damp forehead. "With a smile on your face."

Sam pulled Abby's hand from her pants and patted the table behind Abby. "Sit."

Abby hopped up on the table and Sam worked the buttons loose on her coat. Gently pushing Abby's legs apart, Sam stepped between them.

"Are you cold?" Abby replied with a shake of her head. Sam removed Abby's coat, unbuttoned her blouse and slipped it off her shoulders. She traced her fingertips from Abby's neck to her cleavage, leaned in and kissed her neck as she released the front clasp of Abby's bra. She covered Abby's breasts with warm hands. "So beautiful," she murmured against Abby's now heated skin. Sam's lips moved over Abby's collarbone, down to her breast where her tongue teased a nipple before sucking it into her mouth.

"Oh...yes..." Abby gasped.

As Sam's lips and mouth continued their exploration of Abby's breasts, her hands walked Abby's skirt up her thighs. She stopped and moved her lips next to Abby's. "Lie back. I want to taste you," she whispered breathlessly.

Any concern Abby may have had about where they were and what they were doing dissolved in an instant.

"Please Sam...yes."

Sam struggled for a moment with Abby's pantyhose. "Damn," she mumbled and then her tongue was stroking Abby's swollen flesh.

Abby laced her fingers into Sam's hair and held on as Sam slowly took her over the edge. Abby bit her lip to keep from calling out to Sam as she climaxed. Sam kissed her legs tenderly until they stopped quivering. She rested her head on Abby's stomach. When Abby raised her head, Sam's eyes sparkled back at her like two stars in the night. She stroked Sam's hair.

"That was..."

Sam smiled as she stood. "Yeah, it was." She took Abby's hands and helped her to a sitting position. Sam's expression changed suddenly to a look of guilt.

"What?"

Sam lowered her eyes. "I'm pretty sure I tore your hose," she said softly.

Abby laughed. "Honey, you can tear my hose off anytime you want." Abby gathered Sam in her arms.

"Really?" Sam leaned back and flashed a naughty grin.

Abby brushed her finger over Sam's lips. "Maybe…probably." Abby kissed her briefly. "A pair of hose is a small price to pay for what you do to me."

Sam tilted her head. "I am really sorry."

"You're so cute. Don't worry, sweetie."

She eased off the table and gingerly worked the hose back over her hips. If she were lucky, she might get to the car before they ran all the way to her ankles. They put themselves back together and peeked before re-entering the hallway. Abby couldn't wipe the smile of satisfaction off her face to save her life.

"I've honestly never done anything like that before," Abby said as they waited for the elevator.

"What?" Sam asked, looking puzzled.

"Had sex, you know, in a public place." Abby felt a blush creeping into her cheeks. "It was daring, and…well, exciting." She bumped her shoulder into Sam's.

"Maybe I should come to your work and sneak you into a supply closet." She snickered when Abby's eyes went wide. "Relax, I'm kidding," she said as the elevator arrived. She laughed as they stepped inside.

"Of course you were." Abby leaned in close and whispered, "But I do have a half a dozen closets in my loft."

Sam grinned.

* * *

"Am I interrupting your dinner or anything?" Sam asked when she called at about seven o'clock that evening.

"Not at all." *Not that I wouldn't lie if you were.* "I was trying to decide what to wear to work tomorrow."

"Hmm…" Sam paused. "How about you wear a little black skirt and some kind of silky blouse."

Abby slid hangers across the rod until she found the outfit she wanted. "How did you—"

"Abby, I've seen you after work at the hospital enough times to have an idea what kinds of clothes you wear. Like what you were wearing the other night, you know, when we toured the laundry area of the hospital.

Abby pulled a black skirt and red and black print blouse out and slipped the dry cleaner's plastic off. "That was easy. Thanks." She hung them on the door.

"You know..." she paused again. "You could wear something else to work tomorrow and save whatever you just picked out to wear to dinner with me Friday night. Will you have dinner with me Friday night, Abby?"

"Are you asking me on a date, Sam?"

"Uh...yes. I'm asking you on a date. There's somewhere special I'd like to take you, so you have to say yes."

Abby guessed Sam was fidgeting with nervousness. "Well... okay. I'd like very much to have dinner with you."

"Not just dinner, a date."

Abby giggled. "Sorry. I'd love to go on a date with you, Sam."

"Wonderful!" Sam responded. "Will you wear that outfit?"

"Sure," Abby replied, assuming they weren't going out for pizza or spaghetti.

"Terrific! I'll be at your place around six thirty."

"I'll be waiting."

"Great! I've got some errands to run before I go into work tonight, so I need to get going."

Abby hated to end their conversation so soon. "Have a good night."

"I'm sure I will. I'll be thinking about you in a sexy little skirt."

Abby set the phone down, thinking the outfit would make her look more like a dressed-up school mom. But, if it was what Sam wanted to see her in, Abby didn't want to disappoint her.

She didn't hear from Sam again until around ten o'clock on Thursday night.

"It's not too late, is it?"

"Honey, I told you, you can call me anytime."

"Are you in bed yet?"

Abby took her time to answer, searching the street below. "No. Why?" She wished Sam had stopped on her way to work, but the street was empty.

"You'll never guess where I am right now."

"Well, it's not here so I don't know."

"I'm in the laundry room."

"Okay." She couldn't guess why Sam thought she might know that Sam was doing her laundry.

"At the hospital." Abby heard a grunt. "I'm on the table. Where are you?"

Realization dawned. Abby closed her eyes, tipped her head against the window frame and sighed. "I'm standing between your legs."

"Mmm...are you touching me?" Sam asked her voice low and deep. Abby lost all train of thought for a moment. "Abby?"

She'd never considered having phone sex but threw caution to the wind. "I'm unbuttoning your shirt and kissing your neck." Abby held her eyes closed as she recalled every tiny detail of Sam's body. "Your breasts are in my hands and my wet, hot lips are kissing your shoulder." She paused. "Your collarbone." Sam moaned again. "My tongue is painting a wet trail over your chest and, oh... What's this?" She held her breath and listened to Sam's ragged gasps. "Your nipple is in my mouth." Abby ached to touch herself.

"Oh, God. Abby," Sam rasped. "How do you do this to me?"

Abby chuckled. "You started this."

"I know. I know."

Abby heard noises. "Should I even ask what you're doing?"

"Going outside to cool down. Where exactly are you?" Sam asked, her voice still low and sultry.

"Where would you like me to be?"

"Hmm...in your bed."

Leaving the window, Abby went and stretched across the bed. "I'm in my bed."

"Are you naked?"

Obviously Sam wasn't going to be satisfied until they were both tortured with desire. She quickly discarded her clothes and climbed between the cool sheets.

"Sam…"

"Yes."

"I'm naked in my bed. Where are you?"

Sam emitted a low moan. "I'm naked on top of you, between your legs. I'm touching every part of you with my hands, my lips." She paused a long moment. "You're so incredibly beautiful."

Abby's skin tingled as Sam's words swirled around her head. She didn't want to simply imagine Sam pressing down on her, or Sam's hands touching her burning flesh. She wanted Sam, in the flesh.

"Sam?"

"Yes."

Abby sighed. "You should probably go to work."

"I know." She exhaled a long audible breath. "You're probably right."

"I'll see you tomorrow evening for dinner."

"Our date," she corrected. "If I can live that long without seeing you."

"I certainly hope you do. I'll be waiting."

"Six thirty. Sweet dreams."

"After what you just did to me I'm sure you can count on it.

CHAPTER TWENTY

Abby was anxious all day Friday. After Tuesday night at the hospital and the foray into phone sex the night before, she was starved to touch Sam and be touched by her. She hoped dinner would go quickly, and they'd have time to stop back at the loft before Sam had to go into work. Minutes before six thirty a knock sounded on the heavy door.

"Well, hello!" Sam said in greeting, stepping past Abby as she closed the door. Sam immediately swept Abby into her arms, gazed intently into her eyes and lowered her lips to claim Abby's. Sam ended the kiss after a moment and took a step back.

"You look good enough to eat. Maybe I should cancel the dinner reservation."

"Oh no, you don't." Though the smile Sam wore made Abby want to rip her clothes off. She looked Sam up and down. "You look pretty yummy yourself."

Sam was wearing the dark suit she'd been wearing at the fundraiser with a blue shirt that highlighted her eyes perfectly. She pulled the jacket open revealing how fitted her shirt was over her breasts.

"As you might have guessed, my dress-up wardrobe is pretty limited."

"You look perfect." Abby touched her cheek and brushed a kiss over her lips. "Should we be going?"

Sam turned over her wrist. "Actually, we have a few minutes. The restaurant isn't far from here."

Abby stepped toward the kitchen. "Would you like something to drink?"

Sam parked herself on a stool. "I have to go into work later, remember?" When Abby started to return the wine bottle to the fridge, Sam caught her arm. "I'll have a little sip if you will."

Abby poured a small amount into a wineglass and then stood between Sam's knees. She lifted the glass and Sam took a tiny swallow. Abby's mind wandered to last night's phone call for the hundredth time. She set the glass aside and ran her fingers through Sam's hair. She kissed her again. This time Sam's lips tasted sweet from the wine and Abby wanted to devour her on the spot.

"We should probably go before we end up missing our reservation," Abby said. While waiting for the elevator, Abby put her keys in Sam's hand. "Let's take my car." Sam nodded.

Abby trusted Sam and felt safe with her. Something she now realized she wasn't sure she'd always felt with Selena. On the drive Sam relayed a conversation earlier in the day with Nurse Erika Walker, in which Nurse Walker had outed Sam.

"The tap dance was over. I had to confess, but I told her I couldn't go out because I was already dating someone." She glanced at Abby as she turned into the underground garage for the familiar office tower.

"This place came highly recommended and I hope you'll like it."

Abby simply smiled. When they stepped up to the mahogany doors, Sam pushed a button below the electronic key pad. Moments later the same woman that had greeted her and Blair greeted them.

"May I help you?" The woman who opened the door eyed Abby.

"We have a reservation. Dr. Christiano."

She nodded to Sam and gave Abby a smile that said, "Nice to see you again." She then referred to the small notebook she removed from inside her vest.

"Right this way, Doctor."

Once they were seated, Sam said, "This is a private club. Someone told me about it, but don't worry about us being seen together. It's very discreet."

Abby smiled across at Sam. "Why would I worry?"

Sam propped her chin in her hand. "Because I will probably stare at you all evening." Sam fixed Abby with her gaze.

The waitress arrived and Sam said, "Coffee for me and a glass of your best white wine for my date."

"Sam, I don't—"

"Just a glass with dinner. It's a special occasion." The waitress nodded and smiled at Abby with the same familiarity as the hostess. "I guess I shouldn't be surprised you've caught the eye of both the hostess and waitress, Sam said when she'd gone. "Should I be worried that someone might sweep you off your feet tonight?"

Abby shook her head. "You're the only one here I'm interested in." She didn't want to begin whatever this relationship may become with secrets. "But I have a confession to make."

Sam gazed at her intently. "You're not really a lesbian?"

Abby laughed. "No, silly. I think I've been this way all my life."

Sam cocked her head. "Really?"

"Really. I knew back when..."

Sam raised a hand. "Let's not get off track. You were about to confess something."

Abby nodded. "I've been here before."

Sam's bright eyes lost some of their luster. "So much for introducing you to the city's best kept secret."

Abby placed a hand on Sam's. "It was only lunch and it wasn't a date."

Sam's brows rose. "Oh! Well, do tell."

"It was with my boss." Abby suddenly felt ashamed.

"As in Blair?" Sam asked rather loudly.

Abby glanced around. Fortunately they hadn't attracted anyone's attention. "Yes, it was with Blair, and again it wasn't a date," Abby whispered.

"You never mentioned she was a lesbian. She's a lesbian?"

"I only just found out myself, and believe me, it caught me completely off guard."

Sam sipped her coffee. "So, you and Blair. Huh." She looked around. "Who would have guessed?" Sam's tone sounded tinged with jealousy.

"It was nothing." She touched Sam's hand again. "Unlike it is with you." Abby gave a smile, hoping it reassured Sam. "There is and never has been anything between Blair and me."

"I believe you." She squeezed Abby's hand. "I'm just disappointed this place wasn't a surprise for you."

Abby twined her fingers in Sam's. "Coming here with you is a surprise, and I have never been disappointed for a single moment since I met you." Sam grinned. "You're one surprising woman, Dr. Sam, and I really like you. In case you couldn't tell."

Sam lifted Abby's hand and brushed her lips over it. "Well, I can honestly say that since I met you…" Her words fell away as the waitress appeared.

When she'd left with their order, Abby asked, "You were saying?"

Sam casually sat back in her chair as she did so often when they would sit and talk. "Have I told you how incredibly beautiful you look tonight?"

"I believe you alluded to that earlier." Abby felt a blush coloring her cheeks.

"Of course you always look beautiful."

"That's because you haven't seen me at my worst yet."

Sam shook her head. "Not possible."

They talked easily throughout dinner, Abby having never felt so comfortable with anyone. Sam truly made her feel safe. *She has to be my one.*

"Would you dance with me tonight?" Sam asked after the table was cleared.

"I'd love to." Abby sighed with a smile. She would dance with Sam every night for the rest of her life.

Sam offered Abby her hand and led them through the dining room toward the bar. She never broke contact with Abby. Where the aisles were too narrow, she took Abby's hand and guided her ahead, returning Abby's hand to her arm as soon as she was again beside her. It seemed as though all eyes were on them. Once in the bar area, Sam led them to a table and then went to the bar and returned with a coffee cup and a champagne flute.

"You're not plying me with alcohol so you can take advantage of me, are you?" Abby teased.

"It's sparkling cider, not alcohol, but I wouldn't mind taking you tonight. If only there was time." She wiggled a brow.

"I bet there's a closet around her somewhere." Abby wet her lips before sipping the cider.

"Who would ever guess Abby Collins to be a bad girl?"

Abby propped her elbow on the table and rested her chin in her hand. "I hope my secret is safe with you." She batted her lashes.

"Are you kidding? If that got out, I'd have to beat women off with a stick." She sat back and crossed her legs.

God, I really love this woman. "You'd do that?"

Sam sat forward. "In a heartbeat, my darling." Sam placed her hand on the table and Abby reached across to lock their fingers together. It was hard to say how much time passed as they sat gazing at each other lustily. A slow song began to play and Sam squeezed her fingers.

"Dance with me?"

Abby moved into Sam's arms on the dance floor. When Sam lowered her head, her lips brushed Abby's ear. "I've been dying to feel you this close all evening."

Abby tightened her arms around Sam's shoulders. Sam leaned back slightly looking into Abby's eyes. Sam's eyes were a deep indigo that Abby could feel herself falling into—mind, body, and soul. She yearned for the feel of Sam's lips, but she wasn't sure if Sam would be comfortable showing such affection in front of so many observers.

"I wish I could take you home with me."

Sam touched her forehead to Abby's. "Not half as much as I do."

Abby laid her head against Sam's chest, their bodies hot against one another as they swayed to the music. When the song ended and Abby looked up, Sam brushed her lips across Abby's.

"Thank you."

Abby touched a fingertip to Sam's lips. "You are so very welcome."

Back at their table Sam checked her watch. "I should get you home so I can go to work."

The evening had been amazing, and Abby wasn't ready for it to end. The snippets of time she had with Sam went too quickly.

"I would never have guessed that you belonged to that club," Abby said as Sam drove them toward home.

"I don't. This was a 'try it and see if you like it.' I wanted to go out with you somewhere where we didn't have to worry about who saw us and I didn't know… I wasn't sure if you went to any local gay establishments."

"I don't. When it comes to my personal life I like to keep it private. I don't want my sexuality to define me. Besides the only time I went to one of the bars here in the city they played music I'd never heard before and, I ended up running into someone from work."

"I've only been to one gay bar a few times and that was back in my college days. Anyway, I heard about this place, and I immediately thought Abby Collins. It was described as classy and that's you all the way around."

"Such the charmer." Abby rested her hand on Sam's thigh.

Sam slipped her fingers between Abby's. "If you like the place, we could join." She looked briefly at Abby.

Sam had used "we" again like they were a couple. Abby more than liked the thought of that. "It's something to consider."

Back at the loft, Sam dropped Abby's keys on the table and helped her off with her coat.

"I hate for this evening to end," Sam said, taking Abby in her arms.

"We'll have more." Abby touched Sam's cheek, smiling up at her.

"Promise?"

"I promise."

CHAPTER TWENTY-ONE

When she opened the door at seven thirty the next morning, Sam looked positively worn out. Abby pulled her inside and kissed her as Sam fell back against the door. Sam moaned, wrapping Abby in her arms. Abby ended the kiss and gazed into her tired eyes. She pushed Sam's loose locks of hair behind her ears.

"Sweetie, you look like you're ready to drop."

"You promised food and anything I wanted." Sam pouted.

Abby narrowed her eyes. "What is it you want?"

She pulled Abby tightly in her arms and murmured against her neck. "You…all of you."

Abby pulled free and tugged Sam into the kitchen. "Sit," she ordered. "I'm going to fix you breakfast and then put you in a hot bath. We'll see what comes next."

Sam gave a weary smile. "I told you not to spoil me."

Abby stepped over to her and took Sam's face in her hands. "Not spoiling." She kissed the top of Sam's head as Sam wrapped her arms around Abby's waist. "I want to take care of you."

While Sam ate with a gusto Abby didn't think she could possibly have, she ran the bath. As she helped Sam off with her clothes, Sam started on Abby's, but Abby stopped her.

"I've already had my shower."

Sam frowned. "You're not getting in with me?"

Abby shook her head. "I'll wash your back."

When Sam had settled in the tub, Abby pushed up her sleeves and soaped a washcloth. She moved it across Sam's shoulders and then up and down her back.

"Lean back."

Sam submerged herself to her neck and Abby slid the cloth over her arms, her chest and breasts. When she started down Sam's stomach, Sam grasped her wrist.

"I want you so much."

Abby stroked her cheek and her eyelids fluttered.

"Sam, honey, you can barely keep your eyes open." Sam held on to Abby's arm and sat up.

"Will you at least come to bed with me?"

Abby smiled at her sleepy expression. "Of course, sweetie. Come on."

They climbed under the covers. Abby held her, kissing her forehead, and she was asleep in no time. She didn't want to let go. Sam in her arms, in her bed, felt too right.

She slipped out of the bed and in the laundry room held Sam's shirt to her face, breathing in the faint scent of Sam's cologne nearly masked by the smells of the hospital. *God, Sam, I'm so in love with you.*

Abby felt a kiss on the back of her neck later while she was sitting in the office upstairs at the computer. "Mmm...I hope that's you, Sam, and not some stranger in my home." Sam's hands cupped her breasts.

"It's the big bad wolf come to devour you," Sam said, her voice husky from sleep. She nipped at Abby's neck and a shiver raced through her. The computer clock read one-twelve p.m.

"You didn't sleep very long."

Sam spun the chair around and pulled Abby out of it. "Sleep is for sissies and is highly overrated." She again kissed Abby's neck, letting her lips linger there. "I go on a lot less on a regular basis. Besides, I want to spend my time with you, not sleeping the day away."

Abby threaded her fingers in Sam's hair and tipped her head to look into her eyes. "I was only going to give you two more hours, and then I was going to jump you in the bed."

"Ooh…not only a bad girl, but a rough one." Sam grinned. "You may be too much for me to handle."

Abby laid her head against Sam's chest. "Somehow I doubt that, but maybe we should find out." Abby guided Sam backward to the couch where she sat without resistance. Abby straddled her lap and lifted Sam's arms above her head. Sam closed her eyes.

"Please be gentle with me."

Abby placed her lips to Sam's ear and whispered, "What I'm about to do to you won't hurt a bit." Abby leaned back and when Sam opened her eyes, she winked. "I promise."

She pulled the sweatshirt over Sam's head and her nipples puckered. Abby lowered her head and circled one with the tip of her tongue, sucking it gently between her lips. Sam emitted a throaty groan and her hips rose to Abby. Abby moved to her knees on the floor and worked the boxers over Sam's hips to her ankles. Sam gripped the back of the couch when Abby pushed between her thighs and touched her mouth to Sam's center.

"Abby," Sam growled with the last shudder of orgasm.

Abby crawled back onto the couch beside her, laying her legs across Sam's lap and pulled the throw over them. Sam rolled her head to the side looking completely satiated. Her piercing gaze fixed on Abby.

"I could so easily get used to being with you, Abby."

Abby traced a finger over Sam's full and inviting lips. "I think I'd like you getting used to me." Sam sucked Abby's finger into her mouth, pulling it out slowly.

"I want you all the time. I can't get enough of you and I can't get you off my mind. Do you think it will always feel like this?"

"Anything's possible." Abby rested her head on Sam's shoulder. "Is that what you want?"

"That's what I want." She raised Abby's hand and pressed it to her chest. "My heart beats for you."

"Then I am yours for as long as you want me."

"Forever?"

"Yes, forever."

Abby set a plate with a turkey sandwich and fruit in front of Sam, standing close with her arm across Sam's shoulder. "You know, I've been thinking." Abby took a quick breath and forged on. "Maybe you could keep a few things here." She rubbed her hand across Sam's back. "So you're not limited to my old boxers and sweatshirt." Abby kissed Sam's neck. "Although, I must say you are adorable in this outfit."

Sam wiped her mouth and washed the last bite of sandwich down with a swallow of tea. "You keep putting all this healthy food in me and I'm going to live forever." She turned on the stool so she could get her arm around Abby's waist.

"That's the idea."

"You know, you must be reading my mind." Her eyes sparkled with a smile. "When I was putting on these comfortable old boxers and sweatshirt, I was thinking maybe I should start keeping some clothes in my car." Abby smoothed a hand through her hair and kissed the top of her head. "I'm going to have to get up extra early in the morning so I can run home and get clean clothes."

"I washed what you were wearing this morning, but I don't imagine you want to wear the same thing tomorrow."

She shrugged. "They'll just think I've been on for twenty-four hours."

"Honey, I'd offer you some of my clothes, but the only thing I have that would fit those long legs is a skirt." Sam's nose wrinkled and Abby laughed.

As Abby was clearing off the dishes, Sam grabbed her hand. "Come on, I'm ready for dessert."

"I'm going to see what I have to fix for dinner and check the TV to see if there are any good movies on tonight. Unless…

there's something you want to do." Sam moved her hand up Abby's thigh, but Abby grasped it and held it tight.

"I don't want you to have to cook. Can we order something in?"

"Sure."

"And, I picked up a movie on my way into work last night. We can watch it if you want. It's down in my car."

"What kind of movie?" Abby narrowed her eyes.

Sam blushed. "It's a lesbian romance."

"Oh…"

"Oh?"

Abby lifted a shoulder. "They're usually not the best made movies and the stories are predictable."

"Well, it's probably hard to find good lesbian actresses to make a movie feel real. It's not a typical movie. It's supposed to be artsy. You know, no dialogue, just a narrative. If you don't want to watch it, we can watch something else."

Abby touched Sam's cheek. *What a sweetheart.* "We can at least take a look. If it's not any good, we don't have to watch."

They had pizza delivered later and sat in the living room with music playing while they washed it down with some imported beer Selena had left behind. Well, mostly Sam drank beer and Abby sipped on them.

Sam touched her arm. "You okay?" Abby nodded. "Your cheeks are flushed."

Abby fanned her face. "Must be the beer."

"The two sips you had?" Sam looked at her with a question. "You're not hot all over, are you?" Sam was trying unsuccessfully to hide a grin.

Abby attempted a stern expression. "Eat your pizza."

"Just trying to take care of you."

She had pizza sauce at the corner of her mouth. When Abby wiped it with her finger, Sam caught hold of her hand and stuck the finger in her mouth.

Abby could have melted into Sam's arms. "You take wonderful care of me. Thank you." She leaned in and gave Sam a kiss.

"You're very welcome."

Sam picked up the book lying on the coffee table while Abby cleared off their plates and bottles. She was reading the back cover blurb when Abby returned.

"You like to read romance?" Abby gave a nod. "Do you believe in happily ever after?"

"I do. You don't?" Abby questioned.

Sam shrugged. "I'm pretty sure my parents are happy. I know my grandparents were before my grandpapa died. Grand Momma used to tell me stories. So yeah, I guess it exists."

"And what do you read?"

"Medical journals, case studies, the really good stuff." She chuckled.

At bedtime, Abby set her alarm on the bedside clock for five thirty, but shortly after five in the morning, Sam's phone vibrated on the nightstand. She slipped from the bedroom, the door creaking as she closed it. Abby could hear her trying to talk quietly in the living room. When Sam returned, she searched for her clothes in the dark.

Abby turned on the bedside lamp. "Sam, what's wrong?"

Sam pulled her pants on without any underwear. "They're on their way to the hospital. They think Momma's having a heart attack."

Abby bolted upright in the bed. "Oh Sam, what can I do?"

Sam shoved her socks into her pockets and slipped her bare feet into her shoes. She looked like she felt ill.

"Nothing, but thanks." She leaned over the bed and pecked Abby on the lips. "I've got to go."

"Of course." Abby called after Sam as she disappeared through the door, "Call me."

"As soon as I know something," Sam called back.

Adrenaline made it impossible for her to go back to sleep. She couldn't imagine what Sam must be going through, and she wasn't sure if she would care if her own mother were in the same position. But it upset her that Sam's mother could be in trouble. *Poor Sam.* She and her mother actually had a relationship. Although she'd only been around her on two occasions, it was evident Mrs. Christiano was a wonderful woman and mother. Abby wished she could be at Sam's side, offering support. She guessed, though, that Sam's family probably didn't know of Sam's interest in women. And if Sam had wanted her there, she surely would have asked.

Sam hated being dragged from Abby's warm embrace in bed, and worse, she hated the reason for it. She was so upset driving to the hospital that she ran a red light. Thankfully at such an early hour on a Sunday morning, there wasn't any traffic. She had cried and prayed most of the way and managed only to compose herself as she rushed in from the parking lot. She wished Abby were there, holding her hand as they waited. Sam had a feeling Abby's presence would be calming, soothing, and would make her feel safe and protected. Kind of like her Momma did. She didn't doubt that Abby would make a great mom and she hoped Abby would have that chance.

After what seemed like days of waiting, the cardiologist came out with good news.

"She didn't have a heart attack, but there are a few health issues that need attention or she could suffer heart issues in the future," the doctor said.

Relief washed over Sam. "I can assure you as a fellow medical professional that my mother will strictly follow any diet and lifestyle changes you deem necessary." Sam gave her momma a look and then a kiss when the doctor had gone before she rushed down the hall to call Abby.

"Sam, honey, how is she?"

She heard Sam sigh. "She's fine now. It wasn't her heart, but indigestion complicated by a severe anxiety attack. As long as she follows doctor's orders and takes the recommended medications, she should be just fine."

"And how are you?"

"Tired. I'm sorry for bolting out of there."

"Oh Sam, please don't give it another thought. I'd rush out for your mother too."

"But not your own?"

"I…" Abby didn't want to lie. "I don't know and it doesn't matter at the moment. I wish I could tuck you snugly back into my bed."

"Hmm…not as much as I do. Did you at least go back to sleep?"

"No sweetie. I was worried about your mother…and you. I'll just turn in early tonight. Will you stop by later?"

"I want to, but…" There was a long pause. "I think I should spend some time with my folks. This really scared me. I think I need to see for myself that she is okay."

Abby smiled. She wasn't at all surprised by how Sam was feeling. In fact, she envied her. "I understand, sweetie. I'll be thinking about all of you."

"I'll try to call you later."

And at a little after nine o'clock p.m., the phone rang. Abby could hear what sounded like cars. "Where are you?"

"Sitting on the porch swing at my parents."

"Isn't it cold out?"

Sam chuckled. "I like to call it invigorating. Momma and I sit out here all the time and talk."

Abby could imagine it too. "They don't know do they?"

"Know what?"

"About you…about me."

There was a long hesitation before Sam answered. "I don't think so. I don't know. I know I'm a coward."

"Sam honey, it's okay. You have to do what's right for you and your family. I came out to mine years ago, and let's just say that they are kinder to strangers."

"I want to, I just…I don't know. I'm scared, I guess."

"Really. It's fine. You do what feels right for you."

"In the meantime I have to sneak outside at my parents' house to call my girlfriend. How childish am I?"

She called me her girlfriend.

"And where are you if I might be nosy?"

"I don't think you want to know."

"Why not?"

"Because you're not here."

"Ah, come on, Abby, tell me. Please…"

Abby couldn't resist the plea. "In a tub full of bubbles."

"You're right." She sighed. "I didn't want to know that."

"I told you."

"Gee, and I could be there washing your back or something."

Abby giggled. "I'm thinking the 'or something.'"

"I should let you go so you can finish your bath."

Sam's voice was so soothing to Abby's tired body and mind. "You don't have to."

Sam sighed again. "I don't want to, but if I don't get back inside they'll come looking for me, and I'll be busted." She laughed. "Busted by my parents for sneaking out to call my girlfriend. I'm twenty-eight years old. How juvenile is that?"

"Sam honey, go inside before you catch cold and take care of your mother."

"I'll call you sometime tomorrow."

"You call me anytime you want. I mean that."

"Sweet dreams, Abby."

"Goodnight, Sam."

CHAPTER TWENTY-TWO

Sam worked a day shift through Thursday, calling Abby each evening. She felt the need to look after her mother following the hospital episode and wanted to be sure she followed the doctor's orders regarding her diet and daily routines. She was off on Friday and not due to start a second shift schedule until Saturday. When Abby entered the loft after work, the smell of something wonderful greeted her.

"I hope you don't mind," Sam said as Abby stepped into the kitchen.

In jeans and a sweatshirt, dusted all over with flour, the sight of Sam caused Abby's heart to miss a beat. Sam had let herself in and taken over Abby's kitchen.

"You're always cooking and feeding me so I thought I'd take a turn."

With her thumb Abby removed a smudge of flour on Sam's cheek. "That's very thoughtful and sweet. Thank you." She leaned in for a quick kiss.

"Go change your clothes."

In the bedroom her attention was drawn to the small duffel bag sitting in the corner beside the dresser. She smiled. Her heart did a little dance. She stripped off her work clothes and dressed in jeans and a comfortable old sweater.

"I hope you don't mind that I brought a few things over for when I stay the night and have to go into work."

"Like tonight?" Abby asked and perched on a stool at the counter. Sam handed her a bottle of non-alcoholic beer.

"Definitely tonight." Sam smiled. "I missed you this week."

Abby pulled her between her knees. "I missed you." Sam kissed her. When she pulled back, she asked, "So how is your mother? On the road to healthier living?"

Sam stepped over to the oven and peeked in. "She'll be fine and live forever if she follows her doctor's orders."

"I'm sure you'll see to that."

Sam had made her mother's lasagna recipe and a crisp green salad. After the meal she ushered Abby to the living room with the remainder of her beer while she cleaned up the kitchen.

"I would never think of disobeying doctor's orders." Abby picked up the remote and turned on the sound system. "What's your favorite music?" she called out to Sam in the kitchen.

Sam leaned over the counter. "In high school my good friend's dad said, 'Eighties music is like Schnapps. It's all good.' So we listened to a lot of the eighties music all through high school."

Abby switched the satellite radio to the eighties station and lowered the lights. When Sam joined her, Stevie Wonder's, "Ribbon in the Sky" began to play. Sam set her beer on the coffee table and reached for Abby's hand.

"Dance with me."

Abby's heart fluttered as Sam moved them in front of the windows and began to sway with the city lights as their backdrop.

She touched her fingers to Abby's cheek. "Can we stay like this forever?"

"As long as you want." Abby tightened her arms around Sam's neck.

They danced through several slow jazz numbers and then Sam kissed her, sending off fireworks.

When Abby woke Saturday morning, Sam was lying on her side, gazing at her.

"Good morning," Abby said, with a stretch.

"Definitely." Sam smiled. "I really like waking up with you."

"I can't think of anywhere I'd rather be." She pulled Sam into her arms, stroking her fingers through Sam's hair. "I have a novel idea."

"Oh yeah?" Sam asked, eyes bright. "Would it be a romance?" She laughed.

"Very funny, Dr. Comedian." Abby poked her in the ribs and Sam wiggled. "Let's do something grown-up today, like go to the museum or visit an art show."

"Really?"

Abby nodded.

"I love art, but I'll take a pass on the museum."

"And I know a wonderful little place we can have lunch."

"You know I have to be on at three today."

Abby's lips formed a pout. "I know. Can we forget about it until later?"

"No problem."

In an effort to save time, they showered together, which in the end didn't actually save a lot. Abby had to smack Sam's hand away several times to keep her on task. They grabbed coffee and bagels around the corner on the way to the gallery, and then afterward they headed to a diner for lunch. Abby did not want to let Sam go, and only did so with a promise from Sam that she would return after work since neither had to get up early in the morning. Abby tried to wait up for her, but she woke with Sam placing little kisses across her face at just after one a.m.

"I'm sorry I'm so late," Sam spoke quietly. She scooped Abby into her arms.

"I'm glad you're here now." Abby touched Sam's lips then kissed them.

"It's so romantic," Sam said of the candles that still burned beside the bed and on the dresser. "And you are so beautiful." She traced a finger down to Abby's breast, her eyes following.

Abby tipped Sam's chin up. "And you look dead tired."

"But..."

Abby pressed her finger against Sam's lips. "There's always tomorrow." She patted the bed. "Undress, blow out the candles and come sleep with me." Once under the covers, Abby snuggled against Sam's side. Sam kissed her forehead. "Goodnight, Sam."

Sam mumbled something incoherent and in only a few minutes, Abby could tell that she was asleep from her deep even breaths.

At first Abby had thought the sound was a dream. Then she got an eerie feeling someone was in the room. She rolled away from Sam and sat up. When her eyes adjusted in the darkness she saw the silhouette.

"Well, well, what have we here?" the cold voice said, sending shivers through Abby.

"Shh, be quiet." Abby moved gingerly from the bed, pulling on her robe.

"You didn't waste any time warming up my side of the bed."

Abby grabbed her arm and whispered, "Shut up and get out of here." She shoved Selena toward the door.

"What's wrong, Abby?" Sam rolled over, her voice raspy.

She pushed Selena through the door. "Everything's fine, sweetie, go back to sleep."

Abby pulled the door closed quickly to minimize the creak. Selena pinned Abby to the door the second she turned around.

"Who is she?"

Abby smelled the alcohol and blinked, thinking she could make the image go away, but it didn't. "None of your business." Selena grabbed Abby's arm and tried to kiss her. Abby bristled and beat her fist against Selena's chest. "Get your hands off me!"

"Geez, don't beat the crap out of me." Selena let go.

"Shh...keep your voice down." Abby's eyes narrowed to slits. "And don't touch me."

Selena stumbled to the kitchen. Abby put the counter between them, glanced at the bedroom door and prayed that Sam went back to sleep.

Abby crossed her arms over her chest. "Why are you here?"

Selena reached down into the cabinet, pulled out the tequila bottle and took a drink. "Well, you know I didn't think after all the things you said to me that I'd miss you for a minute." She took another drink. "But damn it, I do." She wiped a hand across her mouth.

"I thought I made it perfectly clear we're over. You don't miss me... You miss being taken care of and I told you, I'm not doing it anymore. Now please, get out of my home." The bedroom door creaked and when she turned, Sam, fully dressed, walked to her side. She looked bleary-eyed and confused.

"Are you okay?" Sam asked and Abby nodded.

"Well, well, Abs, you gonna introduce us?" Abby glared at Selena, and then Sam faced Selena for a look. "Wow, doll." Selena gave a snide smile. "You recruiting at the college now? She's a real cutie."

Sam's face turned crimson and she took a step away from Abby, but Abby caught her arm.

"No...don't."

Selena laughed. "Better mind the Mrs. or she'll kick you out like she did me."

"Get out!" Abby spat through clenched teeth.

With an evil smirk Selena stared Sam down. "Let me guess here. She lured you into her lair with the promise of, oh let's see, maybe a family?" Sam looked back at her and Abby shook her head. Selena threw her head back with a hellish laugh and an expression to match. "You gonna help her get pregnant, right?"

Abby's patience was spent. "Get the hell out of here!"

"Easy there, doll." She raised her hands.

Sam leaned close and whispered, "Will she hurt you?"

"Physically, no..." Abby lowered her head, "but emotionally, she'll torture me until she runs out of steam."

"It sounds like you two have some things to work out," Sam said without emotion. She squeezed Abby's hand. "I'll talk to you later."

Sam hurriedly moved to get her coat. Abby stood in shock, as if she were watching a scene in a movie where the plot twists and then everything moves in slow motion. She remained stunned and silent, unable to get her feet moving to go after Sam. The sound of the steel door closing stung. Her ears started ringing, and her fury built like a pressure cooker. Then she lost it.

"For the last time, get out of my home!"

Selena took another swig from the bottle. "Come on, doll. You can't tell me you'd prefer that over what we had. You can't tell me you don't miss it." She grinned. "You know, in bed."

Abby raced around the counter, snatched the bottle from her hand and turned it upside down in the drain. "Get out, Selena." Selena reached for Abby's face and she slapped her hand away. "Don't ever touch me again."

Selena leaned a hip against the counter. "Aw baby. She can't possibly do for you what I can."

The smell of the tequila reached Abby and she thought she'd throw up. She stepped back.

"If you don't leave right now, I'm going to call the police and have you removed."

She eyed Abby with a look of defiance.

"I will have you removed, arrested, and I'll get a restraining order."

Selena let loose a laugh.

"Have you forgotten who my boss is? I won't hesitate to sic Blair on you."

Abby didn't doubt for a second that if she gave Blair the opportunity, she would go after Selena with her claws sharpened. Blair would rip Selena's life apart, ruin her name, her dignity and leave it all in shreds. Blair would do anything for Abby if she thought Abby needed saving, and Abby wasn't above using that if necessary. It would probably amount to sleeping with the devil, but weighing the alternatives, Abby decided it was worth the sacrifice to get Selena out of her life for good.

"She likes me and I'm pretty sure she hates you. She just doesn't know your name…yet." Selena didn't need to know that Blair already knew who she was. "When she gets done dragging you through the mud, you won't be able to get a job in this town. Hell, you probably won't even find anyone to talk to you."

Selena's smile vanished and she shook her head. "Well, don't come crying to me when your little girl can't keep you happy in the sack."

Abby held out her hand.

"What?"

"Give me the key you got in with."

She laughed. "It's under the pot where you keep it. That steel door isn't any good when you leave a key out for anyone to use. Well doll, maybe I'll see you around." She turned her back on Abby.

"You won't. Take my advice, Selena, and stay away, or I will make your life hell."

She slammed the door on her way out. Abby's hands shook and the tears started, then a sob tore from her lungs.

"Oh God, Sam…" She fumbled for the phone and punched the speed dial number for Sam. When her voice mail picked up Abby said, "Sam, I'm so sorry honey. Please call me."

The tears resumed when she set down the phone. It hadn't been twenty minutes since she'd left. Abby reassured herself that Sam would be calling any minute, but an hour later Sam still hadn't called so Abby called her cell phone and left another voice mail.

By the time Sam reached her car, sirens were going off in her head, and she couldn't hold back the tears. As she drove off in the darkness with no particular destination in mind, she wondered how it was that she had misread Abby. There was obviously still some involvement with her former lover. She was there like she owned the place. It made Sam feel used, yet again by a woman. She struggled to understand how she'd so easily given herself to another beautiful woman who wasn't who she thought she was. She'd followed her heart instead of listening to the warnings in her head. She lacked the experience to have and build a healthy and lasting relationship. The only relationship that she'd had with Brittany was proof. Doubt crept in. Maybe she wasn't meant to share her life with a woman. Her stomach churned.

She wasn't due in to work for almost twelve hours, and she didn't want to go home. She drove toward the hospital and entered the parking garage across the street. She parked on the roof level and leaned her head back, hoping for sleep but knowing it would never come.

Forty-five minutes later her cell phone rang, and the screen showed Abby's name again. She didn't answer. It was after four thirty in the morning. All she wanted was sleep, but she couldn't turn her mind off. She kept hearing that woman's words, over and over. "Lured, lair, family, recruiting, getting pregnant." They all tumbled around in her head like clothes in the wash. Her phone rang again about an hour later with another call from Abby. It was going on six o'clock. That woman had obviously been Selena, the one whose name she remembered from the boxes in Abby's laundry room. She'd been right, the name fit. She was exotic looking, either Latina or Hispanic, and definitely the kind of woman that would never look twice at her. But this woman and Abby, yes, they made a beautiful couple.

Sam continued to beat herself up for her involvement with Abby. Why did she let it happen? She knew that answer. Abby radiated charm and she stirred Sam's libido, the first woman to do that in many years and she couldn't stop herself from satisfying the urge. She was no better than one of the horny male residents at the hospital who bragged about their conquests. Only this was worse. Sam had allowed herself to fall in love. Abby wasn't who Sam thought she was. The ringing phone interrupted the beating she was giving herself. Abby again. And again she didn't answer. The phone beeped with another voice mail. She went back and forth, listen, don't listen. After a long consideration, she listened.

There were three messages total. "Sam, I'm so sorry honey. Please call me." She deleted it and the second one played. "Sam, I'm sure you're upset about what happened. Selena let herself in with the spare key you warned me about leaving under the pot. There's no way it will happen again. Please call me." Abby's voiced sounded more worried and upset than the previous message, Sam thought as she dug in her pants pocket. She looked at the key and then dropped it into her console. The third message began. "Sam, I'm not going to quit calling. I know Selena said hurtful things, but none of it's true. I need to talk to you. Please call me."

She deleted the final message and dropped the phone into the console. She leaned her head back to see the sun peeking above the hospital. She closed her eyes for only a moment. She just wanted to sleep, but she couldn't in her car with the sun shining, so she drove to her apartment complex but didn't park in her own lot. She found a space several buildings away where her car wouldn't be easily seen unless someone happened to cruise the lots looking for it. She felt like a criminal on the run as she walked to her apartment. Dropping onto her bed fully clothed, she forced her mind to a serene place, and every tensing muscle to relax.

The persistent knocking on her door woke her, but she didn't get up. Her clock read nine thirty-six. The knocks sounded again followed by her cell phone ringing and the unmistakable voice right outside her door. Abby was pleading from just thirty feet away. Sam closed her eyes tight, trying to block out the sound. She got up and tiptoed to the door, silently leaning against it to hear Abby's muffled voice, and then silence. She returned to the bedroom and peeked through the blinds. Abby's shoulders were slumped as she walked to her car and then sat there. Sam's tears fell again as she crawled back into bed and placed a pillow over her head in an attempt to hide from the world. Hide like she had since Brittany Greer with her perfectly coiffed blond hair and pretty blue eyes. Brittany had too easily entangled Sam into her life of drama and control. The first time Brittany had blown up, she smashed things in Sam's room and slapped her because Sam had gone out with a few friends instead of her. She should have known then how much trouble Brittany was, but Brittany could bat her long lashes and offer a sweet apology and Sam would fall right back into her web. She had been so young with no experience in relationships.

* * *

All the makeup in the world couldn't hide the dark circles or the puffiness around Abby's eyes. She avoided looking at Blair, but once Blair was settled in her office, she summoned Abby.

"Close the door and please come sit with me."

With trepidation, Abby took a seat on the opposite end of the couch, poised with her steno pad and pen.

"So, do you want to tell me what's going on or shall I guess?"

Abby stared ahead. "Nothing that you need to concern yourself with."

Blair exhaled a long breath. "Now I'm pretty sure that's where you're wrong. I don't mean to sound insensitive, but you look like someone very near and dear to you died. I can tell you've probably been crying all night. Something feels amiss. Please Abby, I truly want to be your friend. Talk to me."

Abby blinked back the tears as long as she could, but when she looked at Blair they slid down her cheeks. "Selena let herself into the loft at three o'clock yesterday morning, drunk."

Blair muttered, "Bitch."

"Is it possible for me to file some legal charges against her? I repeatedly asked her to leave and she wouldn't."

"Did she hurt you?"

Abby sighed. "Not physically."

"Did you call the police and report it?"

Abby shook her head in shame. "There was a witness."

"I see." Blair took her hand as if to lessen the bad news. "I'm not sure on what grounds we could charge her, but if she does it again, call the police." She stood to get the box of tissues from the counter behind them. "Hell, call me. I'm sure I can scare her away." Blair rejoined her on the couch.

"I kind of already threw your name out as a threat to get her to leave. She might leave me alone now."

"If she doesn't, will your *witness* give a statement?"

"Yes...I think..." She sighed again. "I don't know. Selena may have scared her off for good." The thought turned on the waterworks again. She stammered and sniffled when she blurted out, "She scared off my new lover."

Blair placed her arm gently across Abby's shoulder. "If you want to talk about this or there is anything I can do to help, please don't hesitate to ask." Abby nodded. "Why don't you take the day off to get yourself together?"

Abby stood. "I don't want to be alone all day today. It will only make me feel worse. I need to stay busy, so let's get to work."

"As you wish, but if you feel like you need to get out of here, let me know." Blair moved to the chair behind her desk.

"That's very kind. Thank you."

"I'm learning." She smiled.

Blair took her to lunch, Abby welcoming the distraction. Around seven that evening after forcing down her dinner, she called Sam, leaving a message. She fell asleep clutching the phone to her chest and one of Sam's T-shirts from the bag Sam had left behind.

As much as she'd looked forward to the ritual with enthusiasm in the past, she knew she couldn't get through reading to the kids Tuesday evening and called the hospital early in the day offering her excuse. She lunched with Blair each day and called Sam every night, only to lay waiting with the phone that never rang. She became an expert at hiding her hurt and pain from Blair. By Friday Abby was convincing.

"Would you like to go out for dinner tomorrow night?"

"I can't. I have plans, but thanks for the invitation."

Blair accepted her reply. Abby convinced herself she'd been honest. She most certainly had plans. She intended to stalk Sam until she found her.

Sam walked around in a haze. Her eyes were wide open, but everything seemed cloudy now...unclear. Sunday when she came on shift, Nurse Walker informed her that the lovely Ms. Collins had stopped by asking her whereabouts. Sam mumbled something and abruptly turned away. Running on short periods of sleep since her last shift had exhausted her, she arrived home and hit the bed only to have sleep elude her. She couldn't get Abby off her mind for a minute, and to further her self torture, she kept envisioning Abby with that Selena woman. Sam knew she didn't have a chance of competing with a woman like her. She just had to convince her heart of it.

Since work seemed the only good distraction, she made herself available for extra hours and shifts. Like medical school all over again. And, like clockwork, her cell phone rang nightly around seven with Abby's caller ID. Each time she received a voice mail alert. Sam prayed the calls would stop so she wouldn't have to take more drastic steps, like move out of state.

When she finally made it home at two a.m. Tuesday morning, there was another new voice mail message for her there.

"Sam, it's me. I told you I wouldn't quit calling, so please call me. We really need to talk about this." Sam erased it and pulled the bottle of Jack Daniels out of the cupboard. After choking down several big gulps, she fell into her bed fully dressed.

It surprised her to hear that Abby hadn't come to read to the kids when she showed up for her shift later Tuesday. She assumed Abby would use the opportunity to track her down in the hospital, but she'd volunteered for some extra hours in the Psych ward. With all the locked doors and extra security, there was no better place in the hospital to hide out. Her cell again rang like clockwork in the evening, followed by a message alert from Abby. Sam had her "Jack" nightcap and hit the bed hard.

She managed the entire week to successfully avoid seeing and talking to Abby. Given time, Sam prayed it would all become a bad memory and she could bury it along with the others. She worried Abby might get lucky and catch her over the weekend, but with all the changes to her schedule, she hoped that wouldn't happen.

There was a close call Sunday around noon, but Sam heard the familiar voice as she neared the corner of the main hall on her floor. She peeked around and saw Abby talking to one of the nursing assistants and quickly ducked back down the hallway and into the stairwell. A moment later the page sounded for her. She walked up a flight and to the end of the hall where she could see the parking lot. There she stood for almost half an hour before she saw Abby crossing the lot. She turned away returning to the distraction that work provided.

CHAPTER TWENTY-THREE

Normally Abby would feel relieved to work with someone other than Blair, but that was no longer the case. She felt isolated and lonely. Blair checked on her early Monday and they made lunch plans. She continued her evening ritual of calling Sam, which now included the hospital, but to no avail. She showed up to read to the kids after work Tuesday, and it was all she could do to get through the time without crying. While she packed her bag, her gaze repeatedly went to the back of the room looking for that familiar face. Abby's heart was in a million pieces. Losing Selena didn't come close to how she felt now. Sam hadn't simply been her lover. Sam was her friend. On the way out, she asked at the nurses station, but they were clueless. She called Sam's number as she sat in the hospital parking lot before driving home to spend another miserable night. Her life was a scratched record.

"Abby, we've been lunching every day for a week and a half, which by the way, I find highly unusual," Blair shared on their

Wednesday lunch date. She leaned forward. "Please tell me Selena isn't bothering you."

"No." Abby didn't want to pour her heart out to Blair.

"I can't help but worry about you." Blair placed her hand on Abby's.

"Thanks." Abby forced a smile.

At lunch on Friday, Abby knew she couldn't spend another weekend hunting for Sam, and then being alone if she couldn't find her.

"Take me out somewhere this weekend."

"Really?" Blair asked.

"Don't get so excited. I'm not talking about a date, just two gals hanging out."

"Okay." Blair's head bounced. "I can do that. Where would you like to go?"

Abby shrugged. "Surprise me. I only need a few hours notice so I can dress appropriately."

Blair wore a schoolgirl grin as they stepped off the elevator at their floor. Abby hoped she hadn't opened herself up to something she would regret.

"I'll call you tomorrow," Blair said with a wave and headed off in the opposite direction.

Abby made every attempt to reach Sam that evening without luck. She was beginning to think Sam wouldn't ever be calling her back. She made her drive around to the usual places Saturday about noon, but she couldn't find her. Blair had left a message on her home number while she was out, which said to dress nice, have an appetite, and she'd see Abby at seven thirty. Sitting in the tub late afternoon, out of the blue she burst into a sob. The idea of drowning seemed a good solution, although, she knew the only thing she was likely to drown in was her own tears. Even when her entire family had turned their backs on her, she'd never given up. But without Sam... Well, she wasn't sure how she would ever survive.

Blair had said dressy, and while dressy for Abby typically meant a dress, she opted for a pair of slacks and a cashmere sweater. Blair arrived on time, and when Abby opened the door, she thought she might faint or throw up, or both. Her head and stomach swirled. Blair was wearing a tailored dark suit over a gorgeous blue blouse and if she imagined a different face, it could have been Sam standing in her doorway. Blair quickly stepped inside and caught hold of Abby's arm.

"Abby, you're pale as a ghost. Are you all right?"

Because I've just seen one. "I must have gotten up too fast. I'm fine." She stepped away from Blair. "Let me get my coat."

Blair followed her in. "No rush, we have a few minutes. In fact, time for a drink if you want."

The words were like a roundhouse blow to Abby's stomach. The same words Sam had spoken to her on their last date. She clamped her hand over her mouth and ran for the bathroom where she dry-heaved. After a moment she dropped to the floor and sat trance-like until she heard Blair's voice and a soft knock.

"Abby, is everything okay?" Abby could hear her, but her brain wouldn't let her respond. Blair knocked again. "You're scaring the hell out of me. I'm coming in." And suddenly she was squatting beside Abby. "Hey." Blair's voice was soothing as she waved a hand in front of Abby's face. Abby blinked at her when she pushed Abby's hair back. "What's wrong?"

She blinked again. "I'm sorry. I felt sick." With all the strength she had, she pushed up from the floor.

Blair guided her to the side of the tub. "You look very pale. Maybe we shouldn't go out."

"No, no, I'll be fine. Just give me a minute."

She handed Abby a wet washcloth. "If you're not out of here in a few minutes, I'm canceling dinner and putting you to bed or taking you to the hospital."

"I'll be out in a minute." She went to the sink once Blair had gone. "There's a bottle of wine in the fridge. Pour yourself a glass if there's still time," Abby called through the closed door. When she emerged, Blair smiled and handed her a glass.

"You look much more like yourself." Blair tipped the glass to her lips and sipped.

Abby only pretended to take a drink. "I don't know where that came from. I suddenly felt nauseated."

Blair placed her glass on the counter. "Are you sure you want to go out?"

"Absolutely. I'm ready to get out of here for a while." Blair helped her on with her coat. "You don't like wine, do you?" she asked.

"No, I never quite acquired a taste for it." She slid her hand across Abby's back as she stepped around her.

When Blair opened and held the door for her, Abby was reminded that she still needed to get the lock changed so if Selena had managed to get a duplicate key, she couldn't make any more surprise appearances.

"That's right," Abby said as they stepped into the hall, "your taste is for ancient whiskey or something."

"Scotch," Blair corrected.

Abby had a good idea where they were going when Blair turned up Front Street.

"I hope you don't mind if we go back to the club."

"No not at all. I really like the place."

"I thought you might relish the privacy."

"So why aren't we dressed to the nines tonight?"

"I hoped we could sit at the bar and eat where we can enjoy the music."

Abby's mind flashed back to the evening that she and Sam had shared there, gazing at each other the entire night. *Oh God, Sam. I miss you.* Abby hoped for strength to get through the evening. The hostess eyed her suspiciously when they entered. She could hardly blame her. For all that the poor woman knew, Abby could be a high-priced escort. Several times while they ate, Blair mentioned Abby's "witness," which was her name for Abby's mystery woman. Abby quickly changed the subject. She didn't want to think about Sam's absence. She had only a couple of tiny sips of wine through dinner, knowing full well she shouldn't be drinking, but she wanted to give Blair a sense of normalcy. Blair absolutely did not need to know that she could be pregnant. After the meal, they moved over to a table closer to the dance floor and the music.

Blair emptied her second drink and reached a hand across the table. "Dance with me, Abby."

Abby took deep breaths and after a moment, relaxed in Blair's arms. She laid her cheek against Blair's shoulder and closed her eyes. The memories of how it had felt in Sam's arms flooded her mind. She willed Sam to appear in her arms, but she opened her eyes and saw Blair gazing down at her.

"This is so comfortable. I could dance with you all night," Blair said.

Abby again felt lightheaded and closed her eyes, fighting a feeling of darkness that was closing in around her. *Where are you Sam?*

Abby opened her eyes and saw Blair hovering over her. She felt disoriented and fuzzy in her head. "Where are we?" she asked, her own voice sounding far off.

"In the ladies' lounge. You fainted in my arms on the dance floor." Abby tried to sit up but Blair held her down with a gentle hand. "Just lie still for a few minutes. You're still white as a sheet." Abby looked away, embarrassed, and saw the hostess standing behind Blair. "I think she's okay, thank you," Blair said to the woman, who then left. She touched a cool wet cloth to Abby's forehead and then her neck. "I must say I've never had quite this effect on a woman before." She smiled and gave Abby a wink.

"I don't know why that happened."

Blair rewet the cloth and returned to Abby's side, a position Abby didn't think she'd ever find herself in with Blair.

Blair touched her hand to Abby's cheek. "I'm not sure if I believe that. I'm worried about you, Abby."

Abby grasped Blair's hand and moved it away. "I'm fine." But Abby felt all the fight leaving her. She sighed.

"Let's get you home. You think you can stand?" When Abby nodded, Blair took hold of her hands.

Blair guided her to the car and insisted on walking her up to the loft.

"You're not going down on my watch," was Blair's comment as they rode the elevator up. Once inside Abby's door, Blair released her arm and Abby leaned against the wall.

"I'm sorry for ruining this evening, Blair."

She took Abby's hand. "You didn't ruin anything." She tipped her head and gazed intently into Abby's eyes. "I only hope everything is okay with you." Blair's expression showed only compassion.

"Thank you for taking care of me." She squeezed Blair's hand. When Blair attempted to step away, Abby held tightly to her hand, inhaled sharply and closed her eyes. She leaned forward and pressed her lips firmly to Blair's.

Blair pulled back in a rush, an unreadable expression on her face. "Abby...this is not a good idea. You are a beautiful woman and I may be a lot of things people say that I am, but I'm not about to take advantage of your vulnerability. I..." She exhaled loudly and shook her head. "I should go."

"Yes, you should go," Abby whispered.

Blair lifted her chin. "Are you sure you're okay?"

Abby averted her eyes. "Please...I'm fine," she mumbled.

"You will call me, if you need anything at all, please?" Abby gave a nod and stepped away from her. "I mean anything."

Abby glanced at Blair before Blair opened the door and left. Abby slid down the wall and cried like a baby until she felt she would be sick, so she sat in the bathroom and continued to cry.

She managed to drag herself out of bed reasonably early Sunday morning and by nine o'clock was speaking with a locksmith. He stressed how expensive his services would be on the "Lord's Day," but with Abby's agreement, he arrived an hour later. He left her with a shiny new door lock and half dozen keys. Not long after, she grabbed a notepad, envelope and went in search of Sam. Abby didn't find her at the hospital or at her apartment. She called Sam and left a message that she was leaving something under her door. The note read, "Sam, we can't allow things between us to end this way. Please at least call me. Abby." She put a key with the note, sealed the envelope and slid it under the door.

Dropping her phone in her purse she leaned against the door. "Sam honey, I need you." Guilt clawed at her for kissing Blair last night, and the tiny thread of hope she'd been clinging to was crumbling. She left and drove past Sam's parents' house. No Sam. But several blocks away she turned around, parked across the street and watched for a bit. She didn't see any movement through the front windows. It was a little after two in the afternoon, so she didn't think she would be interrupting their Sunday dinner.

"Well, well, look who has come to visit," Sam's father announced boisterously when he opened the door. He turned and called down the hall to Sam's mother, who came out of the kitchen. "Momma, we have company."

Mrs. Christiano stepped around Sam's dad, wiping her hands on her apron. "My, my, what a surprise. Come in, child, come in." She pulled Abby through the door and Mr. Christiano closed it behind them. "Samantha is not here."

Abby nodded. "I wanted to stop and see how you are."

She eyed Abby suspiciously. "Come to kitchen. I make us tea." She slipped her arm through Abby's and pulled her along to the kitchen where she directed Abby to a chair.

When Mrs. Christiano sat down with their tea, Abby swallowed and mustered all the courage she had left. "Honestly, I was hoping to catch Sam here, but when I saw that she wasn't, well, I thought I might speak with you."

Mrs. Christiano abruptly pushed up from her chair. "Come child." Picking up her cup, she led Abby from the kitchen, grabbed a sweater from the coat tree by the front door and went outside to a swing hanging at the end of the porch. She patted the worn wood next to her. "Sit."

Abby realized this was where Sam sat when she had called from her parents. They sat in uncomfortable silence until Abby finally found her nerve. "I wanted to talk to you about Sam."

Mrs. Christiano started the swing moving. "Hmm..." She nodded her head. "You and Samantha have disagreement."

Abby chose her words carefully. "A disagreement yes, not with Sam but with someone else. Unfortunately Sam was hurt by the lies this person told."

She gave the swing another push. "Hmm..." She sipped her tea. "You really like my Samantha?" The possessive use of the word "my" made Abby continue with great caution.

"Mrs. Christiano, Sam and I have become very good friends." Abby had to clear her throat to keep her voice from shaking. "As a matter of fact, she's the best friend I've ever had, and she's so upset that she won't speak to me."

"Girls," she shook her head, "sometimes I trade the lot of you for boys."

"Really?"

She shook her head again. "No, I just say so. I love my girls. Samantha is special."

"She certainly is."

"My special girl doesn't come around the last few weeks." Abby could feel Mrs. Christiano's eyes upon her. "She hides from her own momma."

Abby met her eyes. "If I could just talk to her." She couldn't stop an errant tear from escaping and took a long breath. "I could explain things to her. I need her to understand, but most of all, I need her friendship."

She brushed the tear from Abby's cheek and took her hand. "I see in your eyes how you care for my Samantha. I will talk to her, but I can no promise she will talk to you." She squeezed Abby's hand. "Try is all I can do."

"Thank you, Mrs. Christiano."

"Mrs. sounds old, child. You call me Momma." Abby nodded and they sat silent a while longer before she thanked Sam's mother for the tea.

Standing on the top step, she cupped Abby's chin. "You too skinny, child, you need to come more for dinner and let Momma feed you."

Abby said a silent prayer that Mrs. Christiano could help before driving away.

* * *

Sam's week sucked. They had a seven-year-old car accident victim they couldn't save, but who could have been saved by the grieving parents had they used the proper child car seat restraint. She needed to be held and to cry on someone's shoulder. She'd never been so emotional before at losing a child in the ER, but letting her guard down with Abby had made her heart vulnerable. The last time Sam had allowed herself to be so vulnerable the worst thing imaginable had happened to her.

She'd gotten home only hours before, had her nightcap and fallen asleep on the couch. She didn't hear the knock on the door, but the ringing phone woke her. Sam tiptoed to the door and pressed her ear to it. "Sam, I left something under your door. Let's talk, please." Touching her hand lightly to the scarred wood, Sam could feel Abby's presence as the envelope slid underneath the door, and faintly heard Abby mutter something.

The ringing phone woke Sam at three forty-five. She made no move to answer it, assuming it was Abby being as persistent as she had promised. But it wasn't. It was Momma.

"Samantha, call Momma immediately." Her mother's voice boomed in her ear as she listened to the message. Click. Her voice sounded urgent and Sam launched herself in a panic from the couch. She hurriedly punched in the number.

"Momma, what's wrong?" Sam asked the second her mother answered.

"Samantha?" Her momma gasped her name. "My long-lost daughter."

"Yes, Momma." Sam knew she was in trouble.

"My goodness, child. I think you run off somewhere and forget the family."

Relief washed over Sam and she began her excuses. "I've been very busy at the hospital Momma, and…" She couldn't come up with any more excuses.

"You work too much, Samantha. Not healthy. When is last time you eat real meal?"

Sam didn't have to think long or hard to remember it was dinner with Abby at the club, but she didn't feel the need to share that with Momma. "I don't know, Momma."

"You come for dinner five o'clock," her momma ordered.

"But Momma—"

"No, Samantha. Your Grand Momma is old and gone too soon. You come to dinner, see your family."

"I have to be at work—"

"You don't call your Momma so I call your work to find you. They say you no work til seven. You have time to sit for dinner with family."

Sam knew she'd never win this battle. "All right Momma, I will be there for dinner at five."

It ended up only being her Momma, Papa, and Grand Momma for dinner, and Sam couldn't figure out what all the fuss was. After dinner, though, her momma said they should have coffee on the porch. Sam knew it was serious. She just didn't know what she'd done to warrant "a talk" with her momma. And Momma didn't waste any time. The moment they were seated she leveled her eyes on Sam.

"Why you hide from Momma?"

The slow rocking of the swing started. Sam knew she wouldn't be able to escape without providing some kind of answer.

"Momma, I told you I've been very busy with work. I've been working a lot of extra hours."

Momma's brow lifted to a sharp peak. "This why you no call for weeks?"

Sam shrugged. "I have big school loans to pay off." Her momma's gaze intensified and Sam looked away.

"This is all? Why you stay away from your momma?" Sam could no longer meet her eyes. "Samantha?"

She wasn't prepared to do this. She couldn't share with her momma how broken she felt.

"How is Abby?"

Sam choked back the hurt that the mention of Abby's name inflicted. When she didn't answer, Momma took her hand.

"Abby stop and see Momma. Abby worry about you. That make Momma worry about you."

Sam was terrified by the thought of what Abby may have shared with her momma, and it started emotional waves that Sam wasn't ready to wade through.

"Samantha, what happens you must face like we teach you." She squeezed her daughter's hand. "Nothing worse in life than what you leave undone."

Sam pinched her eyes shut against the tears forming behind them. As if sensing her daughter's distraught and fragile state, Momma put her arm around Sam and pulled her to her ample bosom, stroking her short locks in the comforting way she always had.

"Samantha, I don't judge for what you choose. I know you like Abby, that way. Momma's okay." She gave Sam's shoulder a squeeze. "I only want for my children to be happy."

The floodgates opened and Sam cried in her momma's embrace. Later as she prepared to leave, her momma hugged her tight and kissed her forehead.

"You find what make you happy, Samantha. Nothing matter more. This will matter most."

On the drive across town, Sam played her momma's words over in her mind. What would make her happiest in life? The answer was so simple. She had fallen for Abby Collins the moment she first laid eyes on her. And, she'd known from the pull in her chest it wasn't a schoolgirl infatuation, but an all-consuming, heartbreaking love of the kind that could crush her. She recalled now how Brittany's betrayal had crushed her all those years ago.

CHAPTER TWENTY-FOUR

Abby's new week started off feeling lonely and physically sick about losing Sam. Although Mrs. Christiano had promised to talk to Sam, Abby knew there was nothing more she could do…except wait. She stopped the phone calls and messages, and was leaving it all up to fate.

"Have lunch with me?" Blair asked when she showed up at lunchtime.

"I can't."

"Abby, I don't mean to sound critical, but you don't look so hot. You need to get past whatever's been keeping you down. Is your witness upsetting you?" She arched a brow.

"Blair, please just stop with the questions." Abby buried her face in her hands.

Blair put her hand on Abby's shoulder, gently kneading it. "I'm sorry. Is there anything I can do?"

Abby pushed her hand away. "Yes, you can quit treating me like one of your witnesses."

Blair walked back around the desk and dropped into the chair. "Got. It. Loud and clear." She gave Abby one of her "press shot" smiles. "But I do think you should reconsider having lunch with me."

She avoided Blair's gaze. "And I think you should let me worry about me."

Blair glanced over her shoulder at the door. Abby guessed she wanted to be sure no one had heard her last comment.

"Ouch!" Blair's eyes settled back on Abby as she pushed up from the chair. "Must be that time of the month so I will leave you to wallow in that on your own."

Abby knew that the wreck her life had become wasn't Blair's fault and she shouldn't have been so snarky with her. When she looked up, Blair was gone. Blair was right. She needed to pull up her bootstraps and get a life.

It surprised her when Blair stopped back again on Tuesday with another lunch invite.

"I apologize for my inexcusable behavior yesterday. You must be a glutton for punishment," Abby said.

"When I think of some of the behavior you've put up with from me, it will be some time before we are even. So don't worry about it," Blair said with a genuine smile.

There wasn't any mention of the Saturday night incident, and things seemed to go back to what they'd been between the two of them. Abby simply wanted to forget because…because there were times when Blair was her boss and that would make for more discomfort than she could see herself enduring.

Abby worked on adjusting her mood during the drive to the hospital and even spent a few extra minutes reading to the kids. She congratulated herself for resisting the urge to ask about Sam at the nurses station. However, once out in her car, she sat for a long time thinking about how it was here that it all began. She debated going back inside to try to find Sam and make this the place where it all ended. She'd gotten a feeling that Sam was there tonight, somewhere. If she were, she would have known that Abby was there, and she had chosen to avoid her.

* * *

Sam knew Abby would arrive soon when the aides and some of the nurses started taking the kids to the activity room. Considering her momma's pearls of wisdom, she knew what she needed to do, though, finding the nerve was something else entirely. When she heard Abby's voice around the corner, she didn't feel like tonight was the right time. She called the nurses station to tell them she was headed down to the ER and disappeared off the floor.

She sat in the residents' lounge on the surgical floor drinking coffee until she thought story time would be ending. Then she walked to the window out in the hall that overlooked the parking lot. Watching and waiting paid off when she saw Abby exit the building and make her way to her car. Even bundled up and hunched against the cold, Sam would recognize Abby anywhere. She recalled the first time she had stood at the window on her floor watching the same beautiful figure walk with a purpose and ooze confidence. Abby exuded the same confidence now, and Sam wondered since her phone had quit ringing with Abby's number, if she was already over their little tryst.

Sam's neck flushed with heat at the thought that maybe Abby had gotten what she wanted from the affair and moved on. But then logic made her ask herself why Abby had gone to the trouble of visiting her momma and asking for her help in reaching out to Sam. And why had Abby given up her vigil of phone calls and messages since visiting her momma? "If you'd quit being a chickenshit and face her, you might get some answers," Sam mumbled to no one but herself.

Whipped after her shift, and hurt from seeing Abby, even Sam's old buddy Jack wasn't able to help her to sleep. She paced a rut in front of the couch. Since Abby had stopped calling and leaving her messages, she picked up her cell to call that voice she missed hearing, but she disconnected the call before it finished dialing. Granted, Abby had told her she could call anytime, Sam worried that two o'clock in the morning might scare Abby out of her skin. She tossed the phone on the coffee table and paced some more.

Why did something that had happened so many years ago still haunt her? She'd graduated college with honors, breezed through medical school compared to a number of others, and she was a resident. She was a grown-up, a doctor, and it seemed childish to let some part of her past continue to rule her life. But it was probably too late to fix things. She didn't think there was a chance in hell that Abby would want to talk to her now. After all, Abby had been relentless in reaching out to her for weeks and she'd hidden from her. She dropped onto the lumpy couch and switched on the TV. Utter exhaustion finally claimed her sometime after four in the morning.

Sam managed to sleep until noon and planned to go into work early, so after a shower, she headed to her favorite little Italian restaurant for lunch. It seemed like everyone had a cheerful greeting to offer, but she wasn't feeling social. She said hellos, not stopping to chat, and made her way to a booth in the back. Sipping strong black coffee, her eyes settled on the table in the middle of the room, which she had shared with Abby on their first unofficial date. Abby had been breathtakingly beautiful that evening, and on the way out of the restaurant, Sam noticed in the mirror behind the bar that they made an attractive couple. Abby made her feel special. Sam stared down into the cup, wondering how she ever thought she could hang on to a woman like Abby. Her chest ached, her heart broken.

She needed to resolve things with Abby. She couldn't keep living the way she had been. The following morning after several cups of coffee, Sam decided it was time to face the music. Seated on her couch she dialed Abby's work number. She planned to only ask if Abby would agree to meeting sometime over the weekend so they could talk. Well in truth, Sam wanted to spill her guts and hopefully Abby would listen open-mindedly.

"Please hold. I'll transfer you to that office," the bubbly and energetic voice told her.

The line rang and rang, so many times that Sam thought for sure it would go to voice mail. Then a perky, young female voice answered. "Edward Carlton's office. How can I be of assistance?"

"Uh…I was trying to reach Abby Collins." Sam's stomach dropped at the sound of an unfamiliar voice.

"She's on her lunch break. Can I take a message?"

Damn. Do I, don't I?

"Hello…"

"Uh, no. Thank you." Sam sighed and disconnected the call. Was Abby out somewhere having lunch with someone new? Why wouldn't she be? Abby was a charming, intelligent, and beautiful woman. She was sure to have more lady friends than Sam could hope to amass in her lifetime.

* * *

"I have to say that you look much more like the Abby I recognize from a month ago," Blair said at lunch. "Problem solved or aborted all together?"

Blair's comment didn't come off at all like a come-on, but her choice of words caused Abby to feel ill.

"Not up for discussion, Blair."

"That's exactly what I'm talking about." Abby knitted her brows. "The way you're responding to me is more what I expect from you. That scorching fire."

Abby glared. "I admit to being under the influence of something rather foreign to me lately, but rest assured, you won't ever see me in such a vulnerable state again."

"In any case, welcome back."

Abby had given up. Her persistent attempts hadn't even garnered a nasty note or angry call from Sam to tell her to leave her the hell alone. At this point, she didn't believe that even Sam's own mother could change Sam's mind about what Sam thought she'd witnessed that night in Abby's loft.

CHAPTER TWENTY-FIVE

Abby had gone from having a Latin lover, and then a loving doctor, to being alone. Standing at the kitchen counter looking out into the darkness that blanketed the city, she'd never felt more alone. Worse than alone, she was lonely—for a touch, a soothing voice or simply a face to smile at her. Lonely for something, anything that would pick her heart up from its despair. Life shouldn't ever be this miserable.

She looked at the plate in front of her and forced herself to take another bite. This was her ritual now. Having to make herself eat. It shouldn't have been a surprise when Blair told her she looked like crap and she'd passed a street dweller in the parking garage who looked healthier than Abby did.

"Should I call your mother and tell her what you're doing to yourself?"

Abby had glared until Blair left her office.

She stabbed a green bean and piece of chicken. The process of eating dinner could take as long as an hour sometimes, but she stuck to her healthy diet. The knock sounded as Abby absently chewed and stared off into the night. She grabbed her napkin and glanced at the clock on the microwave on her way to the door. It was a quarter of eight. She peered through the peephole and froze. She chewed ravenously, putting the napkin over her mouth when she opened the door.

"I'm interrupting your dinner. I can stop back another time."

Abby quickly swallowed and wiped he mouth. "I was finishing." She stepped back and held the door open. "Would you like to come in, Sam?"

Abby held her breath as Sam stood motionless just across the threshold. Sadness darkened her eyes. When she finally gave a nod, Abby stepped aside, but Sam only entered far enough for Abby to close the door. She didn't recognize this Sam. She seemed so misguided, as though waiting for someone to offer her direction.

Abby returned to the kitchen, scooped up her plate and set it in the sink. Her stomach in knots, she definitely wouldn't be eating anything more. She dropped her napkin over the remaining dinner.

Sam sat on the same stool where she'd sat the first night she came to dinner. On that night she'd looked adorable and carefree. Tonight though, Sam appeared troubled and Abby feared she was about to push her out of her life for good. She leaned a hip against the counter by the sink and crossed her arms. She took slow even breaths to settle her upset stomach. Whatever Sam's reason for being there, Abby wasn't about to fall apart in front of her. Sam sat silent for a long time, but Abby waited. This was Sam's show and Abby merely her audience.

"I…" Sam cleared her throat and began again. "I ran away…I hid from you." She only stared at her hands, fidgeting in her lap.

"I can't say that I didn't notice."

"I'm sorry." She rubbed her palms over her pants before resting them on her thighs. "I'm such a coward." She inhaled a deep breath, exhaling slowly. "Can you ever forgive me?"

Abby shrugged. "I don't know, Sam." She sighed audibly. "I don't know what to think anymore." She struggled to keep a torrent of emotions out of her voice.

"Momma told me you came to see her." Sam glanced up, but not at Abby. Ah, so Sam was there out of some obligation or guilt placed on her by her mother. "Momma really likes you—hell, my whole family really likes you." Her smile was fleeting.

Abby liked Sam's family as well, especially Sam's mother. She recalled how Mrs. Christiano held her hand and spoke with the kind of compassion mothers were supposed to have for their children. And Abby was practically a stranger. Mrs. Christiano was the kind of mother Abby wanted to be. When tears crowded her eyes, she blinked repeatedly to hold them back. *I will not be weak in front of Sam or any woman—ever again.* Sam had smashed her heart in a million pieces, and she wasn't about to let it happen again.

"God, this is so hard." Sam clenched her hands into tight fists and pressed them into her legs.

"Sam, whatever it is just say it. We're both adults. Stop acting like a child in trouble." Abby sounded harsh, but she was ready to have this over with so she could get on with her life, whatever that would amount to.

Sam's breaths came in short gasps and after a long pause she finally said, "Something happened to me—in college." She looked up at Abby with more hurt in her eyes than even Abby felt herself at that moment. Sam looked at her fists. "I've never talked to a soul about it." She took another shuddering breath and looked back at Abby. "I had a girlfriend in college." Sam had a faraway look in her eyes. "For almost a year. She was beautiful, and she wanted plain ol' me."

Abby couldn't understand why Sam sold herself short. She was attractive, with her European genes, and had a wonderful personality. And she was so damn smart.

"I'd never really been with anyone…before her, so I didn't know what being in love felt like. But I fell in love with her." Sam stared vacantly toward the dark windows. "It started during my freshman year. She was a senior, and being with her was like being in paradise. She could have convinced me to throw away all my dreams and go away with her anywhere." Sam looked back at Abby, tears lining her lashes.

"Sam, we've all suffered a heartbreak at least once in our lives."

Sam shook her head. "Toward the end of the year, I found out that she had been sleeping around campus and not exclusively with women."

"And you're not the only one to ever be cheated on either," Abby said, her most recent experience still fresh in her mind.

Sam looked away. "She was controlling and manipulative. I didn't even realize the power she had over me until I confronted her about the cheating. She only laughed and said I couldn't leave her because I needed her more than she needed me. After several arguments I finally stood up to her." She balled her hands into fists again. "I told her to get out of my life. I never wanted to see her again. But she wouldn't leave. She kept telling me how much she wanted me and no one else, and she kept trying to kiss me." She swallowed hard and her voice trembled when she spoke again. "I told her I didn't believe her, and that I would never trust her again. When I tried to push her away she got so angry." Tears slipped down Sam's cheeks and she pounded her fists on her legs. "She grabbed me." Her voice shuddered. "I…I couldn't get away from her and she…she…"

Abby was unaware that she had pressed her own fist to her mouth. She stepped over to Sam and placed a hand on her shoulder.

"Oh Sam, I'm sorry." Sam shook, a sob tearing from deep within her. Abby sat beside her and faced her. "She abused you… She beat you?" Sam shook her head and sobbed for a breath. Abby lifted her chin. "Sam?" The tears flowed steadily down her face.

Sam looked down into her lap. "She forced me." Sam said it so quietly that Abby didn't think she'd heard correctly.

When it hit her, her heart dropped to her stomach and she thought she might throw up.

Sam gasped for a breath. "I felt—so used and sick. I just wanted to die."

Abby stood and pulled Sam to her chest. She pressed her cheek to Sam's head. "Oh God Sam, I'm so sorry." She held tight to Sam. "I'm so sorry for you, sweetie," Abby whispered into her hair. Sam finally put her arms around Abby and cried like a baby. Abby encouraged her to let out her tears, and she held Sam, rocking her in her embrace. Sam cried until she couldn't catch her breath.

"I'm here for you, whenever you need me. I'll always be your friend, Sam. And you can talk to me about anything. Please remember that."

Sam let go and pulled away. She dropped her head, rubbing her sleeves across her wet and bloodshot eyes. "Thanks."

Abby got up and took a step back, not wanting Sam to think she expected anything of her in such a fragile state. When she sniffled, Abby retrieved the box of tissues from the bathroom, and then she stood at the end of the counter while Sam got herself together. It wasn't what she wanted to do. She wanted to sweep Sam into her arms and take her to the bedroom. She wanted to touch and kiss every part of her, until she felt safe, loved, and healed, but Abby knew she couldn't...she shouldn't. If Sam wanted her, Sam would have to tell her.

Sam tossed the tissues in the wastebasket and stood with her hands jammed in her pants pockets. "I promised myself I wouldn't ever let a woman have power like that over me again."

"But Sam, I didn't—"

"Oh but you did..." She lowered her head and practically whispered. "You do." She swallowed hard. "I fell for you the first time I saw you, and when we finally spoke, well, that was it. I was a goner. The first time you kissed me was like a shot of an addictive drug. I couldn't think about anything else and I didn't want anything else, but you. That is until your girlfriend shattered my fantasy." She sighed deeply.

"But she's not...she wasn't—"

"It doesn't matter." Sam looked up at Abby. "I have to get back to work." Her voice now sounded strong and confident.

"Are you okay?"

She worked the toe of her shoe over the space between the tiles. "Yeah. Sorry to drop by and dump this on you."

"It's okay." Abby reined in every emotion she felt. "If nothing else, we're friends."

Sam nodded. "Friends," she said, walking to the door. She hesitated with her hand on the knob.

Abby wanted with all her heart for Sam to turn around and take her in her arms, and never let go.

"I'll see you."

"I mean it. If you ever need to talk, I'm here." It was all Abby could manage to say, her heart breaking all over again.

With another nod, Sam pulled open the door and left. The click of the steel door reverberated through the loft and Abby crumpled to the floor with a sob. She pressed her fists to her chest and cried until her tears ran out.

Sam was the one, her one, and she knew it in every part of her. She couldn't fathom that she and Sam were over. Dragging herself up from the floor, she wandered aimlessly around the loft. In the kitchen, where it had been so obvious to her she was in love with Sam. She brushed her fingers over the stool where Sam had sat. She didn't want anyone but Sam. She went to the window and stared out to find that brightest star to make her wish on, but the city's nightlights obscured any there might be. She thought her tears had run out but they came again. Wrapping her arms tightly around her to hold herself together, she dropped into the chair by the window.

She rocked and cried. Why couldn't she have the best thing she'd ever known in her life? She cried until she was sick and ran to the bathroom, but the feeling of nausea was that, only nausea. Seated on the cool tiles with a wet cloth pressed to her mouth, she somehow found more tears to shed. Around ten o'clock she took her weak, exhausted self to bed where she cried herself to sleep. Would the tears never end?

CHAPTER TWENTY-SIX

Abby had seemed distant, not at all how she would have thought, but then Sam didn't know what to think. She reminded herself that she had pushed Abby away first. She surprised herself by sharing the past that had haunted her for such a long time, since she'd made a promise it was something she would never tell anyone—ever. But Abby had held her and consoled her much the way her momma would have. And maybe if she'd ever talked to her momma about it, she might not be so screwed up that she'd blown the best thing she would probably ever know in her life.

The car's clock glowed twelve forty-one when Sam rounded the corner and saw the darkened loft windows. She hadn't wanted to return to work after leaving Abby's. She hadn't wanted to leave Abby. Her shift seemed never-ending. And to make it more stressful, they'd gotten slammed in the ER with a multi-car, multi-family involved accident.

Abby's demeanor earlier convinced her that Abby had moved on, although, she said they could be friends. Sam didn't think she could live with only that. But why had she come back? What did she hope to have happen now? Deep inside, she knew the answer. She wanted all or nothing. Simply friends would be too much to bear. She parked on the street and looked up at the loft again. Her palms were sweating and her stomach turned over and over.

"Okay, if Abby throws me out, she's justified in doing so since I'm the one who has been acting like a child. Abby pleaded with me repeatedly to talk to her." Sam gave herself a pep talk. "So you spilled your guts about your trauma, but you didn't open your heart and tell Abby how you felt about her." Sam couldn't imagine ever loving someone else so much. Wanting to do and be everything for them...not like she wanted for Abby.

She bypassed the elevator and took the stairs, praying with each step. She prayed for strength and for the right words to express how she felt. She prayed that Abby would see in her heart how much she loved her. Covered in perspiration by the time she reached the fourth floor, she'd also worn a groove in her thumb rubbing the key in her pocket as she climbed. For a long few minutes, she stared at the shiny brass key under the bright hallway lighting, and then after making the sign of the cross, she unlocked the door.

The loft was dark except for the faint glow from the city lights beyond the living room windows. Closing the door gently, she walked as quietly as possible over the tile to the dining room table. She continued to catch her breath as she looked around. There, the counter that separated the kitchen and living room where everything seemed to come together. And the couch facing the windows, with the spectacular view of the city that had been the perfect playground for them. She looked back at the counter and recalled earlier in the evening when Abby had seemed genuinely concerned about her tragic past, but had kept her distance. Sam walked to the windows and looked up into the night. If only she could find a star to wish on.

She took long, calming breaths and walked across the living room. She knew if she opened the closed bedroom door that the creak would surely wake Abby. She hesitated, still unsure. What if Abby felt blindsided by Sam showing up in the middle of the night? She'd been feeling the unrestrained tug on her heart since her talk with Momma after Sunday dinner. Could Abby ever welcome her back?

She loved Abby with every part of her being. She could no longer deny that, and even her momma had known. She stepped into the dark bathroom and carefully made her way to the other door that stood open to the bedroom. She could see Abby's shape in the bed. She stood there surrounded by silence as she went over it all in her head one more time. She didn't doubt that Abby cared about her, a lot, at least she did before Sam had run away with her tail between her legs. Her heart told her as much, and she wouldn't allow herself to believe that her heart had been wrong. Not after so many years of loneliness…not about Abby. Abby wasn't Brittany. She wouldn't use Sam. She wouldn't lie and cheat or abuse her. *Just let it go.*

She stepped back into the bathroom and closed the door. If she turned on the bathroom light and left the door open a crack, Abby wouldn't come out of her skin when Sam woke her. At least she hoped. She felt around for the switch, and when the light came on, she blinked to adjust her eyes. She scanned the room and smiled at the memory of the day she surprised Abby in the bathtub. She'd been embarrassed beyond words, and yet Abby had remained calm as an evening breeze. The memory warmed her heart but did little to relieve her anxiety. When she turned back to the door, she spotted something out of place on the vanity, a pregnancy tester. She stepped over and picked it up. The positive indicator showed as clearly as the love she held in her heart for Abby.

Suddenly more nervous than that first day with Abby, Sam inhaled a deep breath. She knew if she didn't do what she intended right then, she would be tempting fate and karma, a very bad idea on both accounts. Returning the tester to the vanity, she slipped quickly and quietly through the door, leaving it open only enough to make a ribbon of light across the bedroom. She stood at the bed for what seemed like an eternity before inhaling a breath and then lightly touching her hand to Abby's sleeping form.

"Abby, it's Sam," she whispered and sat carefully on the edge of the bed.

Abby moaned and stretched, and then slowly turned over.

She rubbed her eyes to make sure she wasn't dreaming. Sam had come back. Abby's heart danced.

"I'm sorry for coming so late and waking you."

"Are you all right?" Abby asked her voice groggy from sleep.

"I...yes..."

Abby waited, her heart racing, full of hope.

"I am such a fool for letting an old fear scare me away."

Abby couldn't see her face in the shadows.

"You are the kindest, most caring and giving person I've ever met in my life. I know now without any doubt, maybe too late but I sure hope not, that you are my fate, my destiny." She touched her fingers to Abby's cheek. "I've never loved anyone as much as I love you."

At Sam's touch Abby's pulse beat through every part of her body.

"Abby, you are my one and I know that I won't ever find another you. I want you more than I want the air that I breathe."

Abby took Sam's hand and pressed it to her heart. "My darling Sam, you are all I want." She touched a finger to Sam's lips and slid her hand around Sam's neck to pull her close.

"I feel at home with you...safe," Sam murmured against Abby's lips.

Still unable to see Sam's face, Abby could hear her smile in the sound of her voice. "I have something I need to tell you."

Sam took Abby's palm and kissed it briefly. She moved it to Abby's stomach. "We got pregnant on our first try."

Abby put her other hand on Sam's. "We did. Oh God, I love you so much Sam."

When Sam leaned in to kiss her, Abby felt Sam's tears drop on her cheeks. The passion in their kiss told Abby what she needed to know. Sam loved her too.